EASTER BONNET
MURDER

A LUCY STONE MYSTERY

EASTER BONNET MURDER

LESLIE MEIER

THORNDIKE PRESS
A part of Gale, a Cengage Company

LIBRARY OF CONGRESS CIP DATA ON FILE.
CATALOGUING IN PUBLICATION FOR THIS BOOK
IS AVAILABLE FROM THE LIBRARY OF CONGRESS.

ISBN-13: 978-1-4328-9847-2 (hardcover alk. paper)

Published in 2022 by arrangement with Kensington Books, an imprint of Kensington Publishing Corp.

Printed in Mexico
Print Number: 01   Print Year: 2022

For Greg
Love never dies

For Greg
Love never dies

CHAPTER ONE

"Oh, Lucy. I don't know what to do," moaned Rachel Goodman, collapsing on the visitor's chair Lucy Stone kept by her desk at the *Courier* newspaper office in Tinker's Cove, Maine. Tears were filling Rachel's huge brown eyes and she didn't even seem to have the strength to sit in the chair but propped herself on Lucy's desk, leaning on her arms. "I was at the hospital last night," she continued, reaching for a tissue, "and they told me they don't think she's going to make it." She paused to collect herself, took a big sniff, and wiped her eyes. "The nurse told me to prepare myself. How do I do that? I can't imagine life without her."

Lucy Stone, part-time reporter and feature writer for the weekly newspaper, felt her heart lurch and her stomach land with a thud. She sat down hard on her desk chair and met the tearful eyes of her dear friend

Rachel Goodman. "I can't believe it," she finally said. "I suppose it was foolish but somehow I really thought she'd live forever."

Rachel and Lucy were speaking about the town's oldest and most revered resident, Miss Julia Ward Howe Tilley, who had been fighting pneumonia in the ICU at the Tinker's Cove Cottage Hospital for eight days. Rachel, who provided home care for Miss Tilley — only a sadly diminished group of elderly friends dared to call her Julia — had been visiting daily and reporting on her condition. These reports spread through town faster than a Blue Angels flyover, zipping from one increasingly worried citizen to another as the news steadily grew worse every day that passed. Miss Tilley, the long-retired librarian at the Broadbrooks Free Library, was a friend to all and a beloved institution, cherished for the generous heart that she strove to conceal with brisk efficiency and a tart tongue. A tiny person with rosy cheeks and an aureole of fluffy white curls, she loved nothing more than to express outrageous opinions designed to shock those who would dismiss her as a "sweet old lady."

Lucy passed her a tissue, and took another for herself. "How old is she?" she asked.

"I'm not sure, it's a closely guarded secret,

but I do know she's well over a hundred."

Lucy wiped her eyes. "That's a heck of a good run." She studied her friend's face, thinking that Rachel suddenly looked older and tired now that she was too troubled to bother with rejuvenating creams and the mascara and lipstick she used to apply with a light touch. She thought how much younger Rachel looked when her face was lifted with a smile. "How are you doing?" she asked, taking Rachel's hand.

"Not well," she admitted. "You know my mother died when I was in my teens, so I think maybe Miss T filled that empty space for me. I could talk about anything with her, any problems, and she always helped me put things into perspective." She sighed and squeezed Lucy's hand. "They said that anyone who wants to say good-bye shouldn't delay." Her voice broke and she caught a sob. "They say she could go at any moment."

Lucy, who had come to work early to write a recap of the latest selectmen's meeting, which had been more contentious than usual and didn't end until close to midnight, came to a decision. She shut down her PC and got to her feet, gathering up her bag and grabbing her jacket from the coat stand. "I guess I'd better get going, before I chicken out and hate myself forever," she said.

She and Rachel got to the door just as Phyllis, the receptionist, yanked it open and set the little bell on the door to jangling. Words were not needed, the expressions on Rachel's and Lucy's faces told it all, and Phyllis, a dyed-in-the-wool Methodist, raised her eyes heavenward and crossed herself. "Keep praying," urged Rachel. "Amen," added Lucy, as they hurried past. Once on the sidewalk the two women parted. Rachel headed for her husband Bob's law office, just a few doors down, to tell him the awful news, and Lucy got in her SUV for the drive to the hospital.

Lucy drove along the Main Street of the pretty coastal town, too distressed to notice the colorful banners flapping from lamp-posts in the cool breeze that blew off the cove, advertising the Chamber of Commerce's upcoming Spring Fling sales promotion. She also failed to see the gorgeous barrels that dotted the sidewalk, crammed with blooming daffodils and sprays of forsythia, cultivated by the Garden Club. She instead was trying to think of what she wanted to say to Miss Tilley. As she struggled to frame her thoughts, she realized she'd never been confronted with a moment

10

like this and wasn't at all sure what was expected. The truth was that although she'd lost beloved family members before, she'd never had a chance to say good-bye.

Her father was the first to go, back when she was a young mother, too occupied with the endless demands of her growing brood to truly comprehend the gravity of the situation when her mother called to report he'd had a heart attack. She remembered asking her mother if she should come to New York, where he was in Montefiore Hospital, and being reassured that "everything is going to be just fine." It wasn't fine, however, and her father died that very night while she was pacing the floor with a crying, feverish toddler with an infected ear.

Now that she thought about it, she discovered she really hadn't had time or space to grieve for her father. She was entirely caught up in the struggle to meet the needs of three young children, a nursing baby, and a husband struggling to get his restoration contracting business off the ground. She'd been too tired to cry, or, she concluded with a sudden insight, too afraid that if she started she'd never stop. It was safer to stuff her emotions into some back drawer of her brain; if she acknowledged them she feared she would be overwhelmed.

After losing her husband, her mother had gradually slipped into dementia, becoming a vague, confused shadow of her former self. Lucy hadn't really understood what was happening, thinking her mother's confusion was due to her grief, until she'd gotten a phone call from her mother's doctor. By then there wasn't much she could do except arrange for her mother to go into a memory-care facility; it was only a matter of time until she failed to recognize Lucy, her only child, and eventually slipped into a coma. Lucy had dutifully arranged the funeral but hadn't recognized the woman in the coffin as her mother, her mother had slipped away slowly bit by bit until she simply wasn't there at all.

The most recent family member to get his wings, as the obits often paraphrased the cold, cruel and inevitable fact of death, was her husband Bill's father. Bill Senior had also suffered a sudden heart attack, which Bill's mother stubbornly downplayed, denying the seriousness of his condition. He slipped into unconsciousness before Lucy and Bill could reach him in Florida and learned from the doctor that there was no chance of recovery. They watched mutely, day by day in the ICU, as his breaths grew shallower and finally, ultimately, ceased.

Reaching the hospital, Lucy pulled into the parking lot and braked. She rested her head on the steering wheel, still holding it with her hands at ten and two. She was about to lose one of her dearest friends, and the thought was overwhelming. More than a friend, really, Miss T had been a lodestar, a fixture in her life. Not so much a mother figure, as she was for Rachel, but a mentor. It was Miss T who had encouraged her to take the job at the newspaper when she was looking to increase the family income, pointing out that it was work she would find meaningful and absorbing, unlike the other options in Tinker's Cove such as housekeeping at an inn or waitressing. "Those are important jobs," Miss T had told her, "I believe all workers deserve respect, but you need intellectual challenges."

Lucy had shaken her head in denial. "After four kids, my brain is mush," she said, getting a quick retort from Miss T.

"Nonsense. I see the sort of books you borrow from the library, like that new biography of Emily Dickinson.

"I didn't finish that one," admitted Lucy ruefully. "But I sped through a couple of Jane Langton's and Dorothy Sayers's mysteries."

"Further evidence of your good taste,"

said Miss T.

Lucy smiled at the memory, acknowledging that Miss T had been right. She loved working at the *Pennysaver,* now renamed the *Courier* after her boss, Ted, bought the *Gilead Gabber* and combined the two weeklies into a county-wide paper, also adding an online daily edition. She still cherished the moment she saw her byline on the front page for the first time and realized she was getting paid for work she would gladly do for free. Not getting paid much, actually, but in those days every little bit helped.

And Miss T was right about something else. Lucy discovered she was particularly well-suited for journalism, it came quite naturally to her, and she had picked up numerous awards from the regional newspaper association. She'd also broken several stories that had been picked up by the Portland and Boston papers and TV news, even a few that had gone national, and her investigative reporting had uncovered and even solved local crimes. Miss T had given her confidence in her abilities at a time when she needed precisely that sort of encouragement, and as a result she had become a more authentic and happier person.

There was a tap on her car window and

Lucy jumped, then smiled, realizing it was Rachel. "I thought you were going to Bob's office," she said, after opening the window.

"I did, but he was getting ready to go to court, and I didn't want you to have to do this alone. Or me, for that matter," she added. "Are you ready?"

"No." Lucy sighed. "I was just thinking about how much Miss T means to me. She was the first person I got to know when we moved here and she's always been there for me with good advice, no matter what. I can't imagine life without her."

"I know," said Rachel, waiting as Lucy opened the door and stepped out. "And not just us, but the whole town. She's been a sort of moral conscience for the whole community, standing up for good old-fashioned values like honesty and charity and tolerance."

"She was active against domestic violence long before it ever became an issue, remember how she was part of that underground railroad that helped desperate women escape from their abusers?"

"I do indeed. And she always encouraged the high school kids, especially the girls, to raise their expectations and go on to college; she wrote endless reference letters."

"She had that junior librarian program,

my girls, Elizabeth, Sara and Zoe, were all part of it. They helped out with story hour and picked up all sorts of skills. Computers, the Dewey decimal system, people skills, why, they even became neater at home and tidied up their rooms after spending a few afternoons in the library!"

"She was the one who encouraged my Tim to apply to Harvard, we never thought he had a chance but they accepted him." Rachel sighed, somewhat regretfully. "The rest is history."

Lucy knew that Tim had become enamored of ancient Greek pottery at Harvard, a passion that led him to become an authority in the field. Although Rachel was terribly proud of her son, who was now affiliated with Oxford University, she was grieved that he spent most of his time at archaeological digs on the other side of the world.

"He's doing work he loves," said Lucy. "And he's invited you to come visit any time you want. You should go. Imagine all that gorgeous blue water and the white houses and the clear skies; I'd love to go to Greece."

"It's not like that, Lucy. Those digs are hot and dry and dusty. And endless. They scrape away for days and weeks and months and it's a big celebration if they find a teeny little shard of pottery."

The two women had reached the hospital door and Lucy suddenly understood that their discussion of Tim's career choice had been little more than an effort to distract themselves from what came next. Now it was time to face the awful truth that Miss Tilley was going to die, going to disappear from their lives and be no more. It was time to say good-bye.

The two friends reached for each other's hands and held tight as they advanced and the glass doors automatically opened for them. The hospital lobby was empty at this early morning hour, the turquoise and orange leatherette couches sat vacant and a housekeeper in gray scrubs was watering the ficus plants that stood in the corners. The vinyl floor gleamed in the shafts of morning sun, and the woman at the reception desk was sipping coffee from a paper cup. The elevators were waiting, just beyond the desk.

"Up we go," said Rachel, pushing the button on the wall. The doors slid open and they stepped inside for the brief ride up one floor.

Much too brief, thought Lucy, when the doors slid open. They stepped out and Rachel led the way past the nurses' station, where she was greeted with smiles as a frequent visitor, and down the long hallway to Miss Tilley's room. The door was closed.

Rachel stopped and turned to Lucy. "I don't want you to be shocked," she began. "It's like they say in the PBS costume dramas, when the returning relative comes for a final deathbed visit. 'I fear you'll find her very changed.' She's not the Miss T you remember. She's been sick for a long time, she's lost a lot of weight. There's all sorts of wires and tubes and beeping things."

"But she's conscious?" asked Lucy. "Will she know we're here?"

Rachel furrowed her brow. "Frankly, I think that's the worst part. She's only too aware of what's happening. It seems a cruel twist of fate, if you ask me, but it's her choice. They've offered her all sorts of sedatives, even morphine, but she wouldn't allow it. She says she wants to meet her creator with her faculties intact."

"I suppose she's got some issues with him she'd like to discuss," said Lucy. The words hung in the air for a moment, and then the two women burst into laughter.

"I'm sure she does," said Rachel, wiping her eyes. "And she's not going to mince words."

Then they knew it was time. They hugged each other, and Rachel pushed the door open. They stepped into the little entry area, continued past the bathroom, and turned the corner. The sight that greeted them was astonishing.

"Ha! You're here!" exclaimed a nightmarish creature, a spectral figure sitting bolt upright, with unkempt, wild hair. Her face was gray, her cheeks sunken beneath enormous blazing blue eyes. Withered skin dappled with brown age spots hung from her bony arms and her fingers were gnarled and twisted. The hospital johnny was much too large, it had slipped, revealing a jutting collarbone and sharp shoulder. A bank of machines were arrayed around her tiny figure, all with green and red flashing lights. Lucy stood speechless, trying to take it all in. Brief images of zombies she'd seen in ads for TV shows flashed through her mind. Had Miss Tilley become one of the living dead? Was that even possible?

"It's about time you showed up! Don't just stand there like a pair of idiots!" ordered Miss Tilley. "Get me the hell out of here!"

CHAPTER TWO

"You, you seem much improved," stammered Rachel, rushing to Miss Tilley's bedside and taking her hand. "How do you feel?"

"Just dandy and I want out of here, now!"

"We'll have to see what the doctor says," replied Rachel cautiously. "You've been very sick, you know."

Miss Tilley fixed her gaze on Lucy. "And what have you got to say for yourself?"

Lucy closed her mouth, which had been hanging open. "It's wonderful to see you looking so well. . . ."

"I don't look well. I look like hell and I know it. I've been flat on my back, tortured by these sadists for weeks. It's a miracle I survived."

"There, there," said a nurse, entering the room and pushing along a portable computer on a wheeled stand. "You are one of our success stories."

"Against your best efforts," muttered Miss Tilley as the nurse checked her temperature with a hand-held scanner, then turned away to enter it in the computer.

"Well, what is it?" demanded her patient.

"Ninety-eight."

"Hmpf." Miss Tilley snorted her approval, and Lucy and Rachel shared a bemused glance.

The nurse busied herself wrapping a blood pressure cuff around Miss Tilley's withered arm and began pumping it up. "Her fever broke in the night and she's been complaining nonstop ever since," she said, as the cuff began to deflate. "One-fifty over one-ten," she announced, in a rather disapproving tone. "We'll have to take a look at that."

"You should take a look at that breakfast tray," countered her patient. "That's something that deserves investigation."

"I see you didn't like the oatmeal," observed the nurse, lifting the plastic cover and peering at the gluey mass beneath.

"I had a bite of soggy toast, that was all I could manage."

"I see you drank the orange juice."

"Is that what it was?" Miss T patted the sheet covering her thighs. "I wasn't sure but I drank it anyway. And the coffee was truly

21

unspeakable."

The nurse approached with a little plastic jigger full of pills and much to Lucy's surprise, Miss Tilley obediently swallowed them. "There's a good girl," said the nurse, getting a murderous glare in response.

"She's terrible," said the nurse, smiling at Lucy and Rachel. "But we don't mind a bit. We like the fighters, they're the ones who get better." She turned to Miss Tilley. "I'll be back in a bit to check on you. And I don't want to see you getting out of bed. If you need something, just ring."

Miss T shrugged her bony shoulders and bared her yellowed teeth at the nurse in what was either a smile or a sneer, depending on one's interpretation. Then the nurse and her computer departed and a white-coated doctor marched in. She was a small, dark-haired woman with glasses and was peering at a computer notepad.

"So you are Julia, I suppose your friends call you Julie?" she began, in a brisk, heavily accented voice, not raising her eyes from the tiny computer. Lucy was trying to place the accent, possibly Indian, or perhaps Czech, and waiting with amusement for Miss Tilley's inevitable reaction.

"My friends are nearly all dead," snapped Miss Tilley. "Younger people properly ad-

22

dress me respectfully as Miss Tilley, and that" — she pointed a crooked finger at the doctor — "most definitely includes you."

"Ah, Julie," continued the doctor, ignoring her patient in favor of the computer notepad, "I see you have been quite ill but are now recovering."

"I've always had an iron constitution," insisted the patient, scowling at the doctor.

"Well, we are going to have to adjust your medications. . . ."

"I don't —"

"And you are going to need a couple of weeks of rehab before you go home."

"No. Not negotiable." Miss Tilley gave her head a little shake.

"We are already making the arrangements —"

"Absolutely not."

"Now, Julie," began the doctor, "you have been here in the hospital for, umm, let me see here . . ."

"Eight days."

"Umm. Yes. That's right." She glanced at Miss Tilley, recalibrating her original opinion. She took a deep breath and began again. "You are clearly a very intelligent, capable woman. . . ."

"I am. And I have an excellent helper." She pointed to Rachel. "My lovely young friend and companion, Rachel Goodman, who is also a trained home health aide."

"That is wonderful, Julie, you're very fortunate," agreed the doctor. "However, you are going to need physical and occupational therapy, and we also need to monitor that blood pressure of yours. It's clearly much higher than we like to see."

"I think the doctor is right," said Rachel, in a gentle, coaxing voice. "At this stage I think you need more care than I can realistically provide. I can't stay through the night, for example."

Miss Tilley bent her head, sulking like a schoolgirl who'd been caught copying her neighbor's answers.

"Well, that's settled," said the doctor briskly. "We will arrange a transfer to Heritage House as soon as a bed becomes available."

"When some poor old dear croaks is more like it," snapped Miss Tilley. "I know about those places, they're waiting rooms for the hereafter, that's what they are."

"For your information, Julie, Heritage House has a very high discharge rate," said the doctor. "People actually get better there and go home."

"I'll believe it when I walk through my front door," grumbled Miss Tilley. "And you can call me MISS TILLEY!"

"Take care, Julie," replied the doctor, who was already on her way out the door, eyes fixed on that computer notepad.

"Traitor!" hissed Miss Tilley, pointing a crooked finger at Rachel. *Et tu, Brute?"*

"If I remember my ancient history correctly, unlike the Ides of March when the Roman senators murdered Caesar, no blood has been shed here," countered Rachel placidly. "On the contrary, everybody is trying to help you get back on your feet and home to your own house." She paused. "Maybe it's time for you to adjust your attitude."

Lucy bit her tongue, amused and amazed by this exchange which revealed a twist in the power dynamic between the two women. In the past, Lucy had assumed that Miss Tilley was the boss, but now it seemed that Rachel was taking charge, as a mother might correct a difficult child.

Miss Tilley raised her head. "Of course, you're right." She sighed. "I forgot about the nights." She shook her head. "I never thought I'd be one of those sad pusses in the Old Ladies' Home, that's for sure."

"Heritage House is very nice, I think you'll be pleasantly surprised," offered Lucy. "I'm there a lot, covering events for

25

the paper, and I have to say I've been impressed. The staff is very caring, the activities director works hard and comes up with lots of clever ideas. It's really more like a four-star hotel than a nursing home."

"Not five-star?" inquired Miss Tilley with a raised eyebrow.

"I give up," laughed Rachel, picking up her bag. "I'll stay in touch, meanwhile, try to get some rest."

"I'll be back," promised Lucy, following Rachel toward the door, pausing to smile and give a little wave. "See you later, alligator."

"Not if I see you first," quipped Miss Tilley, stubbornly determined to remain her contrary self.

It was a week later to the day when Lucy went to Heritage House to visit her old friend. Miss Tilley had been moved a few days earlier and Lucy had wanted to give her time to settle in. It had been a couple of months since her last visit to the retirement facility and Lucy was surprised to see that there had been some changes.

The large entry foyer, decorated as a large living room, had been refreshed with a lovely Chinese-style wallpaper featuring flowering branches dotted with colorful birds, the huge brass chandelier had been replaced with sparkling crystal, and the wall-to-wall carpet was gone and the hardwood floor now sported a huge coral and blue Oriental rug. The couches and chairs had been re-covered in muted Regency stripes, with a scattering of jewel-toned cushions. Real plants, including a large arrangement of blooming orchids in a blue and white Canton bowl, brought a healthful dash of life and freshness to the room's atmosphere.

Lucy paused by the reception desk, which was empty, taking in all the carefully thought-out details: informational pamphlets in a basket rather than an institutional Lucite holder, a handwritten board on a gilt easel announcing the day's activities rather than an ugly bulletin board, a couple of wicker waste baskets rather than the former plastic bins. There was no sign of the receptionist at the French Country–style fruitwood desk, but a little group of three women came bustling in, trailed by a fourth who wasn't quite with the others and was dressed for the outdoors in a jacket and hiking boots. She wandered off to study the whiteboard listing the day's activities while the three, recognizing Lucy from earlier visits, quickly took charge of her.

"You're Lucy Stone, the reporter, aren't you?" asked the tiniest and most vivacious member of the group. She was barely five feet tall, had a carefully coiffed head of white hair and a broad, freshly lipsticked smile that matched her bright pink tracksuit. "I'm Bitsy, you interviewed me . . . dear me, when was it?"

"It was some time ago," said her friend, a rather tall, stern-looking woman with short, steel gray hair, dressed in a beige cardigan, checked shirt, and brown polyester pants.

"That's right, Dorothy," said the third member of the group, a chubby woman with a double chin and a pair of reading glasses on a string that rested on her ample, gingham-covered bosom. "It was at Christmas, I think."

"No, Bev. I was at my daughter's at Christmas, remember? I was gone all month because Susie had her knee replaced."

"It was in February, for Valentine's Day, remember?" said the fourth woman, who was now on her way to the door and had overheard the conversation. "You took pictures of us all, making Valentines for Vets," she offered.

"Oh, Agnes is right!" exclaimed Bev. "What a memory!"

"I suppose you're heading out to bird-watch?" asked Dorothy.

"Sure thing," said the woman, not missing a step. "I've heard there's a pink-footed goose out at Salt Bay."

"Well, good hunting," said Bitsy.

"Maybe I'll get a photo," said Agnes rather tartly.

"I didn't actually mean shooting the creature," retorted Bitsy, speaking to Agnes's departing back.

Dorothy deftly turned the conversation to the earlier topic. "It's so important to remember the veterans, especially the Greatest Generation, and now so many are fading away over at the VA hospital," offered Dorothy piously.

"You took a photo of the three of us," reported Bitsy, smiling happily. "It was in color, right on the front page. I liked it so much I bought a bunch of copies and sent them to my kids and grandkids. . . ."

"You could've just photographed the paper and emailed it," advised Dorothy.

"I never thought of that. Aren't you clever?" She turned to Lucy. "Isn't she amazing? She knows all about computers and things."

"It's a new world," offered Lucy, looking about for a rescuer and seeing the activities director, Felicity Corcoran, entering with an armful of papers.

"Ah, Lucy!" she called out merrily. "You've saved me a trip!"

"Super. Always happy to help."

"It's about our Easter bonnet contest, we have it every year," said Felicity, joining the group. She was a tall, capable-looking woman, who tended toward brightly colored sweaters, trim black slacks, and sensible shoes. She wore her hair in a neat pageboy and had a ready smile.

"I love the Easter parade!" declared Bitsy. "Everyone looks so lovely in their hats! Don't you wish women still wore hats? I remember as a little girl, we always had our hats and our white gloves when we went to church."

"I hated those gloves," recalled Dorothy.

"I had a boater with a big black ribbon, I loved it but the wind caught it and, well, no more hat," laughed Beverly.

"Now, now, ladies, it's lovely taking this little walk down memory lane, but I need to talk to our friend Lucy, and give her all the details." She fingered the pile of printed announcements she was holding. "And I know you don't want to miss the morning pick-me-up, today it's cranberry muffins and apple juice."

"Muffins!" declared Bitsy, leading the

charge to the elegant floating stairway that was such a feature of the room, and provided graceful access to the second floor where the activity and dining rooms were located.

"Honestly," whispered Felicity, "they're like children. Easily distracted, thank goodness."

"They're a cute little group," said Lucy. "I've met them before, they love seeing their pictures in the paper."

"Well, they'll be front and center at the Easter bonnet competition, believe me. It's cutthroat, mind you, because the winner not only gets her photo in the paper but there's also a giant chocolate bunny." Felicity grinned mischievously as she handed over one of the announcements. "Here's all the information. I hope you'll cover it. . . ."

"Wouldn't miss it for the world," promised Lucy. "Now, I've got a favor. I'm here to visit Miss Tilley, a new arrival. . . ."

"She's over in skilled nursing, you know the way?"

"Indeed I do," said Lucy, carefully tucking the announcement in her purse and heading for the bank of elevators.

When she found Miss Tilley's room up on the third floor, she was surprised to see the patient had a visitor: Howard White. Lucy knew Howard well, she had interviewed him extensively while covering an earlier story. He reminded her a bit of a rooster with his thick thatch of white hair, his stiff-legged strut, and his usual flock of admirers: Bitsy, Beverly, and Dorothy. The trio followed him constantly and Lucy was impressed that he'd managed to escape them to visit with Miss Tilley.

"Ah, Howard, I just saw your fan club downstairs," she said, smiling.

He gave her a rueful grin. "They are lovely ladies all, but sometimes it's nice to get away and visit an old friend like Julia."

"I've known Howard for years and years," said Miss Tilley. "I remember when he was fresh out of law school. . . ."

"And your father was the judge for my very first trial. They teach you a lot in law school but most of it is useless. Judge Tilley taught me the really important stuff, the way the law actually operates." He paused, thinking. "Our justice system has its flaws, for sure, but Judge Tilley was absolutely incorruptible."

"He was a stubborn old bird," said Miss Tilley. "I think of him as the last Victorian, and he expected me to be a proper Victorian maiden."

"He didn't encourage you to go to college?" asked Lucy.

"Oh, no. That was a battle royal."

"A battle you won," said Howard, "unlike mine. I lost most of my trials before Judge Tilley."

"Valuable learning experiences, nonetheless," said Lucy.

"Fortunately for me he moved on to the state's Supreme Court early in my career and I went on to be more successful with other judges and juries."

"Weak, lily-livered judges no doubt," said Miss Tilley, folding her hands in her lap.

"No doubt," agreed Howard, grinning from ear to ear.

"Well, I have to say you look much improved since I last saw you in the hospital," said Lucy, taking a seat. Miss Tilley's hair had been washed and styled, her cheeks were once again rosy, and she was wearing a lovely blue bed jacket that matched her bright eyes.

"I'm almost feeling like myself, but I will be glad to get home," she admitted.

"How's the food?" asked Lucy.

"Not up to Rachel's standard but quite good," she admitted. "And they do keep me busy with physical therapy."

"What about activities? I understand

there's going to be an Easter bonnet contest."

"I find I resent very much being treated like a child. That sort of thing is fine for kindergarten, but I am an intelligent woman not inclined to snip and glue and gossip."

Hearing this, Howard laughed heartily. "Some of the ladies take this contest very seriously," he said.

"Felicity told me it can be cutthroat," offered Lucy.

"Ah, well, it's the battle of the clans, or rather cliques," said Howard.

"Cliques? Like high school?" asked Lucy.

"Oh, you have no idea," said Miss Tilley. "Various representatives have been trying to recruit me. There are the popular girls who follow Howard around, the crafty ones who knit and sew and glue like crazy, and the card players."

"Always pestering me to be a fourth for bridge," confessed Howard, in the resigned tone of a man who had grown weary of his popularity.

"My goodness. I had no idea," said Lucy.

"It's quite a hierarchy, maybe more like a caste system. Pity the poor soul who sits at the wrong table at dinner," said Howard.

"I've been insulated here, I'm not considered ambulatory so they bring me my meals in my room. But I've heard that the loners have a hard time," said Miss Tilley.

"Loners?" asked Lucy.

"The poor dears whose faculties are slipping," said Howard, with a knowing nod. "It's probably because of fear, nobody likes to think they could be next, but those early Alzheimer's folks are shunned, they might as well have leprosy. And, of course, there are a few brave, independent souls like Julia here and one or two others who prefer to follow their own pursuits." He paused, and Lucy thought of the woman she'd seen following the group of three in the lobby, clearly separate from their tight little club.

"Which reminds me," he said, using his cane for assistance to stand up, "I think my *New York Times* may be downstairs, so I'll leave you two ladies to catch up."

"Save the crossword for me," asked Miss Tilley.

"It's yours," he said, turning to Lucy. "She's a demon, you know, she polishes it off in five minutes. Takes ten for the Sunday version." Then he nodded a courtly farewell and, using his cane, made his way to the door with his odd, birdlike gait.

"He's had knees *and* hips replaced," said Miss Tilley, when he'd left. Her tone of voice implied there was something dishonorable about the surgery, as if Howard had failed to keep his joints in working order, like someone who neglected to follow the recommended service schedule for a car.

"And how are your joints?" asked Lucy naughtily.

"Just fine," snapped Miss Tilley. "And I've got all my original teeth, too. Never even had a cavity."

Lucy chuckled. "I'm not surprised. I'd expect no less."

It was a week or so later, on a day when Lucy was scrambling to finish a complicated school budget story by deadline, when her phone rang. Thinking it was the school district's business manager returning her call, she snatched it up. "Hi!" she began. "Thank goodness. Is it a two percent raise, or does that figure include increased health insurance costs?"

"Uh, is this the *Courier*?" inquired the caller. "I'm trying to reach Lucy Stone."

Oops, thought Lucy, identifying herself, and hoping this call wouldn't take too much time. "I'm sorry. What can I do for you?"

"The thing is, I'm very worried about my mother," began the caller.

Not really my problem, thought Lucy, flipping through the budget packet. "Umm, maybe you should call Elder Services."

"Maybe I should. I don't really know what to do. The thing is, my mother has disappeared from Heritage House."

"Whuh?" asked Lucy, shoving the budget packet aside and focusing on the call. "What do you mean, she's disappeared?"

"She's vanished, disappeared, that's what's happened. I went to visit her like I always do on Wednesdays, we go out to lunch and do a bit of shopping, that sort of thing. Anyway, I got there right on time and she wasn't waiting for me in the lobby like she always does, so I went to her little apartment, and she wasn't there, either. I talked to her neighbors but didn't get any sense from them, and I went to the administration offices and nobody there knew anything about her. . . ."

"What did they say?" asked Lucy.

"Oh, that I shouldn't worry. She'd probably just forgotten I was coming and went out, they said she'd probably show up in time for dinner. And it's true, she does spend a lot of time outdoors, bird-watching, but she's never done anything like this before."

"Is she, uh, you know, mentally sharp?"

"Oh, yes. She's in her seventies, a young seventy. She's healthy and has her wits about her. I tried calling her, she has a cell phone, you know, but she didn't answer and that's when I began to worry."

"Well, this sounds more like a matter for the police. . . ." said Lucy.

"I tried them but they said she has to be missing for twenty-four hours before they can do anything."

"Well, I'm not sure what I can do," said Lucy, fingering the budget packet.

"You're an investigative reporter, aren't you?"

"That may be a bit of an exaggeration. . . ."

"Well, you could put something on the website, right?" The voice was frustrated. "With a photo maybe? Ask if anyone's seen her?"

"I guess I could do that," admitted Lucy. "So tell me: What's your name?"

"I'm Geri. Geri Mazzone. And my mother is Agnes Neal, age seventy-one, five feet six, weighs a hundred forty pounds or thereabouts. She's got short gray hair, brown eyes, drives a Mini Cooper."

"Is the car there? At Heritage House?"

"Yeah. It's there, in her assigned spot."

"Can you send me a photo of her? A nice, clear headshot would be best."

"No problem. I'll do it right away."

"I'll post a notice as soon as I get the photo," promised Lucy.

"Thanks. Thanks so much. I really appreciate it. And Lucy, if she doesn't turn up, you'll keep at it, won't you? I really think there's something weird going on at Heritage House."

Lucy glanced at the budget packet, with its blue cover and fifty-seven pages of finely printed columns of numbers. It sat on her desk, seeming to reproach her, as the clock on the wall above her head ticked toward the noon deadline.

"Okay, okay. I'll do what I can," agreed Lucy, desperate to end the call. "I'm on deadline right now, but give me your number, just in case."

"Oh, thanks," sighed Geri, rattling off the number. "I can't tell you —"

"I'm sorry, but I really have to go." Lucy hung up and immediately called the business manager, mindful of Ted's frequently expressed admonition: "It's not a guideline, it's a deadline."

CHAPTER THREE

After she'd spoken to the business manager, who gave her the information she needed, she quickly finished up the school budget story. With ten minutes to go before the noon deadline for the print edition, she opened up the photo file Geri Mazzone had sent her.

Agnes Neal's direct gaze looked right at her out of the monitor screen; her face was that of a confident, self-assured, mature woman. Not beautiful, but undeniably attractive, a face that radiated confidence and self-assurance. Self-worth. A face that said, *I am powerful, I am a serious person, do not underestimate me.* It was also, Lucy realized, the face of the woman she'd seen at Heritage House when she visited there a week ago. Agnes Neal was the woman she'd seen trailing Bitsy, Bev, and Dorothy, the three women she thought of as Howard White's fan club. She was the woman who she'd thought at first was with the group, but wasn't. She had soon realized that Agnes simply exchanged a few words with them while passing through the room, on her way to spot a pink-footed goose.

She wrote up the brief announcement as she'd promised Geri, and sent it to Ted, her editor, who was working out of the Gilead office. Then she stood up and started to gather up her things, preparing to leave.

"Done for the day?" asked Phyllis, the receptionist who also handled the events listings and the classified ads.

"It's noon," said Lucy.

Phyllis looked up at the clock, peering over the reading glasses that were perched on her nose. "Already? My word. Where does the time go?" She dressed according to the season and today was celebrating the coming of spring with a bright green sweatshirt printed with flowers. Her hair was dyed pink, to match her pull-on pants. Even her duck boots, a necessity this time of year, were printed with pink and yellow flowers.

"It goes, it just goes," said Lucy, who had a lot of errands she planned to cross off her to-do list this afternoon. She leaned over her chair to shut down her computer, which was still displaying Agnes Neal's face. She paused, her hand poised above the mouse.

"Do you know this woman?" she asked, tilting the screen so Phyllis could see it. "Have you seen her?"

Phyllis shook her head. "No. Can't say I have. Who is she?"

"Her name's Agnes Neal. Her daughter says she's disappeared from Heritage House."

Phyllis shook her head. "Poor old dear, probably Alzheimer's. They do tend to wander off."

"No. Not Agnes, not according to her daughter. She's sharp."

"Denial is not a river in Egypt," observed Phyllis skeptically.

"I promised the daughter, Geri Mazzone's her name, that I'd look into it. She sent me a photo and I wrote up a brief announcement that I sent to Ted."

"Well, he'll run it in the paper and the online edition, too. What more can you do?"

Lucy thought of the oil change, the dry cleaning, the package to her grandson in Alaska waiting to be mailed, and the shopping she'd planned to do. She sighed and sat back down at her desk, reaching for her phone. It wouldn't hurt to make just a few phone calls, she decided. How long could it take? So she dialed Heritage House and asked to speak to the nursing supervisor,

Elvira Hostens, whom she'd profiled for the "Good Neighbors" column a few weeks earlier. She'd been impressed then by Elvira's professionalism; in her mind's eye she pictured Elvira in a starched white uniform and nurse's cap despite the fact she had actually been wearing a light gray turtleneck sweater and tailored black pants.

"Hi, Lucy!" Elvira's voice was surprisingly warm and friendly when she answered the call. "People are still congratulating me on that story you wrote. Felicity posted it on the bulletin board and the residents think I'm some sort of celebrity."

"I guess you've beat the average fifteen minutes of fame."

"Thanks to you, Lucy. So what can I do for you?"

"I hope you can help me. Geri Mazzone called, she's worried about her mother, Agnes Neal, who she says has disappeared from Heritage House. She's asked me to run a photo in the paper —"

Elvira cut her off, alarmed, and her voice was no longer warm and fuzzy but had grown sharp. "Are you going to do that? Run the photo?"

"Well, yeah. If my editor has space it will be in tomorrow's edition. And it's probably already online."

43

"You should have checked with me first," said Elvira, scolding Lucy. "Agnes is an independent woman, she's free to come and go as she wishes. She's probably just gone to visit a friend and didn't bother to tell her daughter."

"But doesn't Heritage House have a certain responsibility to keep track of the residents?"

"That depends on the level of care the resident is receiving. Agnes is in the senior living section, in her own apartment. We offer housecleaning services, optional gourmet meals, and a menu of activities for those who choose to participate. The residents are mostly single women who don't want to be bothered with lawn mowing and house maintenance and enjoy the twenty-four-hour security we provide. It's carefree living," she added, which happened to be the promise that appeared in the ad Heritage House ran in the *Courier* every week.

"You should be in the sales department," observed Lucy.

"Well, it happens to be true," countered Elvira. "As nursing supervisor I am responsible for the other two levels of accommodation we provide, assisted living and skilled nursing. The folks in those sections require varying levels of assistance, ranging from meal preparation and supervision of medications all the way on up to skilled rehab or sadly, end-of-life care."

"And Agnes doesn't require any of those services?"

"No. Most definitely not, as she would be the first to tell you." Elvira paused. "A funny thing happens, sometimes, with daughters. When their moms get older, the daughters start behaving like their mothers' mother. The roles get reversed. I think that's what's happened with Geri, and I suspect that Agnes doesn't like it. She probably feels her daughter is too controlling and interferes in her life."

"So the mom becomes like a rebellious teenage daughter," said Lucy, thinking of Elizabeth, Sara, and Zoe and how they resisted parental control as they struggled to establish their own identities and separate lives. Elizabeth had gone so far as to move to Paris, where she worked as a concierge in a fancy hotel. Sara was now living in Boston, working at the Museum of Science, and Zoe was still trying her wings from the safety of the family nest as she finished up her bachelor's degree and began job-hunting.

"We have a saying here we use when we train staff: 'The older they get, the younger they get.' We don't want staff to treat them like children, but they need to adjust their expectations and react accordingly. Some residents might need little reminders about meals and meds, but it needs to be done tactfully; others just need a friendly smile."

"And Agnes is in the friendly smile category?" asked Lucy.

"At most. Agnes is fiercely independent and always on the move." Elvira sounded as if she didn't quite approve of Agnes's attitude. "It's like that song, she insists on doing things her way and she doesn't appreciate any attempts to limit her freedom. She's perfectly able to care for herself, and she'd be the first to tell you."

"Well, I'm sure she'll turn up then," said Lucy, "and we'll be sure to print an update."

"Good. I'll be looking for it."

Lucy hung up, not quite as confident as Elvira that Agnes Neal was simply enjoying her right to life, liberty, and the pursuit of happiness. Perhaps Elvira should be looking for Agnes instead of a correction in the paper, maybe casually chatting up staff and residents who might have seen her leave. But Lucy suspected she was looking at the situation through her mom-glasses, the attitude that began to color her thinking the moment her first baby, Toby, was placed in her arms. That overwhelming sense that from now on she was responsible for this precious, tiny life, and which continued to this day even though Toby was an established professional, a married man, and the father of her adored grandson, Patrick.

She reached for her purse and tossed her phone in, preparing to leave, but then had a second thought and pulled it out. She punched in the number she knew by heart, the Tinker's Cove Police Department, and asked for Officer Sally Kirwan. Officer Sally was the newest member of the force and a member of the Kirwan clan that filled many positions in the fire and police departments and was making inroads into other town departments. As the only female in the department, she was expected to handle matters that weren't necessarily criminal but involved mental health and family issues.

She was also one of the few officers who maintained friendly relations with the media and could be counted on for a comment and even inside information, strictly off the record. Today was no different, she answered Lucy's call with a cheerful "What can I do for you?"

"Well, I had a call from Geri Mazzone. . . ."

"I know, she told me. She called here, too.

Her mother is missing from Heritage House."

So Geri was covering all the bases, thought Lucy. "So are you taking her seriously? Are you looking for Agnes?"

"Not officially, but all units have been notified to keep an eye out, if you know what I mean."

"Why not officially?" asked Lucy.

"Well, you know we have to wait twenty-four hours before opening a missing person case."

"Even for an elderly person like Agnes?"

"That's why it's unofficial," explained Sally. "We're a small-town department, we know most everyone in town, and if we see her we can tell her that her daughter is looking for her. That sort of thing. But we can't start checking out phone and credit card records, that would be an invasion of privacy."

"I see," said Lucy. "So has she been spotted?"

"Not so far, but remember, she's an adult and is free to come and go as she likes. I understand why her daughter is concerned, but I'm confident Agnes will turn up in time for dinner and wonder what the fuss was all about."

"I hope so. Let me know if she does, okay?"

"Will do. Have a nice day, Lucy."

Lucy had spent a busy afternoon crossing errands off her to-do list and was on her way to the IGA to do her weekly grocery shopping when her phone rang; she couldn't use it while she was driving but as soon as she arrived at the store and parked she dug it out of her purse. There was a voice mail requesting a call from Geri Mazzone and, hoping for good news, she returned the call.

The moment she heard Geri's voice, however, she knew there was no good news. "I'm just wondering if you've turned up anything," she asked.

"No. I spoke to Sally Kirwan at the police department but she said it's too soon to open a missing person case but that all the officers have been given your mother's photo and will keep their eyes open."

"Yeah, that's what she told me, too." Geri didn't sound very hopeful.

"And I spoke to Elvira Hostens at Heritage House —"

"That woman is useless," declared Geri, cutting her off. "She's a lot more interested in covering her ass, pardon my French, and protecting Heritage House."

"Well, I'm sure liability is a big issue for them."

"It should be! That place is not as wonderful as they'd like everyone to think."

"What do you mean?" asked Lucy, who knew Heritage House had an absolutely sterling reputation.

"Well, for one thing," began Geri, "they're really short-staffed and there's an awful lot of turnover. Mom said she never knew who was going to turn up to clean her unit, weekly housekeeping is supposed to be part of the deal, but she said sometimes all she got was about fifteen minutes, nothing more than a quick lick and a polish she called it." Geri lowered her voice. "And she started hiding her valuables because a ring she left in a little dish on her dresser disappeared."

"Did she report it?"

"No, and that's what bothered me most. She said she didn't want to make a fuss. It wasn't worth it. It wasn't even valuable, just a trinket she picked up in her travels."

Lucy was puzzled. "Why on earth not report it? I'm sure the management would want to know if they had a dishonest employee who was stealing from residents."

"She seemed to feel there'd be repercussions, that they'd get back at her."

"Who's they?" asked Lucy. "The staff, or

the management?"

"I don't know," admitted Geri. "When I pressed her about it she brushed it off. Nothing she couldn't handle, that's what she said. And I know she felt kind of alienated there. I was hoping she'd make some friends, have a social life, but she said the other residents were either gaga or stuck up."

Lucy chuckled, thinking of Howard's description of the various cliques. "I guess that's par for the course in those places."

"She didn't mind, she's very independent, and she didn't want to be bothered with what she called 'domestic trivia.' She just wanted a roof over her head, she didn't want to have to think about it. . . ." Geri's voice caught and Lucy heard her sniffling. "That's the thing, Lucy. It's getting late, it'll be dark soon, and Mom's never been gone like this. Where could she be?"

Geri's question was still in Lucy's mind the next morning when she went to her usual Thursday morning breakfast with her friends at Jake's Donut Shack. The four women, Sue Finch, Rachel Goodman, Pam Stillings, and Lucy, began their weekly gathering when their kids grew older and they no longer encountered one another at sports practices and school events. The

51

breakfast had soon become a fixture in their lives, offering a regular dose of friendship, advice, and emotional support.

Lucy called out a hello to Jake's veteran waitress, Norine, and headed for the usual table in the corner where her three friends were already sitting and sipping coffee. She'd no sooner joined them when Norine arrived with a fresh pot to fill her mug and top off the others. "Usual all round?" inquired Norine, getting nods from them all.

"Just black coffee for me," said Sue, quite unnecessarily, teasing Norine, who disapproved of her stubborn refusal to order anything more.

"A donut, a piece of toast wouldn't kill you," muttered Norine, unable to resist rising to Sue's bait.

"She's right, you know," offered Pam, watching Norine stomp off to the kitchen. "Black coffee and white wine is not a terribly healthy diet."

Lucy and Rachel shared a glance, acknowledging that Pam was venturing into dangerous territory. Sue, however, remained unruffled. "I take my multivitamin every day," she said, tucking a lock of glossy black hair behind her ear with a perfectly manicured hand. She shrugged. "I'm a medical marvel, according to my doctor."

Then Rachel jumped in and quickly changed the subject. "I have news about Miss Tilley. It seems she's the medical marvel, they say she's recovering more quickly than expected and will soon no longer require skilled nursing care. Just to be on the safe side, however, they're suggesting she move into assisted living for a few weeks before going home."

"How does that work?" asked Lucy. "I thought those assisted living units were unfurnished, so people could bring their own bits and pieces."

"They have several furnished units, for temporary stays," said Rachel. "I saw one and it's very nice. Really quite luxurious."

"It's all about the money," insisted Pam. "Medicare covers her rehab, but they don't pay much. I bet she'll have to pay an arm and a leg for this assisted living."

"No. I was there when she spoke with the social worker," said Rachel. "It's quite reasonable and she can easily afford it."

"Probably a sales gimmick, like those cheap stays they offer at time-shares," said Sue, who had taken advantage of several such invitations at luxury resorts and bragged about her ability to resist the required sixty minutes of strong-arm sales tactics in order to enjoy three nights and four days of five-star pampering at bargain rates.

"I hadn't thought of that," confessed Rachel, furrowing her brow. "They're trying to get her to move in, to stay permanently."

"I wouldn't worry," said Lucy, covering Rachel's hand with her own. "Miss Tilley loves her little house, and she loves you. I'm sure she wants to get home as soon as possible."

"I don't know," fretted Rachel. "They have a fancy chef and twenty-four-hour security and panic buttons in every room in case there's an emergency. . . ." Her voice trailed off as Norine arrived with a heavily laden tray.

"Here we go," declared Norine, thumping down hash and eggs for Lucy, a sunshine muffin for Rachel, and a granola-yogurt parfait for Pam. "I'll be back with more coffee, madame," she added, glaring at Sue, before tucking the empty tray under her arm and marching off.

"I love helping Miss T," continued Rachel, breaking off a bit of muffin. "I really do, but I can't compete with Heritage House. I can't help but think she'd be better off there."

Lucy thought of Geri's concerns for her

mother and shook her head. "No, Rachel, that's not true." She picked up a toast triangle and poked an egg yolk, breaking it. "Definitely not. The sooner she's home, the better."

CHAPTER FOUR

That sense of possibility dissipated when she arrived at the *Courier* office and Phyllis handed her a press release from the Tinker's Cove PD. Chief Jim Kirwan announced that he was putting out an APB and initiating a search for Agnes Neal, who had now been missing for more than the required twenty-four hours. "A housekeeper at Heritage House reports seeing Agnes Neal at six a.m. Tuesday. The employee noted she was wearing binoculars and assumed she was going out to bird-watch, which she did most mornings. Because of that we are concentrating our search in the Audubon sanctuary and other conservation areas including the Salt Bay Reserve. Interested citizens are encouraged to join the search for Agnes Neal, age seventy-one, with short gray hair and brown eyes. When last seen she was wearing a blue windbreaker, a brown cap, khaki pants, and duck boots. If seen, immediately contact the department by text or phone."

"I'll post this immediately on the website as breaking news," said Lucy. "Did we get any response to the photo I posted yesterday?"

"Only that housekeeper," said Phyllis. "I told her to call the cops but she didn't want to do that, probably worried about immigration or something. She gave me the information and I called it in."

"We make a good team," said Lucy, beaming at Phyllis. "If I hadn't believed Geri and insisted on running the photo the housekeeper never would have called, and if you hadn't forwarded her message the police wouldn't have the time she was last seen or that complete description. I bet there were other bird-watchers out there yesterday who must have seen her. They're a pretty chummy group."

"I thought bird-watchers were kind of competitive," said Phyllis.

"When I've seen them they tend to flock together," said Lucy, getting a groan from Phyllis. "But even if they're competing with each other to be the first to spot a red-bellied woodpecker they're observant and would have noticed Agnes."

Lucy's words turned out to be prophetic

as no sooner had the official police announcement of Agnes Neal's disappearance gone online than reports of sightings started to come in. "I saw a gray-haired woman in a blue jacket walking along Shore Road." "A woman with khaki pants and a windbreaker — I'm pretty sure it was blue — anyway, I saw her going into the library." "There was a gray-haired lady exiting the IGA just ahead of me, she had duck boots and a blue jacket, no cap but she did have a brown scarf. Do you think that's what they meant?"

"Wow," observed Lucy, as she forwarded the reported sightings to the police department. "It seems that Agnes really got around."

"I doubt any of those sightings will actually pan out," said Phyllis. "There are a lot of older, gray-haired women in this town, and it's spring which means every one of them is probably wearing a windbreaker, and I bet most of them are blue." She paused to pat her hair, which today was dyed neon green in honor of the spring that everyone believed was coming but hadn't actually arrived in coastal Maine. "Golly, I even have one."

"You do?" This was a surprise to Lucy, who couldn't remember ever seeing the flamboyant Phyllis in anything as boring as a blue windbreaker.

"I do. It's really old and I wear it to take out the garbage, that sort of thing." She fingered the zebra-striped reading glasses that perched on her ample bosom, held by a diamanté chain. "But mostly, as you know, I prefer more colorful, unique clothes."

Lucy smiled. "Well, today you've outdone yourself, what with the bright pink track suit and your electric green hair, and I especially like your purple sneakers."

"I do what I can," admitted Phyllis. "I hope I sort of cheer people up when they see me, and I'm pretty sure they remember me. If you're a woman of a certain age and go around with gray hair and neutral clothes you look like everyone else in this town and you become invisible. Now if Agnes had worn a fire-engine-red jacket and sunshine-yellow pants with a big old sunflower pinned to her hat, well, she'd be found by now."

"Point taken, though I suspect she dresses rather conservatively so as not to frighten the birds," countered Lucy, forwarding five more suspected sightings of gray-haired women in windbreakers to the police department.

Hearing the little bell on the door jangle she looked up and saw Ted Stillings coming in, wearing his usual barn coat and a faded red L. Brackett & Son cap over his gray hair. Ted was the editor, publisher, and chief reporter for the *Courier,* and was also married to her friend Pam. He maintained a desk in the Tinker's Cove office, the antique rolltop he'd inherited from his grandfather, a noted regional journalist whose folksy columns had won a national readership, but Ted only popped in occasionally these days. He spent most of his work week over in the neighboring town of Gilead, now that the two weeklies had been combined under the *Courier* masthead. Daily postings to the online edition were now Lucy's responsibility. She didn't actually appreciate the extra work and constant pressure; she missed the old days when she only had one deadline, at noon on Wednesday.

"Good morning, ladies," he greeted them in a cheery voice. "You're looking very festive today, Phyllis."

"She's aiming for memorable," offered Lucy. "She doesn't want to be invisible."

"And I certainly don't want to be patronized," snapped Phyllis. " 'Ladies'? What do you think this is? A bridge party?"

"Uh, no," said Ted, looking puzzled. "Lucy, great work on that disappeared old la — um, that disappeared woman, Ms.

Neal, I believe," he continued, changing tack. "Thanks to you we had that alert ahead of everybody. Has there been any response?"

"Only one definite sighting which was the call Phyllis took from the housekeeper yesterday," said Lucy, determined to share the credit. "Phyllis immediately sent the info to the police. We're getting lots of reports of sightings this morning, which we've also forwarded to the police, but it's doubtful that any of them are actually Agnes Neal. That's what Phyllis and I were discussing, the way women after a certain age start to look alike. Agnes Neal's description fits most of the women in this town over fifty, which is actually most of the women in this town."

"We're invisible," claimed Phyllis. "That's why I dress the way I do. I don't want to blend into the woodwork."

"There's no chance of that," agreed Ted, smiling. He took off his barn jacket and hung it on the coat stand, added his hat, and then seated himself at his desk and swiveled his chair around to face Lucy and Phyllis. "So, what's on the news budget this week?"

"The library is starting a weekly lecture series on Sunday afternoons," offered Phyllis, who handled the events listings. "That might be worth a preview story to let people know it's coming. And there's the annual Easter bonnet contest at Heritage House."

"I already got a press release from Felicity Corcoran," said Lucy.

"We can run some photos from previous years to announce it, sort of a seasonal photo essay," suggested Ted. "And, of course, Lucy will cover the big event and we'll put the winner's photo on the front page." He jotted down a reminder in his computer notebook. "What else have you got, Lucy?"

"Well," she began, taking a deep breath. "Geri Mazzone, you know, Agnes Neal's daughter, she alleges that Heritage House isn't living up to its reputation. She says there's a lot of staff turnover, which leaves the place understaffed, and that leads to accidents and negligence. I think it's worth looking into, especially after Agnes's disappearance."

"You want to investigate Heritage House?" asked Ted, somewhat incredulously. "Is that what I'm hearing?"

"Well, yeah."

Ted shook his head in disbelief. "Absolutely not, Lucy. That place has an absolutely sterling reputation and, just in case you hadn't noticed, they run a full-page ad every week in the *Courier.* They pay on time, too, and I'm certainly not going to endanger that important revenue stream."

"Ethics, Ted?" inquired Phyllis. "Aren't news and ads supposed to be separate departments?"

Ted snorted. "That was then, this is now. Haven't you noticed that when your *women's*" — he paused to make air quotes — "women's magazines print an article about the healthful benefits of yogurt, there's a yogurt ad on the opposite page?"

" 'I've noticed," volunteered Lucy, "and I don't like it."

"Neither do I," agreed Phyllis.

"Nor I," added Ted, "but that's the world we live in — so get used to it." He sighed and stared at the screen on his notebook. "I see we've got the usual selectmen's meeting, and also a school board meeting on the agenda. Can you cover them, Lucy?"

"Sure," agreed Lucy with a nod, but as soon as Ted left she turned to her PC and found the state department of health's website and began looking for the section on nursing home inspections and complaint investigations. Her research revealed that there were no perfect nursing homes in the state; even the ones with the highest ratings had violations and complaints and Heritage House was no exception. The violations cited were minor, mostly involving missing documentation. Even more troubling, however, was the tale the statistics revealed about the department itself, which often postponed scheduled inspections and didn't provide information about following up on violations or resolving complaints. Determined to get more information than the website provided, Lucy called the hotline number provided and was told her call was very important and wait time was fifty-six minutes.

Typical, she thought, deciding to try calling again earlier in the day, when there was a chance she'd beat the midmorning rush. Meanwhile, she had plenty to do, starting with setting up an interview with the head librarian. The day passed quickly and Lucy was surprised when she noticed Phyllis getting ready to leave. "Is it five already?" she asked.

"Past," said Phyllis. "Almost five-thirty. I wanted to finish cleaning up the classifieds."

"Golly, where does the time go?"

"Time flies when you're having fun," said Phyllis, shrugging into the purple faux shearling jacket that matched her sneakers. "See you tomorrow."

"Right," agreed Lucy, shutting down her computer. She put on her own jacket, a lightweight puffy parka, flicked off the lights, and locked the door behind her. When she looked for her car in its usual spot and didn't find it, she remembered she'd left it at the lot behind Jake's and headed down the street. It was still light, thanks to daylight savings, but the day was fading and she enjoyed walking past the old-fashioned storefronts that made Tinker's Cove one of the prettiest towns in Maine. She paused at Harborside Gifts to admire the handmade pottery in the window, then continued on past the hardware store where snow shovels were on clearance, and cast a speculative eye at the designer clothes on display at Carriage Trade, which had an END OF SEASON SALE banner on the door. Maybe, just maybe, she could afford something. A new sweater perhaps, or a pair of flattering designer jeans. She was about to go in and investigate further when she realized the store was closed for the day.

Nearing Jake's, her thoughts turned to dinner, and what to have. There was half of a lasagna, left over from Tuesday, and also beef stew from Wednesday. She decided to go with the lasagna, rather than have the stew two nights in a row, and popped into

65

the bakery to buy a loaf of Italian bread. Then, realizing time was getting away from her, she hurried on to the parking lot.

When she arrived home at the antique farmhouse on Red Top Road, she found her youngest daughter, Zoe, sitting at the kitchen table poring over a stack of printouts.

"That's very low-tech," she observed, hanging her parka on one of the hooks by the kitchen door. Libby, the family's elderly black Lab, no longer bothered to get up to greet her, but did offer a few tail thumps from her comfy doggy bed.

"Tell me about it. They're printouts from the college's career development office." Zoe was finishing up her bachelor's degree at nearby Winchester College and was looking for a job.

"Anything interesting?" asked Lucy, going straight to the fridge and pulling out the lasagna pan, which she shoved into the oven, setting it at three-fifty. Then she poured herself a glass of wine and started making a salad.

"I've called a few places but the jobs are already filled, which is discouraging," admitted Zoe. "Leanne and I really want to have jobs before we start apartment hunting, but there's a lot of competition out there from other graduates."

"Are you and Leanne still both committed to moving to Portland right after graduation?" asked Lucy, naming Zoe's best friend. "You know you could get summer jobs here in town and save your money. Then you could look in the fall, that's when employers really get serious about hiring."

"We don't want to hang around here waiting to get started on real life," said Zoe, as her phone started playing the loud rap song that served as her ringtone.

Lucy busied herself with chopping some cucumber for the salad, pretending not to listen. She couldn't gather much from Zoe's side of the call, anyway, which was mostly a series of um-hmms and yeahs. She was thinking she would really have to coach that girl about professional phone etiquette when Zoe slapped down the phone and let out a joyous whoop.

"Did you win the lottery?" asked Lucy.

"Almost." Zoe was beaming. "I got an interview with the Sea Dogs."

Lucy knew the Sea Dogs, who had a stadium right next to the highway in Portland, were an AA affiliate of the Boston Red Sox.

"And what would you do for the Sea Dogs? Sell hot dogs?"

"No, Mom. They have a huge PR program. They do a lot of advertising, they have special events and promos, it's a dream job."

"Year-round?"

"Yeah, full-time, year-round, terrific benefits." Zoe sighed dramatically. "There is one drawback, though."

"Oh, what's that?" asked Lucy.

"The guys. So many cute guys," she said, adopting a fake regretful tone, "but they're only there for the season."

Lucy smiled, slicing into a radish. "So you want to be a baseball wife? You're not even blond."

"Who wants to be a wife?" countered Zoe. "I just want to have fun."

"Well," began Lucy, thumping the celery down on the counter and ripping off a couple of stalks, "you've got to get the job first."

CHAPTER FIVE

Ted's carefully crafted news budget, and Lucy's plans to research conditions at Heritage House, as well as the police search for Agnes were all victims of breaking news on Friday when a helicopter carrying famous hi-tech billionaire Josh Hartman crashed into the sea near Quissett Point, the rocky peninsula that sheltered the town harbor. Lucy spent the entire day out on the point, watching the massive rescue attempt involving everyone from the US Coast Guard down to the local harbormaster. Bits of wreckage were spotted floating in the distance, and rescuers plied the water and air searching for survivors but none were found. Rescue eventually became recovery and the crowd of national and local reporters disbanded, seeking warmth and a hot meal. Lucy headed home, where she went straight into a hot shower, then tucked herself in bed and cranked the electric blanket up to maximum. She was still shivering when Bill brought her a bowl of steaming chowder and a hot toddy.

"It wouldn't have been so bad if I'd been dressed for it," said Lucy, sipping the hot drink. "I didn't expect to be outside all day, and once I was there I didn't dare leave for fear of missing something."

"They closed off the road to the lighthouse, they wouldn't have let you back," said Bill, sitting on the side of the bed and rubbing her legs. "I tried to bring you warm clothes but they wouldn't let me through."

"Thanks for trying," said Lucy, spooning up some chowder with a shaky hand. "Any news about Josh Hartman?"

"Nope." Bill shook his head. "You could say he was a victim of his own success. If he wasn't the richest man in the world, and wasn't flying around in a helicopter, he might still be alive instead of somewhere down in Davy Jones's locker."

"There were other people, too," said Lucy. "The pilot and a group of company hotshots. They were supposedly looking at possible sites for a new company headquarters."

"They must've flown too close to the sun," said Bill philosophically, stroking his beard.

"So true. It's better to be poor," offered Lucy, "with both feet on the ground."

"You said it." Bill stood up. "When you warm up, do you think you'll come down? Do you want me to save some dinner for you?"

Lucy yawned. "I think I'll finish this and have a little nap."

He smiled and kissed the top of her head. "Sleep tight."

When Lucy woke up the tray was gone and the bedside clock read five o'clock, which meant she'd slept for an incredible ten hours. It was definitely time to get up, with a much-needed stop in the luxurious en suite bath Bill had installed when he renovated their master bedroom, turning it into a genuine master suite.

Much relieved, Lucy headed downstairs to start the coffeepot but was surprised to discover Zoe was already up and pouring herself a cup. "My goodness, you're up early," said Lucy.

"Don't you remember? I'm going on a spring ski trip with the college ski club."

"Right," said Lucy, who dimly remembered something of the sort. She filled a mug for herself and sat down at the golden oak kitchen table. "Are you sure about this? Don't you have that Sea Dogs interview on Monday?"

"Yeah. It's in the afternoon. I'll have

plenty of time to get there."

"Don't you want to prepare?" Lucy took a long swallow of coffee. "Research the team, study their present PR effort . . . you should praise it but offer some constructive new ideas." Another swig of coffee went down and Lucy was shifting into high gear. "You know what would be really valuable? Do some practice interviews. I could come up with some typical interview questions. You know, like where do you see yourself in five years? That sort of thing."

"Five years!" Zoe laughed. "I haven't got a clue about this summer!"

"Well, maybe you should give it some thought," said Lucy, sensing she wasn't making any headway with her daughter, who was already zipping up her ski pants.

"You know what I have been thinking about? Maybe you and Dad could give me an airplane ticket to Paris for a graduation present? It would be a nice break before I start working and I could stay with Elizabeth, she could show me around. . . ."

Lucy wasn't convinced that her oldest daughter, Elizabeth, who lived in Paris and worked as a concierge at the tony Cavendish Hotel, would actually welcome a visit from her younger sibling. Furthermore, she wasn't at all sure the family checking account was going to cover the mortgage payment this month, much less stretch to an expensive plane ticket. "We'll see," she said, employing the reliable parental response that had become automatic.

"See you later," said Zoe, hoisting her skis over her shoulder and opening the door, letting in a gust of cold air. "Brrr," she said, shivering. "I don't think the weather got the memo, it's supposed to be delightfully mild on the slopes."

"Not too late to change your mind," said Lucy, but Zoe was already gone and Lucy's phone was already announcing a call. It was Ted, sending her back out to Quissett Point. This time she was going to dress for the weather, and bring along a thermos of hot soup.

On Monday morning, Lucy again watched her daughter depart, this time heading to Portland for the job interview. Zoe had only returned home five hours before; Lucy's bedside clock read two-fifteen when she was wakened by Zoe thumping around in the kitchen. So much for her motherly admonition to be sure to get a good night's sleep before her interview, she thought, rolling onto her other side and pulling the covers tighter around her shoulders. Zoe, however, was bright as a button and dressed for success at seven a.m., while Lucy was still groggy when she started on her second cup of coffee. "Good luck," she said, when Zoe waved good-bye, thinking that her carefree daughter would need a lot more than luck to land the job.

The helicopter crash was still dominating the radio news when Lucy drove to work, dressed once again in thermal underwear. She learned with a sense of relief that the helicopter had been recovered, along with the bodies of Josh Hartman and the other occupants still strapped into their seats, which meant she would not have to spend another day freezing out on Quissett Point. Hartman himself was lauded as a technology pioneer, a philanthropist, and a visionary CEO, information that she could use to write up an obit while roasting in her long underwear in the toasty office. Listening to the accolades, she thought briefly of Agnes Neal but assumed she had most likely returned to Heritage House, safe and sound and wondering why anyone had been worried about her. But when she got to the office, Phyllis told her that Ted wanted her to go straight to Blueberry Pond where the police were dragging the icy water for Agnes's body.

"She's still missing?" asked a very surprised Lucy. "How come it wasn't on the news?"

"It's all Josh Hartman, all the time," said Phyllis. Today she was a human daffodil, togged out in green pants and a yellow shirt, and had brought a couple of bunches of supermarket daffs which she set in a vase on the reception counter. "Poor Agnes got lost in the shuffle."

"And I'm going to spend another day out in the cold," said Lucy, sighing as she put her gloves back on.

"Hopefully it won't be all day," said Phyllis.

When Lucy arrived at the pond, there were several police cruisers in the parking lot and an aluminum boat was out on the water. The heads of a couple of divers could be seen bobbing about near the boat, in between dives. The very thought of immersing oneself in the cold water, where bits of ice were still floating here and there, made her shiver.

"Any progress?" she asked Police Chief Jim Kirwan, who was standing by along with Barney Culpepper and a couple of other officers. They were all dressed for the weather in official police cold-weather gear, which reminded Lucy of the one-piece snowsuits she used to zip the kids into when they were small. Neither officer could be called small, however, especially Barney, who was well over six feet tall and whose girth had been steadily expanding through the years. His jumpsuit was definitely showing signs of strain.

"Not yet, probably never. We've got to do it but I don't expect to find anything except somebody's old washing machine," said the chief.

"One year we found a bunch of stolen bicycles," offered Barney, loosening the zipper that was pinching his three chins.

"Why steal the bikes if you're only going to toss them in the pond?" asked Lucy.

"A reasonable question," said Kirwan, "but then again, Lucy, you're not fourteen years old."

"Point taken," said Lucy, watching as one of the divers disappeared beneath the surface of the pond. "How long do you think this will take?"

"Not long, I hope. The visibility is usually pretty good in this pond, especially now since nobody's been swimming or boating and roiling up the bottom."

"I guess since you're dragging the pond there's been no sign of Agnes. No reports of sightings, anything like that?"

Kirwan sighed and Barney shifted his considerable weight from one foot to the other and back again. "No sign of her at all," said Kirwan.

"Phone and credit cards?" asked Lucy.

Barney shook his head, then produced a large cotton handkerchief from one of the suit's many pockets and gave his nose a good blow. "My nose always runs in the cold," he explained. "Maybe I'm allergic or something. Can you be allergic to the cold?"

"I sure am," agreed Lucy, shivering and stamping her feet. "So if you don't find Agnes in the pond, what next?"

Kirwan shrugged. "I'm out of options. We do our best to get the word out but there's a lot of missing persons, and most of them are doing their best to stay that way."

In response to Lucy's puzzled expression, he explained. "A lot of these folks are escaping a bad situation, like crushing debts, or starting a new life. Getting a fresh start, maybe with a lover."

"Somehow I don't think that applies to Agnes," said Lucy.

"No. Folks like her are the most frustrating cases of all. She was a keen naturalist and bird-watcher, and there's a whole lotta nature around here. We've done a foot search of the conservation areas, the places bird-watchers frequent, but if she went farther afield, well, I just don't have the resources to search every bit of woods around here. If she spotted a pileated woodpecker or some such and started following it, she could have twisted an ankle or broke a leg or got lost. She could have had a stroke, or heart attack, something like that, and chances are that if she went far enough, we'll never know what happened."

Lucy thought of the thousands of acres of fields and forests, all undeveloped land, in Tinker's Cove alone. "You mean you might never recover her body?"

The two officers looked at the ground, then Barney spoke up. "Hunting season, in the fall, that's our best chance."

Out on the pond, Lucy noticed the divers were climbing into the boat, which then motored toward shore. The search had come up empty.

Lucy couldn't shake the image of all that emptiness as she drove back to town, keeping an eye out along the road for any sign of Agnes: a scrap of blue windbreaker, the fluttering pages of a bird book, a glint of light reflected from a binocular lens. She thought of the possible mishaps that could have felled her: a broken bone, a twisted ankle, a stroke. How awful it would be to suddenly become helpless and to lie alone in the cold, waiting for help that never came. She hoped that wasn't the case, but feared it was the most likely scenario.

At the office, Lucy was greeted by a fishy aroma. "Sorry about the smell," said Phyllis, who was eating a fish sandwich. "I reheated my lunch in the microwave, I didn't realize it would be so stinky."

"It's not stinky, it's making me hungry," said Lucy, shrugging out of her parka. She had also brought her lunch, a pot of yogurt and a handful of mini carrots, which had seemed a good idea at seven o'clock but wasn't very appealing now, compared to Phyllis's fragrant sandwich. She considered the various options offered on Main Street, which were limited to the high-priced gourmet sandwich shop, the pizzeria, and the pre-wrapped days-old salads and sandwiches at the Quik-Stop, and decided to stick with her yogurt and carrots. She was spooning up the last of the yogurt when her phone rang. The caller was Geri Mazzone.

"Any news?" asked Lucy.

"They dragged the pond."

"I know. I was out there."

"Mom didn't fall into a pond, and if she twisted an ankle or something, believe me, she'd make herself a splint or a crutch and

79

get herself some help. She was a survivor, she was a war correspondent, for Pete's sake. She was shot at, bombed, strafed, you name it, she survived it. She never went out without her survival kit. . . ."

"Survival kit?" asked Lucy.

"Yeah. Bandages, a tourniquet, a knife, stuff like that. And she kept her phone charged. And really, what could happen in these woods the chief keeps telling me about? There's a lot of woods, sure, but most of them aren't actually that far from a house, right? And as for a stroke or heart attack, well, I wish I had my mom's blood pressure." She paused. "Or her energy. I don't know how she did it but I couldn't keep up with her at the mall."

"So what do you think happened?" asked Lucy.

"Foul play, for lack of a better term. She probably got wind of some injustice, something not right, and started investigating, and —" Geri's voice broke, and she struggled a few minutes before continuing, "I have a bad feeling about Heritage House. I think there's something rotten there and Mom found out about it."

In all the years she'd been a reporter Lucy had learned to listen carefully to sources, but not to always believe them. Some people thought they could manipulate the news for their own ends, some people outright lied because they didn't want the truth to be known, and some people wanted to shame or hurt others. "Do you have any proof of this?" she asked.

"Not a shred," admitted Geri. "I just have a bad feeling about the place."

"Well, I'll keep your concerns in mind," said Lucy. "And I hope your mom turns up safe and sound."

"Me too, but I don't think she will," said Geri, sniffing. Her voice broke as she added, "I've pretty much given up hope."

Lucy was thoughtful as she tossed the empty yogurt container into the trash and uploaded the photos she'd taken at the pond onto her computer. They offered a bleak scene of bare trees, gray sky, and slate-gray water that served as a backdrop to the dark silhouettes of the rescue boat and divers. Lucy scrolled through them, picked the best ones, and sent them to Ted.

That chore done, she considered calling one of the selectmen to get a preview of the agenda for the upcoming meeting, or perhaps call the school superintendent, or maybe one of the members of the school board to get a quote about that controversial budget increase, but knew her heart wasn't in it. She impulsively stood up, grabbed her parka and bag, and headed for the door. "Where to?" asked Phyllis.

"Miss Tilley," said Lucy, zipping up her parka.

"Is she okay?" asked Phyllis, concerned.

"Far as I know she's fine and dandy, and I have a job for her."

Lucy found Miss Tilley seated in a comfy recliner in her room, hidden behind the latest edition of the *New York Review of Books*.

"That's pretty heavy reading," said Lucy, announcing her arrival.

Two bright blue eyes peered at her over the *Review*. "Interesting article deconstructing Norman Mailer's postmodern macho persona in light of the Me Too movement."

"Can't wait to read it," said Lucy somewhat sarcastically.

"It's dry as dust," said Miss Tilley, dropping the publication in her lap. "You can imagine how bored I am if I'm reading this." She slapped the paper for emphasis. "There's absolutely nothing for me to do here except my PT exercises."

Lucy perched herself on the side of the hospital bed. "Now, now, that's an exaggeration. There's plenty to do."

Miss Tilley rolled her eyes. "It's like kindergarten. Make an Easter bonnet out of a paper plate. Play bingo. Or how about Scrabble? Some of these poor old dears can't even spell simple words." She let out a big sigh. "I put in 'xiphias' yesterday and got a triple word score, too, but the idiots I was playing with wouldn't accept it." She snorted disdainfully. "Made me take it out."

"And what, pray tell, is a xiphias?"

Miss Tilley looked at her with great disappointment. "A fish, of course."

"Ah, right," replied Lucy. "You know I might have a solution for your problem. Something you could do for me."

Miss Tilley lowered her eyelids and gave her a suspicious glance. "Will it get me in trouble?" she asked somewhat eagerly.

"Not if you do it right," said Lucy, smiling. "Geri Mazzone, Agnes Neal's daughter . . . you know, the woman . . ."

"The lady who vanished."

"Right. Well, Geri keeps calling me and claiming there are problems here at Heritage House. She won't say exactly what, just that there's something not quite right going on."

"I'll say!" exclaimed Miss Tilley. "They're trying to bore us to death."

"Something more than that, I imagine, though Geri wouldn't say exactly what. She did say that she thought her mother had uncovered something amiss."

83

"And you want me to risk vanishing like poor Agnes in order to find out what's going on?"

"No! Just keep your eyes and ears open, that sort of thing. Let me know if anything catches your attention."

"I suppose I could," agreed Miss Tilley somewhat grudgingly. "Would there be something in it for me?"

"Well, I suppose so." Lucy's thoughts ran to a new book, perhaps along with a box of Fern's Famous Fudge. "What would you like?"

Miss Tilley promptly replied, "A couple of bottles of sherry? The dry cocktail kind, of course. Not that disgusting sweet stuff."

"I suppose that sort of thing is strictly forbidden?"

"Not if no one finds out about it."

Lucy smiled. "You got it, I'll bring it next time I come."

"Just call me Miss Marple," said Miss Tilley, with a naughty smile.

Lucy was still shaking her head over her old friend's feisty attitude when she reached the lobby and encountered Howard and his fan club of three.

"Ah, Lucy," exclaimed Howard, greeting her with a warm smile. "Just the person we need." He lowered his voice, and the three women leaned in closer. "I suppose you have the inside scoop on Agnes's disappearance?"

"Isn't that the strangest thing?" asked Bitsy, her eyes huge. "How does a person just disappear? Here one minute and gone the next . . ."

"And in this day and age," added Bev. "We've got astronauts in space, we know where they are, but we can't keep track of people here on planet Earth."

"Two entirely different things, Bev," said Dorothy. "You really can't compare them."

"Of course I can," insisted Bev. "If they can track astronauts, why can't they find Agnes?"

"Because there's no tracking devices on Agnes," fumed Dorothy. "Why would there be? She's not zooming around in space, she's presumed to be safe here on earth in Tinker's Cove."

"Ladies, ladies," said Howard, stepping in to referee. "Maybe Lucy, our intrepid reporter, has some news for us."

"I wish I did," said Lucy. "But as far as I know Agnes is still missing. Her daughter is very worried."

"I'm sure she is," said Bitsy. "She's such a good daughter. She visits every week."

"It must be absolutely awful for her,"

added Bev.

"On the other hand, she's an only child and I imagine she will inherit a tidy sum from Agnes. . . ." offered Dorothy.

"Shame on you, Dorothy!" exclaimed Bitsy.

"The last thing on her mind, I'm sure," exclaimed Bev.

"Now, now," said Howard, "I've heard that Florida Dawkins has come up with a very exciting Easter bonnet idea. . . ."

This did not go over well with the group.

"Are you sure?"

"Who told you that?"

"She must be getting advice from out-side," speculated Dorothy. "Isn't her daughter a fashion designer?"

"Oh, my!" exclaimed Bitsy, shocked to her core. "Isn't that cheating?"

Howard didn't answer, he was studying his cell phone. After tucking it away in his pocket, he turned to the group. "Well, I'm sure you will all want to get to work planning your bonnets, and I have been summoned elsewhere, so I'm afraid I must bid you all adieu." He gave Lucy a nod and a smile, turned, and marched off stiffly down the hallway toward the skilled nursing section.

"She sends him a text and off he goes,"

sniffed Bitsy, linking arms with her friends.

"Honestly, I don't see the appeal. She's well over ninety if she's a day and, like my mother used to say, she's too smart for her own good," observed Bev, as the group started off down the hall, arm in arm. "And we all know that men don't like smarty-pants women."

"And she certainly hasn't taken care of her appearance," said Bitsy, pausing before offering an even more shocking allegation. "I don't think she's ever had a facial, or even uses moisturizer. She doesn't even bother with lipstick."

"Oh, that doesn't matter, at his age," said Dorothy. "He probably doesn't see all that well. I think what Howard finds attractive is her mind, he likes talking about current events and politics."

Lucy watched, amused, as the group moved away, certain that they were gossiping about Howard's new flame, Miss Tilley.

CHAPTER SIX

Next morning, Lucy found herself in the basement meeting room at the Tinker's Cove Police Department, which also served as the town's emergency management head-quarters. That explained the banks of computers and phones, as well as the cello packs of bottled water and neatly labeled boxes of first aid supplies and food. Tinker's Cove was clearly prepared for whatever disaster might arrive, though thankfully it had been spared so far. The worst that had happened in Lucy's memory was the occasional winter blizzard, which folks not only expected but reveled in, eagerly recounting their tales of hardihood and survival. "Yup, the snow went right up over the front door, so we used the back, ha!"

Lucy remembered that a blizzard usually meant the power went out when she and Bill had first moved to Tinker's Cove, but nowadays outages seemed to happen less often, probably because the electric company trimmed the trees along the lines. Furthermore, lots of people had invested in generators, which at least allowed them to keep the heat and kitchen stove going, along with a lamp or two. Mainers were used to foul weather and proud of their ability to carry on despite whatever Mother Nature decided to throw at them.

But today, the sun was shining and the promise of spring was in the air, and the police chief had called a news conference for a different purpose. The announcement, which promised an update on the search for Agnes Neal, hadn't drawn much of a crowd; there were only two other local reporters gathered in the meeting room and Lucy knew them both. She was sitting beside Deb Hildreth, now the news director at local radio station WCOV, and Bob Mayes, stringer for the *Boston Globe,* was only a few seats away, staring at his cell phone.

"Not much of a turnout," observed Deb.

"Old women, even missing old women, aren't exactly hot copy," observed Lucy.

"I'm hot all the time," complained Deb, fanning herself with a floppy hand. "Well, not all the time, but these hot flashes are really uncomfortable. I swear I never wore a sweater once all winter!"

"That must save you quite a bit on the heating bill," said Lucy, who always tried to look on the bright side.

"If only. It's a constant battle in my house. I'm turning the thermostat down and George is pushing it up."

"Tell him to put on a sweater," said Lucy, laughing, remembering that she had said those very words so often that her kids made it into a collage for her one Christmas. She'd framed it and it still hung in the upstairs hall by the staircase, but nowadays there was only Zoe to see it and she tended to wear stylish but impractical sweaters that bared her midriff. Lucy was about to share this bit of youthful folly with Deb when police chief Jim Kirwan made his entrance, along with the fire chief, Buzz Bresnahan.

"Thanks for coming, I'm glad we were able to accommodate the crowd," said Jim Kirwan sarcastically.

"You all know who we are, so I guess we can skip the introductions," added Buzz, passing out a press release. It was brief, merely one sentence announcing the department had ended the search for Agnes Neal.

"I'm afraid I don't have much to add," said Jim. "I'm sorry to say that our search for Agnes Neal, last seen at six a.m. last Tuesday leaving Heritage House, has been unsuccessful and we have found no trace of her. We're calling off the search, pending further developments. The case will remain open, of course, and we urge all citizens to keep her in mind and ask for their help." He shrugged. "I guess that's it."

"Any questions?" asked the fire chief.

"Can you describe the scope of the search so far?" asked Deb.

"We have conducted foot searches of all the areas in town known to be frequented by bird-watchers," said Jim, sounding tired. "As you know Agnes, mmm" — here he paused, clearly unsure whether he should say *was* or *is,* and skipping ahead — "a keen bird-watcher. We asked the public to report possible sightings, and I have to say we've had a terrific level of community support. We received many leads and followed up on each and every one, actually identifying most of the subjects. We've posted missing persons reports on our state and regional public safety networks. . . ." Kirwan sighed and shrugged. "That's really all we can do."

"We also dragged Blueberry Pond and searched the waterfront, but didn't find the missing woman," added Buzz. "Our hope is that she's simply decided to visit a friend or something and didn't tell anyone but I think by now, what with all the news coverage, that's unlikely."

"What about Heritage House?" asked Lucy. "Have you questioned people there?"

"Yes, we have, and no one saw Agnes Neal after she left early last Tuesday morning," said Jim. "And I'd like to add that the management of Heritage House has been most cooperative, offering any and all assistance we requested. We are satisfied they followed all appropriate protocols."

"Have you put out an Amber Alert?" asked Bob Mayes.

"That was the very first thing we did, once we confirmed that Ms. Neal was a missing person," said Jim.

"What about her family? Any conflicts, feuds, violence? What about restraining orders?"

"Nothing like that." Jim shook his head. "We've questioned the family and are satisfied there's no involvement in her disappearance."

Lucy wasn't about to let the safety officials off the hook. "What if Agnes Neal was four years old, instead of seventy-one would you be so quick to call off the search?" she asked, challenging them.

Jim and Buzz both looked uncomfortable and Jim replied, "Agnes Neal is not four, she is not presumed kidnapped, there is no sign of foul play. She is an adult woman described as being of sound mind and in good health. We've gone above and beyond, doing everything our departments can do, and we have exhausted all our options."

"Isn't it true that Josh Hartman's helicopter crash took priority, leaving little manpower and equipment available to search for Agnes Neal?" asked Bob.

Jim Kirwan glared at him. "I assure you that we can walk and chew gum at the same time."

Bob smiled, nothing made him happier than rankling public officials. "I'm sure you can, but that's not what I asked. But I'll bet that the log, which is a public record, will show that over the weekend most, if not all, departmental resources were deployed to the helicopter crash and the search for Agnes Neal didn't even begin until yesterday."

"It's a sad truth, and I'm sure Chief Bresnahan agrees with me, that given our current budget we have to prioritize and make difficult choices," said Kirwan, practically snarling. "I was able, however, to assign one officer to the Agnes Neal case and that officer —"

Bob interrupted the chief. "Only one officer?"

"Sorry, Bob. This is not *CSI: Miami,* it's not even *Murder, She Wrote.* This is real life in Tinker's Cove, Maine, where our citizens keep a close eye on spending. I have a small staff and an even smaller overtime budget. " He shook his head. "That's all."

Buzz stepped forward. "Again, I'd just like to ask folks to let us know if they see anything suspicious, anything at all. Also, we're asking dog walkers to stay on the alert, and if Fido gets kind of excited we'd like to know about it." He sighed. "Believe me, we want to close this case."

"Nobody more than Buzz and I," added Jim, making a quick exit. Buzz gave a gesture of helplessness and followed him.

"Well," said Bob, "that was a whole lot of nothing."

"You said it," agreed Lucy, gathering up her things.

She'd only been back in the office for a few minutes, long enough to drink a cup of coffee, when Geri called. "Chief Kirwan just called me to say they're not going to look for Mom anymore," she wailed. "I can't believe it!"

"I know." Lucy took one last swallow, draining her mug. "There was a press conference."

"He said they've exhausted all leads," said

Geri. "How can that be? I asked if they questioned everyone at Heritage House and he didn't even answer me. He just said they'd done everything they could."

Lucy heard the anger and frustration in Geri's voice and knew she must be feeling desperate, and wished there was some way to ease her anxiety, her grief for her absent mother. "Geri, I know this must be terribly hard for you —"

"Don't! Don't tell me there's nothing you can do, nothing anybody can do. The police simply don't care, nobody cares about a seventy-one-year-old woman! Nobody cares!"

Geri's claim struck Lucy where it hurt most: in her conscience. She had to admit that down deep, awful as it was, she didn't actually care, at least not much. She had problems of her own, Agnes wasn't her problem, and she really couldn't summon up much more than casual interest in the woman's fate. That realization stunned her, even shocked her. She was treating Agnes like yesterday's news, like last week's edition of the paper which she'd already tossed in the recycling bin. But Agnes wasn't an old story, she was a real person and she mattered. Wasn't that what Rev. Marge preached about every Sunday, that every person was precious in God's sight? Shouldn't Agnes matter to her? And Geri, too, who needed to know what happened to her mother? Lucy let out a deep sigh. "Okay, Geri. Tell me what you want the police to do."

"Mom was last seen at Heritage House, so that's where they should start. They should question everyone there."

"Didn't they do that?" asked Lucy, trying to remember Kirwan's exact words at the press conference. She had assumed the police had done a thorough canvass of the employees and residents, but he hadn't actually said that. He'd only said that no one saw her after she'd left early in the morning. "She was seen leaving —"

Geri interrupted her. "Right. We know she went out, but what if she came back?"

"Somebody would have seen her and said something," replied Lucy.

"I asked the chief about that," said Geri. "I asked him if he'd questioned everyone and he said they spoke with staff members who were on duty that morning, as well as residents who were considered pretty sharp, but that there was no point questioning people who were past it, that's what he said, past it."

"So you think she might have returned?"

"I do. She left at six, and normally she would have come back by eight or nine, but she certainly could have come back earlier, especially if it wasn't a good birding day. Very few residents would be up and about that early; Mom often said that most of the residents missed the best part of the day." Geri paused, then continued. "And if they were up, and they saw something that wasn't right, they'd probably forget to report it."

"What do you mean?" pressed Lucy. "What sort of thing?"

"Maybe just an argument," offered Geri, speculating. "Or maybe she witnessed a payoff, or some sort of abuse. Something that somebody didn't want her to see that triggered, or even caused her to disappear."

"That seems like kind of a long shot," said Lucy softly, wondering if Geri was in one of those irrational stages of grief, like maybe denial.

"I know, I know. Everybody says calm down, Geri. Your mom is old, old people die all the time, that's what happens. Accept that she wandered off into the hereafter. But I just can't. I have a bad feeling about Heritage House, I had it right from the beginning. I think there's something rotten there and if anybody was going to discover it, it would be my mom. She wouldn't think of her own safety, that she might be doing something dangerous. She'd just be digging and sniffing around, determined to uncover the truth."

Once again, Geri was hitting her where it hurt. Wasn't that her job? "Okay, Geri. I have to go over there today, anyway. They're having an Easter bonnet workshop. I'll be able to interview some of the residents and I'll see what I can find out." She thought of Miss Tilley. "And I also have an old friend who's recuperating there, she's agreed to do a little inside investigating for me."

"I'm sorry, I guess I underestimated you," said Geri. "You've got suspicions about Heritage House, too."

"I did take a look at the state's inspection record, but that's as far as I got," admitted Lucy. "I was somewhat surprised at the number of violations, but my editor wasn't interested. Didn't think it was worth investigating."

"I have noticed that full-page ad they run every week," said Geri.

"Exactly," said Lucy. She paused, choosing her words carefully. "I've been down this road before, Geri, and I have to tell you that it doesn't always take you where you want to go. Sometimes it takes you to a dead end, and sometimes you end up at a really bad place, learning things you'd rather not know."

"I know," said Geri. "But I have to take that road. I owe it to Mom."

"I understand," said Lucy, but later that morning, when she went to Heritage House for the workshop, she looked at the place with new eyes. Sure it looked very nice with its traditional red-brick architecture and white-columned portico over the glazed double door entry. Stepping inside the newly decorated lobby, there was not a whiff of any unpleasant scent. On the contrary, she noticed, the air was lightly perfumed with a fresh aroma, almost like a breath of fresh air. Fake fresh air, thought Lucy. What else was fake around here?

An attractive middle-aged woman was seated at the antique fruitwood writing table that had replaced the ugly old reception desk and she greeted Lucy with a big smile. "How can I help you today?"

"I'm Lucy Stone, from the *Courier.* I've been invited to cover the Easter bonnet workshop."

"Oh, yes, Lucy. We're expecting you. You can go right up those stairs," she said, pointing to the swooping staircase that was such a feature of the lobby, "or if you'd rather, you could take the elevator."

"I'll climb, thanks," said Lucy, somewhat discomfited to think that someone might think she wasn't fit enough to climb a flight of stairs. Of course, she reminded herself, this was a residence for seniors and the staff was probably trained to gracefully accommodate those with disabilities. Also, many painful disabilities weren't obvious, like arthritis and sciatica and COPD. Of course, she was hale and hearty and determined to show that a flight of stairs, even a double flight such as this, was nothing to her, so she hurried on up.

The staircase was longer than she anticipated, however, and Lucy was slightly out of breath when she reached the large mezzanine overlooking the lobby that served as a gathering space for residents. Today a number of folding tables had been added to the usual sofas and armchairs, and a goodly number of residents, all female, were seated in groups around them.

"Ah, Lucy, welcome," exclaimed Felicity Corcoran, the activities director, who had topped her usual slacks and sweater with a practical smock. "I'm so glad you could come."

"Thanks for inviting me," said Lucy, noticing the various craft supplies on the tables. "Can I make a hat, too?"

"Of course! But I'm warning you, these ladies aren't about to reveal their top-secret plans for their Easter bonnets. We're just going to learn a few nifty techniques, like ruching and crimping and how to safely use a hot glue gun, that sort of thing. Then they'll use those skills to make their amazing millinery creations."

"Super," said Lucy, "looks like I'll get a lot of great photos." She noticed Bitsy waving to her from one of the tables and asked, "Can I sit anywhere?"

"Absolutely," said Felicity, beaming. "Make yourself at home. This is going to be a fun morning, just one of the many activities we offer our residents. Activities, I might add, that engage them mentally and also help them maintain what we professionals call *digital dexterity.* It's very important to keep those finger bones working."

"Ah, there's method to your madness," said Lucy, smiling and making her way over to the table where Bitsy, Bev, and Dorothy were seated. That required passing several other tables, each filled with three or four women, chatting among themselves but not with the women at the other tables. It reminded Lucy somewhat strangely of her high school cafeteria, where the popular girls reigned at a table by the windows, the sporty girls had the other window table, and the student council members settled in a rear corner, plotting world domination. It was certainly not the sort of activity that would interest Miss Tilley, and she was not surprised to see her old friend wasn't present.

"Hello, Lucy," exclaimed Bitsy, proclaiming to the room that she had snagged an important guest for her table. "Sit right down, dear," she encouraged, patting an empty chair.

"Thanks," said Lucy. "Do you mind if I snap a few photos?"

"Please do," chirped Bev, with a big smile. "Will we be in the paper?"

"That's the idea," said Lucy. "So fill me in, who all is here?"

"Well," said Bitsy, "see that woman in the coral twinset?" Lucy nodded.

"She's Laura Whitcomb, her son is the president of Seamen's Bank. You can't talk to her for five minutes before she finds a way to bring it up," said Bitsy.

"Did you notice her necklace? South Sea pearls," added Bev.

"But," offered Dorothy, tapping her temple, "she's losing it. The other day she got lost trying to find the dining room."

102

"Oh, dear," said Lucy. "That's too bad. I suppose her friends will help her out," she said, referring to the three other women at the bank lady's table.

"Not that bunch. Believe me, when you can't remember which suit is trump, you're out on your own."

"They like to play bridge?" asked Lucy.

"Yes," hissed Bev. "And they've been after our Dorothy."

Dorothy smiled rather smugly. "I do play, you know."

"But you wouldn't desert us for that crowd, would you?" asked Bitsy.

"Well, neither of you play," protested Dorothy. "I could play a rubber or two, we'd still be friends."

Bev and Bitsy shared a glance. "I guess it would depend," said Bev finally.

There was a bit of a flurry by the door and a wave of excitement spread through the room as a tall, rather handsome silver-haired man in a navy blue suit stepped into the room. "That's Peter, Peter Novak," whispered Bitsy. "He's the boss."

"The boss?" asked Lucy.

"He's in charge here, he's the head honcho," said Dorothy.

"And he's sooo handsome," added Bev.

"Shhh," cautioned Bitsy. "He's coming

over here."

Lucy watched as Peter made his way through the room, pausing at each table to charm and flatter the ladies. When he finally reached their table, the three women gazed up at him as if he were a Greek god who had dropped in from Mt. Olympus to grace them with his favor.

"Ah, ladies, I can't wait to see what lovely creations you come up with this year. And who," he asked, speaking in a lightly accented voice, "is your charming companion?"

"I'm Lucy Stone, from the *Courier*. Felicity invited me to cover the workshop."

"Marvelous, marvelous," said Peter, dazzling them all with his smile and perfect but lightly accented English. "Isn't Felicity wonderful?" He turned to face the room and raised his voice. "I was just saying, isn't our Felicity absolutely marvelous? She arranged this workshop for you all, and I know, this year you will all make such beautiful bonnets that we'll have to have chocolate bunnies for everyone!"

Hearing this, the women burst into applause, beaming and smiling at Peter.

"Of course," he added, grinning naughtily, "there can only be one winner who will receive the big, giant chocolate bunny, so I encourage you all to put on your thinking caps and dazzle the judges with your ingenuity and creativity."

The ladies all cooed and clapped and buzzed as he left the room, and one lady in particular seemed to be quite overcome.

"Oh, no," exclaimed Dorothy. "It looks like Helen's fainting."

"Oh, not again," said Bev, as two nurse's aides hurried to the slumping woman's side.

"Poor Helen. She has a weak heart or something. When she gets too excited, she faints."

Concerned, Lucy watched as the two aides quickly pulled some chairs next to Helen's and maneuvered her onto her back. Once they'd positioned her and checked her airway, they massaged her hands and spoke to her gently.

"The Black one is Vera," whispered Dorothy. "And the other is Juliana, she's Mexican, I think."

"They're angels," said Bev.

"Even if they're brown," added Bitsy.

The room remained hushed as everyone watched and waited for Helen to recover, which she did in a matter of minutes. Once she was conscious the aides helped her into a wheelchair and whisked her out of the room, to regain her strength in privacy.

Once gone she was quickly forgotten as Felicity tapped a glass with a spoon to get everyone's attention and began demonstrating various techniques for creating paper flowers and other decorative elements for their bonnets.

The women were soon involved in following Felicity's instructions for making ribbon rosebuds, Lucy included. Her rosebud looked rather droopy and she laughed, showing it to the others. Much to her surprise, however, they didn't see anything at all funny about the droopy bud and urged her to try again. Checking out the other tables, Lucy noticed there was a definite air of competition, which culminated when a woman at another table proudly displayed her perfect pink rosebud, complete with realistic leaves.

"Oh, that Frances!" muttered Bev. "She's done it again."

"She must be very crafty," said Lucy.

"You can say that again," growled Dorothy. "She's a quilter, you know." From her tone, Lucy gathered that Dorothy didn't consider quilting a worthy pastime.

"It's better than hooking," joked Bitsy, with a naughty smile. Seeing that Lucy didn't get the joke she added, "Rug hooking. They call themselves hookers."

"So there are some active crafters here," said Lucy, thinking of possible future stories.

"I guess they've nothing better to do," said Bitsy, with a sigh.

"Well, people have different talents," offered Lucy. "By the way, who won the bonnet contest last year?"

There was an awkward silence as the three women seemed to deliberate about replying, then Dorothy spoke up. "It was Agnes," she said.

"It was a nest, a bird's nest, with a mother robin sitting on some eggs," remembered Bev.

"And the daddy robin was flying about on a wire," added Bitsy.

"It was very clever," admitted Dorothy.

"Indeed," agreed Lucy. "So do you have any idea what might have happened to Agnes? Any clues at all?"

"Not really," said Bitsy, with a shake of her curly head.

"We weren't close," offered Bev, with a shrug.

"Why are you asking us? Why do you think we know anything?" queried Dorothy somewhat defensively.

"Oh, I don't know. You seem like one big family here," suggested Lucy, who was beginning to think Heritage House wasn't

107

like a family at all, it was more like a girls' school with competing cliques.

"Do something for me?" she urged, producing her phone. "Smile for the camera?"

The three women snuggled together, pleased as punch to be photographed. Then Lucy thanked them for a lovely time, gathered her things, and began to make her exit. She made a point of thanking Felicity for inviting her, chatted with a few of the residents, and snapped their pictures on her way to the door. They were all pleased to be photographed, but when she asked for information about Agnes they didn't have much to say apart from observing that it was very puzzling. When she stepped out into the hallway she was met by Vera.

"Ah, you're leaving, I see," said Vera, who had a big smile and a lilting Jamaican accent.

"Duty calls," said Lucy. "I have to say, I was very impressed by the care you and your colleague . . ."

"Juliana."

"You took such good care of that poor lady."

"Like you said, duty calls. It's our job."

"There's something that struck me, maybe you have some insight? I was surprised that none of the other women seemed very concerned about her. And when I asked about Agnes, the lady who disappeared, they didn't seem very interested. Why is that?"

Vera gazed down the hallway for a long minute, then replied, "Ah, in a place like this you get used to losing folks. Here today and gone tomorrow. It may seem cold, it bothered me, too, at first, but then I understood it's really self-defense. They have their activities to keep their minds busy, they have wall-to-wall carpeting and gourmet meals, but they're not fooled. They all know the grim reaper is just around the corner, waiting for them."

"Of course," said Lucy, realizing the truth of what she said. "Thanks."

"Have a nice day now," said Vera, going on her way.

What an image, thought Lucy, starting down the stairway and imagining death lurking behind the lush potted plants, behind the comfy padded sofas, behind every freshly painted six-panel door.

CHAPTER SEVEN

Back in her car, Lucy sent the photos of the bonnet workshop to Ted, along with lengthy captions naming all the participants. Then she realized with a shock that she was done for the day since the rest of the stories on her news budget had already been filed. If there were any questions he could always call her, but that rarely happened since she was so careful about her work. Weird, she thought, starting the car. At first she'd resented the way the computer had transformed her workweek, turning it from thirty-six hours into a twenty-four-seven affair, but now she was learning there were advantages, too. She wasn't chained to a desk, or an office; now she could file a story with a few swipes and taps on her cell phone.

What to do with the unexpected gift of a free afternoon? Shop for new shoes? Poke about in the library for a new book? Take the dog in for her annual veterinary exam? None of those options really appealed, she decided, turning onto Red Top Road and heading for home. No, as it happened, now that she finally had her own lovely private closet she was itching to organize it. She'd had to share with Bill before; this was the first time she'd had a closet of her own, but she hadn't had time to set it up properly and had simply mashed all her things together and shoved them in any which way. She had even bought beautiful French toile accessories: a shoe rack, a hanging gizmo to hold sweaters, shelf dividers to organize her purses, and velvety hangers in a matching shade of blue. Today she was going to dig in and follow Sue's advice to toss out anything she hadn't worn in a year.

She was visualizing the gorgeous closet she was going to create, a closet filled with clothes she loved that would bring her joy every morning when she opened the door and the interior light automatically turned on, when she turned into the drive and saw Zoe's little Toyota back in its usual place along with her friend Leanne's brand-new Civic. That meant Zoe was back from her job interview in Portland and she was either celebrating with her best friend, or had turned to her for comfort and consolation.

The answer wasn't immediately obvious when she entered the kitchen, unnoticed. Libby was happily curled up under the table, snoozing and occasionally flicking her ears, reacting to the girls' chatter and much too comfortable to bother greeting Lucy. The girls also were completely absorbed in themselves, munching on an array of snacks while poring over the real estate section of the Sunday paper.

"What's up?" asked Lucy, dropping her bag on a handy chair and shrugging out of her jacket.

"Mom!" exclaimed Zoe, jumping up and hugging her mother. "I got the job!"

"Wow," said Lucy, who hadn't expected this. She had been prepared to offer advice, consolation, and patience to help Zoe cope with rejection and was caught completely off guard. "That's great," she said, giving Zoe another hug. "When do you start?"

"Right after graduation, so Leanne and I are apartment hunting. Did you know they have all these apartment ads in the Sunday paper? Leanne's mom told us about it and gave us this big section full of them."

"Yeah. There's houses and condos and apartments," offered Leanne, completely amazed. "This way you can see them all and compare them, it's easier than those little listings on our phones."

"They even have big color photos, Mom. Look at this loft. It's got exposed brick and big huge windows and it's only twenty-one hundred a month, right downtown."

Amused, Lucy leaned over her daughter's shoulder and studied the attractive photo. "Big windows will need some sort of curtains or shades, that's going to be expensive," cautioned Lucy. "And you need to know if heat is included because those windows will let the heat out and you'll be heating all of downtown Portland."

"It's got all sorts of amenities," said Leanne. "We'll save on gym memberships because they've got their own gym, and a pool, too."

"And, get this, Mom. The first month's rent is free!"

"Don't forget, they'll still want a security deposit and your last month's rent, that's over four thousand dollars. And you'll need renters' insurance, sometimes there's a charge for parking. . . ."

"It says free parking, Mom. And free Wi-Fi and cable hookups."

Lucy pointed to the small print. "You're just starting out, you'll need to budget carefully. The general rule is that you shouldn't spend more than thirty percent of your income on rent. It says in the ad that rents *start* at twenty-one hundred, that's probably for a studio. You'll need a bigger place, preferably with two bedrooms. . . ."

"Well, I think we should definitely put it on our list and look at it," insisted Zoe.

"Absolutely," agreed Leanne.

Shaking her head, Lucy went on upstairs to rendezvous with her soon-to-be gorgeous, perfectly organized closet, the closet it had taken decades of scrimping and saving, not to mention all that sweat equity spent painting and scraping and hammering, to finally achieve.

Next morning, Lucy had her moment of joy when she opened her closet and gazed at the neat rows of clothing organized by color and type. Her shoes were lined up in the shoe rack, her sweaters were neatly folded in the hanging rack, next came pants on special hangers, followed by skirts and shirts, and at the far end, out-of-season items. She could hardly stand the wonderfulness as she decided what to wear today, finally deciding on her favorite jeans and a green-and-white-striped shirt she'd forgotten she had until she found it stuck behind Toby's old Cub Scout uniform. That sentimental artifact was now neatly folded and stored along with other items she couldn't bear to part with in her mother's old hope chest, which stood at the foot of the bed.

Pleased with her spring outfit — she'd topped the shirt with a green crew neck sweater she'd bought a few years ago at an end-of-season sale at the town's fanciest boutique, the Carriage Trade — Lucy was confident that even Sue couldn't find anything wrong with her outfit today. Or Zoe, who'd already left to apartment hunt with Leanne in Portland. She did have second thoughts when she got to work and Phyllis, togged out in a sweatshirt featuring a glittery multicolored sequin-covered unicorn, complimented her on the bright green sweater.

She found a new message from Geri on her voice mail and decided she might as well get it over with and returned the call. If she didn't, she told herself as she listened to the phone ring, Geri would hound her with messages all day. Besides, she really did want to ask Geri about the bonnet contest, which she had been surprised to learn that Agnes had won.

"Oh, that!" answered Geri in a dismissive tone. "Nobody was more surprised than Mom when she won. But that was last year, water under the bridge. You can't possibly think one of those old biddies did her in over a silly hat contest!"

"Not even for a giant chocolate bunny?" asked Lucy, half joking. "There are days when I'd kill for a piece of chocolate."

"Me too," admitted Geri, "but face it. Most of them are old and frail, they couldn't commit a murder even if they wanted to, and I can't see why they'd want to."

"They may be old, but that doesn't mean they don't have strong emotions, even rivalries. I was just there to cover a bonnet-making workshop and I have to admit I was surprised at the competitive atmosphere. One lady fainted and nobody seemed very concerned, and when I asked about your mother's disappearance there wasn't much interest."

"That doesn't surprise me," said Geri. "Mom didn't really have any friends there, she didn't have much in common with the others. For one thing, she was probably one of the youngest residents and was quite likely the strongest and fittest. She moved there because she despised cooking and cleaning and enjoyed leaving that to some-one else. She told me she didn't want to be tied down with the responsibility of a house, she wanted to enjoy maximum freedom in the last part of her life and to pursue her own interests." Geri paused. "Also, she

116

didn't admit it, but I think she didn't want to be a burden to me if her health did begin to fail. But that seemed really far off, believe me. She treated Heritage House like a luxury hotel, she loved being free as a bird, that's what she often said."

"I know she loved bird-watching," said Lucy.

"You said it. She was out every morning at dawn, that's when the birds are most active. She was so excited when she heard the first redwings calling, she rang me right up and made me listen on her cell phone. She said it meant spring was really coming."

Lucy wondered if this was a clue. "Was that the day she disappeared?" she asked, thinking that the call might place Agnes in a particular location.

"No, it was a few weeks before. Red-winged blackbirds are the first spring migrants. The last bird alert she sent me was a photo of a killdeer, and that was the day she disappeared."

"Where would that have been? Any idea?"

"I'm not sure. Probably that sandy area where the old brickyard used to be, and you know, it's not far from Heritage House."

"The police chief didn't mention searching out there," said Lucy.

"I don't know why I didn't think of this

sooner! I've got to get out there! Mom might be hurt, drifting in and out of consciousness. . . ."

Lucy thought this was highly improbable and felt awful about raising false hopes. "It's been days since she disappeared," she cautioned.

"If she's out there, Mom very well could be injured but alive. Believe me, she knows how to take care of herself. And she's strong, like I told you. She was climbing the White Mountains, the Presidentials, until a few years ago. She adored staying at those AMC huts. She said being up above the clouds made her think there might really be a God after all."

Hearing the hopeful, excited note in Geri's voice she felt an overwhelming sense of responsibility. There was no way she could drop the matter, she had to follow through, no matter how awful the consequences. "Do you want to go out there and take a look?" she asked.

"Would you do that?" asked Geri.

"Sure," said Lucy. "And I know someone who might like to come along, someone who has the perfect dog. Connor found a body in the Great Bay conservation area last year." Lucy bit her tongue, belatedly realizing this was not the image she wished to

118

convey, and quickly added, "If she's hurt or injured, if she's out there, Connor will find her."

Connor's owner, Mickey Woods, quickly agreed to bring Connor along for a walk by the shore, if her mother would agree to watch baby Sophie. "Now that Sophie is older it's a lot harder for me to get out for walks, and Connor's been sort of depressed lately. Sophie's grown a lot and I can't manage her comfortably in a baby carrier, not like the days when she was a newborn and I'd pop her in the Snugli. Now she wants to walk and you can imagine how that goes!"

"I remember those days," said Lucy, who had been shocked when Sue commented one day that babies were 90 percent boredom and 10 percent panic, but over the years had come to agree with her. "Let me know what time to meet, okay?"

It was just after ten when the three women met at the trailhead, each one dressed for the windy spring weather in hats and gloves, warm jackets, and duck boots. Connor was wearing a jaunty bandanna around his neck and was exhibiting doggy delirium, smiling a toothy, tongue-lolling smile and holding his tail aloft, dashing ahead and circling back to check on Mickey.

"It's terrible about your mother," said

Mickey, speaking to Geri.

"Thanks for doing this," said Geri, who wore a perpetually anxious expression these days. "I really appreciate it."

"I'm happy to help, though I have to warn you that Connor isn't exactly a trained search dog." That was proven when he returned with a stick in his mouth and dropped it at Mickey's feet, then sat, inviting her to throw it for him to retrieve. "No, Connor. No fetch today."

Watching him, Lucy felt a pang of regret. Once upon a time Libby loved walks and fetch but now that she was older she preferred to spend her days snoozing in her dog bed near the kitchen stove. Maybe, she thought, she should get a puppy.

Then, noticing Connor hunched over to produce a very large amount of doggy business, which Mickey quickly picked up in a plastic poo-bag, she reconsidered. Puppies were a lot of work, almost as much work as a baby.

"Tell me about Sophie," urged Lucy as they walked along. "I remember that day when Connor found that poor girl's body, and you had her in the Snugli, tucked under your chin, sleeping like a little angel."

"Like I told you, she's walking and talking, she's a real handful. She gets into everything, things you don't even think of, like the bathroom trash can. I have to watch her every minute, but" — Mickey's face softened — "I'm sure I'm not exactly impartial but I do think she's the cleverest, most beautiful, most adorable child on earth."

Lucy and Geri chuckled. "I'm sure you do," said Geri.

"Do you have kids?" Mickey asked.

"No. It was just me and Mom, but there wasn't really all that much of Mom because she was always off reporting in distant places, so I spent most of my childhood with my aunt and uncle."

"I hadn't realized," said Lucy. "That must have been tough."

"It was, and I was a really resentful kid. I did all the stuff that angry, rebellious kids do: sex and booze and drugs and dropping out of college, I did it all. It was a professor, a guy I was having a completely inappropriate affair with, who told me I was too smart to waste my life and got me to straighten out. And then Mom got pretty seriously traumatized — I don't know the details but she said she couldn't go back. That's when she came home and took up bird-watching and we really got to know each other."

The three women were walking along a

narrow strand of beach, dotted with boulders and sprinkled with old bricks, broken and rounded by the constant action of the waves. The pine forest was on one side, the lapping waves on the other. Just ahead, Lucy knew, there was a bigger sandy area where a little stream trickled down to the bay, where it was likely that Agnes saw the killdeer. It was there that she saw Connor leap ahead, jumping over a fallen tree, black tail held high like a signal.

"Do you think . . ." wondered Lucy.

"What's he after?" asked Geri, hesitating a moment and then running after the dog.

"Connor! Connor!" yelled Mickey, and the dog's head popped up over the log.

Geri stopped in her tracks, halfway down the beach, and Connor trotted up to her, eager to show his trophy: a battered seagull's wing.

Geri, out of breath, bent over and gave the dog a pat on his head. Lucy and Mickey soon caught up with her, and Lucy gave the exhausted woman a hug. "False alarm."

"I'm relieved and disappointed," confessed Geri. "I didn't want it to be her, but I did."

"There comes a time when you just want to know what happened, even if it means she's gone," said Lucy.

Geri nodded, and the three women continued their walk, solemnly, no longer chatting but following the dog's lead. They eventually picked up the trail again, and circled back through the woods to the parking area, where they paused to drink some water and Lucy distributed granola bars.

"Well, thanks for trying," said Geri, her voice breaking. "I really appreciate it."

"Don't give up," urged Mickey, opening the hatch so Connor could jump into her SUV. Then with a wave she slipped behind the wheel and drove off, leaving Lucy with Geri.

"I'm not giving up," said Geri, "but I honestly don't know what to do next."

Lucy had a thought. "Her car's still at Heritage House, right?"

"Yeah."

"So she must have returned, right?"

"She could have walked from Heritage House, she probably did. She preferred walking, she liked being out in the open air, and she covered miles every week." Geri snorted. "Made me look like a lazy bones."

"I know you said she didn't bother to make friends at Heritage House, but isn't there anyone she had an interest in?"

"Not really. I guess Howard, Howard White, was the one she liked best. She disagreed with him on politics, though. She thought he had a conservative streak she didn't approve of."

Lucy chuckled. "I know Howard. I'll pay him a visit, see if he's come up with any new ideas about your mom." She replaced the cap on her water bottle. "I did try chatting up the ladies at the Easter bonnet workshop, but like I told you, I didn't get anywhere."

"Thanks, Lucy," said Geri, stuffing the last of the granola bar in her mouth and crumpling the wrapper in her hand. When it was a tight little ball she continued to squeeze it, unwilling to give it up.

"Take care," said Lucy, holding her in a long hug, then releasing her and getting in her car. She caught a glimpse of her in her rearview mirror as she drove away down the unpaved road, a lonesome figure in a black parka against the bleak scrap of windswept shore. She could be a Wyeth painting, thought Lucy, bouncing as she hit a rut.

Lucy's thoughts were scattershot as she drove home; at one moment she pictured Agnes in a tropical jungle peering through her high-power birding binoculars at a colorful parrot, the next she was dead in a ditch, or lying in a distant hospital with no memory of how she got there. Jim Kirwan was right, she decided, when he told her that disappearances were the most frustrating cases.

When she arrived at the old farmhouse on Red Top Road she noticed Zoe's car was again parked in the driveway, along with Leanne's, which meant they'd returned from apartment hunting. Lucy was curious to learn if they'd been successful when she again found them both sitting at the kitchen table. "What's up?" she asked, giving Libby a pat on the head in response to the dog's rather subdued welcome. Noticing Libby's stiff-legged walk as she returned to her doggy bed, Lucy considered giving her one of the pain pills prescribed by the vet.

"We found the cutest apartment, Mom," enthused Zoe. "And it's affordable."

"Right," agreed Leanne. "Only nine hundred a month."

"What sort of shape is it in?" asked Lucy skeptically, as she wrestled with the child-safe cap on the pill bottle. She was picturing cracked windows, stained wallpaper, and peeling linoleum in some dank, dark cellar.

"Look for yourself!" invited Zoe, offering her cell phone.

Lucy finally removed the cap with a pop, took out a huge tablet, and proceeded to coat it with peanut butter. "Yum, yum," she said in a coaxing voice, which didn't impress Libby in the least. The dog dropped her chin on her forepaws and sighed. Nothing for it, decided Lucy, but to pry the dog's mouth open and shove the pill as far inside as she could. That task completed, she apologized. "Sorry, old girl."

Then she washed her hands free of doggy slobber and peanut butter, before accepting the phone and studying the photos Zoe had taken of the apartment. What she saw was a pleasant surprise. The photos depicted a dormered attic apartment with two very tiny bedrooms, a roomier living area, and a very cute, albeit retro, kitchen.

"I'd die for that stove," she said, admiring the gleaming white vintage Amana with its high back panel and curved corners. "Does it work?"

"Like a charm, the lady made us tea on it," said Leanne.

"She said we have to keep the red Formica table and chairs, that's nonnegotiable since she doesn't have any place to store them," said Zoe.

"Yeah, she was all apologetic about it," added Leanne. "Like we wouldn't want them!"

"They are real cute," agreed Lucy. "What about the bathroom? Is it in good shape?"

"Yes, Mom. It's basic, but it's got a sink, shower, and toilet, and it's very clean. No cracks or dripping faucets, no rust spots. You'd approve."

"How many flights up?" asked Lucy, who knew that she and Bill would be dragooned into helping them move.

"Two flights. Both outside," admitted Zoe.

"Good exercise for us. We won't need a gym membership," said Leanne.

"And it's near the ballpark and the hospital, we can both walk to work."

"It sounds perfect," admitted Lucy, who was already thinking about red-and-white-checked gingham curtains for the kitchen, and finally getting rid of her mother's Early American love seat and braided rugs she'd been storing in the basement.

"Yup, Mom. We're going to go boho. It's going to be so cute!"

"Right. Bead curtains, lava lamps, shag rugs, and Peter Max posters!" declared Leanne, swiftly demolishing Lucy's dream of finally emptying her basement.

CHAPTER EIGHT

Finding herself with a few free hours when the usual Thursday morning gathering at Jake's was moved to Friday because Rachel was at a Chamber of Commerce breakfast honoring Bob, Lucy decided to pay a visit to Miss Tilley to keep her promise about the sherry, and perhaps have a chat with Howard White. Geri had told her he was pretty much Agnes's only pal at Heritage House and Lucy wondered what he might have to say about her disappearance.

As she made her way through the lobby and along the corridors to the skilled nursing wing Lucy realized she'd come to feel quite at home at Heritage House. She'd been there so much lately and was beginning to find her way around, and she had also come to recognize a good number of residents and staff members who greeted her with smiles. "Beautiful weather today," they'd say, or "Good to see you," greetings that made her feel good. She was also cheered by the fact that Miss Tilley's recovery had truly been remarkable and her old friend was now chafing at the bit, feeling quite well enough to return home. In the meantime, the bottle of Tio Pepe sherry she was bringing disguised in a tote bag would make her stay more enjoyable.

She wasn't entirely confident that alcoholic beverages were allowed in the skilled nursing section, however, so she became somewhat uneasy when she spotted Elvira Hostens coming toward her in the corridor. "Hi, Lucy," said Elvira, giving her the once-over. "I suppose you're here to visit Miss Tilley?"

"That's right," said Lucy. "I'm bringing her some crossword puzzles."

"More than crossword puzzles, by the look of your bag," observed Elvira. Today she looked more than ever like a 1950s-era nurse, with her hair pulled back in a severe bun and wearing a starched white shirt buttoned right up to the neck. Her only jewelry was a name tag positioned squarely over her left breast. All that was missing was a white cap.

Lucy's mind was awhirl, wondering if the nursing supervisor was entitled to examine the contents of her bag. Wasn't that a violation of her constitutional right to privacy? Or were private institutions entitled to make their own rules? She smiled and shrugged. "You know how it is," she began attempting a diversion. "I'm always accumulating things throughout the day. I've been growing more forgetful so I just throw everything in my bag and deal with it later."

Elvira raised a skeptical eyebrow. "Really? You're kind of young to start losing your memory, aren't you?"

"I think it's just having too many things to remember," said Lucy. "I'm a working mom, I help my husband with his business, it's details, details, details. If I didn't make lists I'd be lost."

"Well, if you say so," said Elvira, narrowing her eyes and looking down the hall. Lucy turned her head and noticed a housecleaner dusting the chair rail that lined the hallway walls in a rather half-hearted way. "I'd better attend to that," she said, marching off to confront a new victim.

Lucy was only able to enjoy her sense of relief until she reached Miss Tilley's room, crowded with two aides and the facility's doctor, who was dashing the old woman's hopes about returning home. Instead, he informed his patient that she was indeed moving, but only to the assisted living wing, before making a quick departure.

"You'll have a nice little apartment there," explained Juliana Gutierrez as she packed some books into a plastic tote. "More room and more privacy."

"But you'll still have the support you need," advised Vera Crimmins, handing her difficult patient a little plastic cup containing a couple of pills. "Meds, meals, cleaning, personal care, all that good stuff."

"I have a wonderful helper at my own home," protested Miss Tilley, pausing to cough before taking the pills. "Rachel takes very good care of me."

"I'm sure she does, but can she be there twenty-four hours, love?"

"My name is Miss Tilley," snapped the patient, angered at Vera's familiarity and glaring at her.

"I wouldn't mind moving into assisted living," offered Lucy, by way of announcing herself. "I could use a nice rest."

"All I do is rest," complained Miss Tilley with a sigh. She was sitting in a chair, anxiously watching the aides packing her things. "What brings you here, Lucy?"

"I came to visit you, but I see this isn't a good time." She glanced at her tote and winked, signaling she had brought the contraband sherry. "I'll come back later, when you're settled in your new place."

"Probably a good idea," admitted Miss Tilley. "If you see Howard, please tell him I'm being relocated."

"Any idea where I might find him?" she asked.

"He likes to sit in the café in the morning and check his investments," said Vera. "If you take the elevator down to the lower level, it's right there."

She turned to Miss Tilley. "See you later," she said with a smile and a wave.

"Not if I see you first," replied Miss Tilley with a naughty grin.

Lucy followed Vera's directions and, when the elevator doors opened, saw a faux French café, complete with striped awning and cute little bistro tables and chairs. That's where the resemblance ended, she discovered, as the coffee drinks were all decaffeinated and the pastries low-fat. But Howard was indeed there, seated in a corner and studying his laptop. "Mind if I interrupt?" she asked, approaching him.

"Not at all," he said, standing up. "Please sit down. May I get you something?"

"Just some information," said Lucy.

"The Dow is up but the Nasdaq is down," he offered, seating himself. "Standard and Poor's is holding steady."

"Not that sort of information," confessed Lucy. "I want to ask you about Agnes. Her daughter says you are her best friend here."

Howard nodded. "Not much of a recommendation, I'm afraid, since I'm really her only friend here."

"Birds of a feather, perhaps," suggested Lucy, quick to add, "because you're both quite independent."

Howard acknowledged her little joke with a wry smile. "In a way, I guess. Sometimes I think we are the only residents here who see beyond these walls. Who watch the news and get out and about." He shut the lid on his laptop. "Also, I have to admit, we both have the advantage of good health. Good genes and solid constitutions."

"Even so, I know Geri worried about her mother. She thought she was a mite too independent."

"Agnes knew her daughter loved her and only wanted the best for her, but she did find her too controlling. She often said that her daughter treated her as if she was the child, not the mother. She said Geri was a daughter trying to be a helicopter parent."

"I imagine Agnes resented that?"

"She wasn't used to having to account for her time, having to explain what she was doing and where she was going. She found it extremely irksome and resented it."

"She sounds like my twenty-something daughter," said Lucy, laughing.

"It comes to all of us, you know. We're not as young as we used to be. That's what I used to tell Agnes but she disagreed. Insisted she was every bit as young as she ever was."

Lucy gazed at the mural on the wall picturing a colorful Parisian street scene. There was a row of colorful boutiques with French names: *Boulangerie, Libraire, Banque, Bureau de Poste,* a curvy art nouveau Metro arch identifying an underground station, and a busy café on the corner of the cobble-stoned street. The sidewalk was filled with pedestrians, including a chic lady walking a poodle, a curate in a black robe and hat, a white-faced mime in a striped shirt, and a little girl with a jump rope. "I've been to Paris and Paris is nothing like that," observed Lucy.

Howard chuckled. "If you want to know what I think . . ." he began.

"I really do," coaxed Lucy.

"I think Agnes simply decided to up and leave, to take a break, and didn't tell anyone. That would be just the sort of thing she'd do."

Hearing this expression of wishful thinking made Lucy feel horribly sad, like hearing a stage-four cancer patient making elaborate plans for a future that was not likely to materialize. "I wish that, too," she said, "but the police have checked her phone and bank records and found no activity at all, and her car is still in its parking spot."

"Doesn't mean a thing," insisted Howard with a wave of his hand. "She could have arranged to have a friend pick her up. Maybe she's a houseguest somewhere tropical, staying with a generous host. Doesn't need money, they flew in on a private jet and they're busy catching up and adding rare species to their life lists of birds."

"I suppose it's possible," admitted Lucy, thinking of her mother-in-law Edna's visits, when it was a point of pride to make her guest completely comfortable by providing everything she could possibly need, even politely rejecting Edna's offers to buy groceries or treat the family to a restaurant meal.

"Don't forget, Agnes worked for the CIA, you know. If anybody would know how to disappear, it would be Agnes," added Howard. "They have safe houses, y'know."

"So I've heard," said Lucy, wondering if Howard was onto something, or if he'd seen too many spy movies. "Well, I guess I'd better disappear myself, right to the office, and let you get back to the stock market."

He shrugged. "It's ridiculous. I feel good if it's up and bad if it's down, but it's just numbers after all." His face dropped, and Lucy realized he wasn't nearly as optimistic as he claimed to be. "Family, friends, good health, those are the really important things and now, at my stage of life, well, they're slipping away."

Lucy grinned. "Don't forget, you've got your fan club," she teased. "Bitsy, Bev, and Dorothy think you're the cat's pajamas."

He nodded and smiled naughtily. "Lord love 'em."

"By the way, they're moving Miss Tilley to assisted living today. I brought along some things she wanted. Perhaps you could drop them off later?"

"I think I could manage that," he said, accepting the tote and peeking inside. Seeing the contents, he gave Lucy a naughty smile. "I see this is high priority and will act accordingly." He snapped the clip on the bag. "With all due discretion."

"Thanks so much," said Lucy, confident she was leaving the Tio Pepe in good hands.

Lucy thought about Howard's theory that

Agnes was simply taking a bird-watching vacation in a remote location with a friend as she drove back to the *Courier* office, wondering if it was simply wishful thinking or had some basis in reality. She tried to imagine how she would feel if, as was likely someday far, far in the future, she were widowed and aging and becoming increasingly dependent on her kids. Well, she thought, good luck to her. Elizabeth was by now more French than American, happily living a carefree life in Paris. Toby, with his wife, Molly, and son, Patrick, had settled in far-off Alaska, where they had enthusiastically adopted the sporty, outdoors lifestyle. Sara and Zoe, she hoped, would remain close by in New England, marry and produce many more grandchildren for her to spoil, but she knew their focus would rightly be on their own families. She didn't want to be a burden, but she didn't want to be sent out to sea on an ice floe, either. It was a tricky balance, she realized, acknowledging that she would want to keep her independence for as long as possible.

Already her girls seemed to view her and Bill as fossils, pointing to their ignorance of social media phenomena like TikTok and Spotify. She was quite sure she would resent it terribly if someday the kids took it upon themselves to lecture her about her living choices, her finances, or worst of all, tried to get her to give up her driver's license. They believed they would be motivated by concern and love, but it would be very difficult to accept such a reversal of roles. It was her job to nag and offer unwanted advice to them, not vice versa! If that had truly been the sort of situation Agnes faced with Geri, she might well have decided to take French leave.

Phyllis, dressed head to toe in beige, was at the reception desk when she arrived at the office. "What's with your outfit?" demanded Lucy, realizing too late that perhaps she'd let her surprise get the better of her.

"Elfrida said I should start acting my age," said Phyllis, naming her niece. She said I was going around looking like a fat, middle-aged kindergartener. So I got this outfit from a catalog, forty percent off."

"That's very middle-aged of you," said Lucy, shrugging out of her parka and hanging it on the coat tree. "The neon green hair kind of spoils the look, however."

"Elfrida tried to wash it out but it turned out to be permanent." Phyllis smiled. "I hadn't realized, I didn't have my glasses on when I bought the stuff."

"What does Wilf think of your new look?"

asked Lucy, referring to Phyllis's husband.

"He hasn't said. He knows better by now than to comment on my clothes."

"Well," said Lucy, sitting down at her desk and powering up her computer, "you look very nice, very professional, but personally, I think you look great whatever you wear." In her heart, Lucy preferred Phyllis's collection of seasonally themed sweatshirts, coordinated with her ever-changing hair colors and reading glasses.

The computer was slow today, groaning and popping and then grudgingly producing a white circle that went round and round. This was par for the course, and Lucy knew she'd have to give it time to do whatever it was doing, so she decided to call Geri and ask her about Howard's theory.

Geri answered quickly, a hopeful note in her voice. "Any news, Lucy?"

"Sorry, no."

"I'm in the conservation area, but there's no sign of her here. I ran into a couple of birders but they said they haven't seen her lately, which they found quite surprising because there's a rare Eurasian pink-footed goose that's visiting." Geri's voice broke as she added, "Mom certainly wouldn't want to miss a rare sighting, that's for sure."

Lucy thought Howard's theory might offer some comfort, and began, "I was over at Heritage House, talking to Howard White. . . ."

"He's quite the character, isn't he?" offered Geri, quick to gain control of her emotions. "A rooster in the henhouse."

Lucy chuckled. "He was hiding in the café, no sign of his fan club. I asked him about your mother and he said he suspected she'd simply gone off to take a break, probably staying with a friend. That, he said, would explain the lack of phone and credit card activity."

"I've been through her entire address book," said Geri somewhat defensively. "I did it first thing."

"Of course you did," admitted Lucy. "What if she decided to go off on her own? Like those aborigines who go on walkabout, I think they call it. Take some time for themselves. Howard said she'd certainly know how to disappear for a while since she'd been in the CIA."

Geri laughed. "Where did he ever get that idea? Mom in the CIA? That wasn't her at all! She was all about uncovering secrets, not hiding them. She was a reporter, a war correspondent. She traveled all over the world to expose the horrors of war, corruption, ethnic cleansing, famine. She believed in finding the truth and making it known." Geri paused and took a breath. "It really got to be too much for her, all that cruelty and inhumanity. After Bosnia she was quite disillusioned. She came home and got a job in Portland, she said she was going to work where she could actually make a difference, where people cared if the building inspector was getting kickbacks. That's when she took up bird-watching. She said birds just went about their business being birds, they simply followed nature's plan, and she found that very comforting."

"It didn't bother her when a Cooper's hawk swooped down on a baby bunny?" asked Lucy.

"No. She was tough that way. Not sentimental. Hawks have to feed their babies, too."

"She was always a reporter at heart?" asked Lucy. "Always wanted to get at the truth and make it known?"

"Yeah. Even at Heritage House she discovered the podiatrist who took care of the old folks' feet was double billing or something. She went after him, reported him to Medicare." She chuckled. "It didn't make her very popular with the other residents who absolutely adored Doctor Foot."

"I know you think she might have been conducting another investigation at Heritage House, maybe something that was a bit more serious than Doctor Foot? Perhaps something that was dangerous?"

"I really don't know, Lucy. It's hard to believe that she was silenced because she was getting too close to something or someone . . . like what? It's a retirement community, not Putin's Russia. What could she possibly uncover that would be worth her life?" Geri paused. "If something happened to her at Heritage House, I'm inclined to think it was some sort of horrible accident that they wanted to cover up."

"I'm sure you're right," conceded Lucy. "I was just, umm, speculating. What if, you know? Crazy stuff. Forget I ever said it."

"Wow, Lucy. Talk about déjà vu all over again . . . I can't tell you many times my mother said those very words to me: 'Just speculating.' "

"Goes with the territory," said Lucy. "You don't have to be in the news business for very long before you start thinking the worst of everyone. Not a pleasant trait, I'm afraid."

"Out here in the woods, listening to the birds, I feel close to Mom and I'm beginning to think this is all the answer I'm going to get." She paused and Lucy heard the insistent call of a redwing blackbird, the chirp of a sparrow. "I think I'm going to have to be okay with that."

"I understand. Stay well, Geri," said Lucy, ending the call and reaching for a tissue.

The day dragged on for Lucy, whose thoughts kept wandering as she tried to focus on the account of the selectmen's meeting she was writing. Somehow the matters the selectmen had been debating — whether to change private Gull Cove Way to a town road, whether to accept the tree warden's advice to cut down an ailing but much-loved maple tree on the library lawn, how to fund costly repairs to the bandstand on the town green — all paled in comparison to Agnes Neal's disappearance.

She finally threw in the towel an hour early and headed home, hoping to clear her head by taking Libby out for a walk in the woods behind her house.

That idea was immediately abandoned when she opened the kitchen door and found Zoe collapsed in tears at the kitchen table. "What's the matter?" she asked, sitting beside her daughter and stroking her arm. The arm that held her cell phone.

"It's Leanne," she said, wiping her eyes with a crumpled cloth napkin that needed a wash. "She's bailing on me, she doesn't want to be my roommate anymore."

"Did you have a fight?"

Zoe sniffled and shook her head. "She's moving in with some girls from Alpha Pi, that fancy sorority. They've got one of those fancy loft apartments and invited her to join them."

"I suppose they need her to afford the rent," said Lucy.

"Leanne said they've invited me, too," said Zoe, showing Lucy a text she'd received on her phone. "But that since I was a townie on scholarship, she didn't think I could afford the higher rent." She paused to sniff again. "And then Jenna, she texted me, too, saying that her mother's best friend is a decorator and she's offered to fix the place up for them at a discount, and I'd only need to chip in four thousand dollars but she'd need it right away. Was that a problem?" Zoe fumed. "Like, really?"

"Kind of raising the bar."

"It gets worse, Mom. Then I got another text, from Lexie, which I wasn't supposed to get but she sent by mistake. Mistake, ha ha, saying how they'd never really feel comfortable living with me because you work for the newspaper and I might tell you something about them or their families that would end up on the front page."

"Wow, that stings," admitted Lucy, feeling insulted.

"That thread continued, Mom, all about how what if they went out to a club or something, would I fit in? Would I look right, since I don't have the right clothes? And what about my relationships? You know I've been hanging around with anarchists and climate change freaks . . . I'm not really their sort."

"Who are these girls?" asked Lucy.

"Lexie and Jenna? They're legacies, their mothers went to Winchester and were in Alpha Pi, too. I never really thought about it but I guess they're kind of rich, they both have cars and wear Canada Goose jackets and Le Chameau boots, like Duchess Kate. They're in that Greek orbit, go around with frat boys and their sorority friends. I always thought they were okay, I worked with them on a food bank project." She sighed and crumpled the napkin. "I didn't realize they were looking down on me the whole time."

"It's not about you," said Lucy, giving her a hug. "It's a tactic to break up your friendship with Leanne."

"Why Leanne? What's Leanne got?"

"I don't know. If they're as well off as you say they don't need her to help with the

rent. Maybe she fills some parental require-
ment, like 'you can have the apartment but
you need someone sensible and more mature to keep an eye on you.' Leanne's getting a nursing degree, right? She might fill
the bill." Lucy paused. "Whatever it is,
they're using her."

"And wrecking my life. What am I gonna
do? I can't afford the apartment by myself."

"We'll figure something out," promised
Lucy. Then she offered the same advice
mothers have been giving their broken-
hearted daughters since time began: "You're
probably better off without Leanne. She
really wasn't a very good friend after all."

Zoe responded with a similarly timeworn
answer: "I know you're right, but it doesn't
help much." She picked herself up and went
upstairs to her room, leaving Lucy alone in
the kitchen.

What was it with women, she wondered,
taking a package of ground chicken out of
the fridge and dumping it into a bowl. Why
can't they just lead their own happy lives,
why do they have to scheme and plot against
each other? she asked herself, dumping in
the breadcrumbs. She cracked an egg and
dropped it in the bowl, too, along with some
Italian seasoning, and began mixing it all
up. As she rolled the mixture into balls and

set them on a baking sheet she wondered if Agnes had been bullied by some clique or other at Heritage House. Had Agnes been made to pay for winning that bonnet contest? Had some sort of mean trick gone awry? Or had she gone off to lick her wounds in private?

CHAPTER NINE

Friday morning Lucy was out of the house by eight and on her way to Jake's Donut Shack for the belated Thursday breakfast gathering. She was especially eager to hear what her friends had to say about Leanne's breakup with Zoe. As usual, she was the last to arrive and found Sue, Pam, and Rachel already seated at their usual table in the back corner. Norine, the server, was filling their mugs with coffee and, seeing Lucy enter, filled one for her, too.

"Thanks, Norine," she said with a grateful smile as she slid onto the leatherette banquette. "You're the best."

"Regulars for everyone?" inquired Norine, expecting nods all round and getting them. "I'll get your orders right in."

Then she was gone and the group got down to the business at hand. "I'm thinking of painting my kitchen white," said Sue, sipping the black coffee that was all she ever ordered at Jake's. "Bunny Williams says kitchens should always be white."

"Who's Bunny Williams?" asked Pam.

"The grande dame of interior designers," said Rachel. "Like Charlotte Moss."

"Never heard of either of them," admitted Lucy. "But don't you think white might get kind of dingy?"

"I like yellow in a kitchen," offered Pam. "Nice and bright."

"The problem is that there are so many whites, I couldn't pick one," complained Sue.

"Really? Isn't white white?" asked Pam.

"No." Sue shook her head and tucked a stray lock of hair behind one ear with a perfectly manicured hand. "There are zillions of shades of white. It's mind-boggling."

"Well, I'm sure you'll pick the perfect one," said Rachel. "You have great taste."

"Aw, thanks," said Sue, putting on a show of false modesty. It had long been agreed that Sue was the group's fashion and decorating trendsetter.

"Well, at least you have a kitchen to paint," said Lucy, looking up as Norine arrived with their orders and began distributing a yogurt parfait for Rachel, a sunshine muffin for Pam, and hash and eggs for Lucy. "Zoe found a cute apartment in Portland

and was planning to share it with her friend Leanne, but Leanne was poached by a couple of other girls, leaving Zoe homeless. She can't afford it on her own."

"That stinks," said Norine. "What's she gonna do?"

"Look for a smaller place, I guess," said Lucy. "Or try to find another roommate."

Norine nodded approvingly. "That's the spirit. Pick yourself up and get on with your life." Then she was off to tend to other customers.

"Is she terribly upset?" asked Rachel. "It can be devastating when a friend turns out to not be a friend."

"The thing is," said Lucy, "these two girls also trashed her on Twitter or Facebook or something, stuff like pretending they would have invited her to join them but didn't want to embarrass her financially, stuff like that."

"That is such a classic mean girl tactic!" exclaimed Sue. "Pretending to be concerned about you when all the time they're stabbing you in the back."

"Stealing a friend, that's the worst," agreed Rachel. "We look to our friends for self-affirmation and when a friend turns away and chooses another it's very damaging to one's self-image." Rachel majored in psychology in college and never got over it.

"I told her that Leanne really wasn't the friend she thought she was, but I know that didn't help much."

"That's for sure. I remember when my college roommate, a girl I really thought was my best friend, stole my boyfriend," recalled Sue. "It made for a very awkward sophomore year since I had to live with her in such close quarters, and it still rankles, just thinking about it."

"These girls, Jenna and Lexie, claimed that Zoe hangs out with anarchists and climate change activists, and added that she couldn't be trusted to keep secrets because I work for the paper."

"Well, Lucy, we know you can't be trusted, don't we?" teased Pam. "We don't tell you everything, now do we?"

The others all laughed and Lucy felt hurt, left out of the joke. "That's not funny, Pam," she said, dropping her fork. "Especially since I work for the paper you and your husband own."

Pam's face fell and she was quick to apologize. "I am sorry, Lucy. I didn't mean anything, really." She paused. "You know, I think I was a mean girl back in high school."

The other three all looked at her. "Really?" asked Sue.

Pam nodded. "I was a cheerleader, I dated a football player, I absolutely shunned any kids who weren't part of my circle." She continued, "Anybody who was the least bit different."

"But you didn't actively try to hurt them, did you?" asked Rachel, offering Pam a lifeline.

"Actually, I did. I remember giggling and whispering with my friends when Dennis the Dork walked by, and we all knew he heard us call him that." She paused. "And other stuff."

"Why did you do it?" asked Rachel. "I'm asking in a purely academic sense. Research."

"Insecurity, I guess. I was desperate to be popular, to be in the right clique, to have the right clothes and the right boyfriend, even though that quarterback I dated was actually a lot dorkier than Dennis." She sighed. "He ditched me one night to watch the NFL draft, left me without a date for a big dance."

"But you're not really a mean girl anymore, apart from occasional slips," said Lucy. "What made you change?"

"Real life, I guess. Once I got out of high school I started working, I lived at home and took courses part-time, that's all my folks could afford. I didn't have the old clique anymore and had to learn how to make friends on my own." She gave her yogurt-granola parfait a stir. "I guess I'm still learning."

"We're all learning as we go," offered Sue, spreading out an array of paint chips on the table. "So which white should I pick for my kitchen?"

When Lucy was leaving Jake's Rachel took her aside and asked her to check in with Miss Tilley over at Heritage House and see how she was settling in at the assisted living apartment. "Bob wants me to lobby with him in Augusta, he thought I was a big hit at the Chamber of Commerce," she explained, her cheeks growing pink at the memory. "He's trying to get them to increase the tax break for electric cars. Otherwise I'd go myself."

"No problem," said Lucy. "I was heading over there anyway. Chief Bresnahan wants me to cover this big fire drill he's organized to show off these special techniques they've been working on for mass extractions, something like that. I was hoping to chat with Miss T and see if she's uncovered any interesting information about Agnes Neal."

"Give Miss T my love," said Rachel. "Tell her I'm watering the plants for her, keeping the house ready for her to come home."

"Will do," promised Lucy with a wave as she headed to her car. Driving the short distance to Heritage House she wondered if Miss Tilley was adjusting to the change, or if she was still eager to get back home. She admitted to herself that she had some nagging suspicions about the senior residence, but she couldn't exactly pin down the cause. Maybe, she decided, as she approached the double-door entrance, it was because everything was so perfect that it became unbelievable to her. It seemed phony, not quite what it seemed to be.

Maybe that revealed more about her, she realized, than Heritage House. Maybe she needed to step up her game, maybe she should be thinking about painting her kitchen, instead of dreaming about a big, expensive reno, and while she was at it, there was a long list of things she ought to do but never got around to. Cleaning out the cellar came to mind, she was pretty sure that any storage areas at Heritage House were organized and immaculate. And what about her garden? The dead plants from last summer were an unsightly mess in her garden, while the planting beds at Heritage House were freshly mulched and starting to show bright green shoots. And, she noted as she walked through the beautifully decorated lobby that boasted abundant displays of white phalaenopsis orchids in Canton bowls, there were never dirty plates and mugs, scattered newspapers, or stray shoes left behind in the inviting lounge areas at Heritage House.

"About time you made an appearance," muttered Miss Tilley, by way of welcome when Lucy followed the instruction card pinned on her door which advised her to "knock and then enter." She smiled, seeing Lucy, and winked. "Thanks for the sherry, Tio Pepe no less! Excellent choice. Howard brought it, very hush-hush about the whole thing." She was seated in a recliner in a modestly sized, but very pleasant, living room. Lucy took in the small apartment in one glance: the sunny living area with a small kitchenette, and a separate bedroom with en suite bath. The windows had expensive custom curtains, the furniture was all freshly reupholstered, the wall-to-wall carpet was spotless.

"So how do you like it here?" asked Lucy, seating herself on the love seat and shrugging out of her jacket. "It's a lot homier than the skilled nursing unit, that's for sure."

"It's done very well," admitted Miss Tilley. "You wouldn't know it, but the bed is like a hospital bed. You can make it sit up, or raise your feet. It's adjustable."

"That must be nice," said Lucy. "Especially if you like to read in bed."

"I might get one for my house, if they're not too expensive," confided Miss Tilley. "Juliana told me you can get them at any furniture store." She patted the book she was holding in her lap. "And the bathroom is fitted out for handicapped people, you could bring a wheelchair in there if you had to, and there's a fancy walk-in tub. There's grab bars everywhere and a red string you can yank if you fall and somebody will come."

"That must be very reassuring," speculated Lucy. "Do you think you might move in permanently? You could bring your own furniture and books and all, you know."

Miss Tilley was quick to dismiss that notion. "I really don't think it's for me. I'd miss Rachel, you know, and I like my independence. Last night, at dinner, it caused quite a stir when Howard sat with me instead of that group of women who are always hanging around him."

"The fan club, that's what I call them."

"Well, he is one of the very few men here, and I suppose he's quite attractive, but it's all rather juvenile if you ask me. I ran into one of them, the little one with fluffy hair. . . ."

"Bitsy?" coaxed Lucy.

"I think so. We were both checking our mailboxes and I greeted her with a pleasant 'good morning,' but she didn't answer, she just turned on her heel and walked away."

"Maybe she's hard of hearing," suggested Lucy.

"No, I think she's just rude, because later in the day, when I was sitting in the lounge area, working on a crossword puzzle, I heard the three of them talking about me." She giggled. "They called me an intellectual snob."

"I'd take it as a compliment," said Lucy, grinning. "I don't think those three together have half your smarts."

"I don't know, Lucy. I don't think I'm as quick as I used to be," she said with a rueful shake of her head. "I couldn't finish that puzzle, first time ever that I couldn't complete the Sunday *Times*."

"I've never been able to do it," confessed Lucy. "Have you heard anything about Agnes Neal? What are people saying?"

Miss Tilley raised her large, clawlike hands in a gesture of emptiness. "Nothing. Not a word. Isn't that odd?"

"I don't know," admitted Lucy with a

shrug. "One of the nurse's aides told me that there's a lot of turnover here and folks don't like to think about it. She said something about the grim reaper lurking around the corner, something like that."

Miss Tilley fell quiet and Lucy wondered if she'd misspoken, if perhaps Miss Tilley didn't like to think about death either. She was about to apologize when Miss Tilley broke into a big smile. "You can run but you can't hide, isn't that what they say? As for me, when he comes for me, I'm going to give him a fight. Like the poet says, I'm not going gentle into that good night. I've got a lot of living yet to do. And besides, I'm endlessly curious. I want to see what happens next."

"Good," said Lucy, checking her watch and realizing the fire drill was about to begin. She was about to mention it to Miss T, advising her to be ready, but remembered just in time that surprise was an important part of the exercise. Instead, she stood up and planted a kiss on the top of her old friend's head. "We need you to keep us all on the straight and narrow."

When Lucy made her way back to the lobby she was met by Felicity Corcoran, equipped with a clipboard and a walkie-talkie. "Thanks for coming, Lucy. I think you'll be impressed. My team has been working with Chief Bresnahan and other members of his department to develop an evacuation model that takes into account the various abilities of our residents." She handed Lucy an information packet and continued, "As you'll see, we strive to offer an exceptional level of care here at Heritage House, and we're aware that despite the most strenuous precautions, the unforeseen can happen. That's why we've developed this plan to go into effect in case of fire, flood, or any emergency situation." She looked up and smiled as the fire chief's red pickup truck was seen turning into the drive. "Well, we're off and running. I'd suggest you pick a spot in the circle outside."

"Will do," said Lucy.

"And be sure to take plenty of photos of our residents," added Felicity, spotting Chief Bresnahan entering the lobby, kitted out in boots, heavy coat, and white chief's helmet.

Lucy snapped a photo of the two of them, then took up the suggested position in the grassy circle outside. Minutes later she heard the fire alarm ringing inside the building and watched as the department's full complement of trucks began to arrive: the hook and ladder, two engines and the newly acquired special Bull Dog Extreme 4x4 off-road truck equipped to handle brush and forest fires, as well as the ambulance. Soon the entire crew of firefighters took up positions, some running inside the building, others unloading hoses and other equipment.

The first to leave the building were the patients from the skilled nursing unit, who were transported on gurneys and wheelchairs. Each patient was tended by at least one caregiver and was wrapped in warm blankets. They were greeted by firefighters and EMTs who quickly assessed their condition before moving them to a designated section of the parking lot.

Next to be evacuated, Lucy noted from the information packet, would be the assisted-living and senior-living residents without mobility issues. Because the elevators would be too dangerous in a fire they would be guided, the packet informed her, to the emergency staircases, which would be opened to facilitate "a prompt and well-supervised exit for all, with assistance for those residents who require support."

Lucy stood with her phone in hand, ready to capture the stream of residents she expected to begin issuing from the entrance, but as the minutes passed, nobody came. This was not the plan, she realized, as the

EMTs and firefighters began looking around and conferring with one another. Spotting Police Chief Jim Kirwan, she approached him. "What's up?" she asked.

"Dunno, they're at least ten minutes behind schedule."

"Ten minutes, that's plenty of time for a fire to get out of control."

"You said it. Something's wrong." Then he was off, running inside to see what was happening.

Lucy moved closer, trying to peek through the doors, but was stopped by a petite firefighter, dwarfed by her coat and helmet. "Sorry, ma'am, but you can't go any closer."

"What's going on?" she asked.

"Beats me," she answered. "But this is definitely not going according to plan."

Left with no choice except to wait, Lucy waited, hoping that whatever was wrong was a minor glitch. She couldn't help worrying, however. What if the residents panicked, or one of them had stumbled and fallen down the stairs? What if it was Miss Tilley? She took a deep breath and sent up a little prayer: *Please, please let everyone be okay. Please.* Then, all of a sudden, the doors began to open.

CHAPTER TEN

First to come through the door, *so typical,* thought Lucy, was Bitsy. She was supported on either side by her two friends Bev and Dorothy, and seemed ready to collapse. "Oh, my, oh, my," she kept repeating, rolling her eyes dramatically and gasping for breath. Seeing Lucy snapping photos, she found the strength to utter a few words. "The stench, oh, dear me, the stench! It was awful."

"What happened?" Lucy directed her question to Dorothy, who seemed the most composed member of the group.

"Keep moving, keep moving," urged the firefighter, and Lucy realized the three friends were causing a bottleneck, as other residents behind them were anxiously waiting to make their way through the door.

"This way," she said, relieving Bev, who seemed a bit unsteady on her feet, and taking Bitsy by the elbow. Together, they all made their way to the decorative stone wall that bordered the walkway and sat down. Bitsy began fanning herself with her hand, Bev's chest was rising and falling with her struggle to breathe, and Dorothy had closed her eyes, perhaps resting them, or even, thought Lucy, praying.

Other residents were straggling out in a rather disorderly way, looking about nervously like deer caught in headlights, and were directed to also seat themselves on the wall. A few were ushered to the ambulance, and Lucy could hear sirens in the distance that indicated mutual aid had been requested from neighboring towns.

"Is there a fire? A real fire?" asked Lucy, thinking that perhaps the planned demonstration had become an actual alarm.

"No," said Dorothy, patting Bitsy's hand. "There is no fire. There was an announcement saying the bells would ring and it was only a drill, and we should follow the directions of the employees, who would help us exit the building safely through the emergency stairs."

"That's when it happened," interjected Bitsy, eyes round as saucers. "They unlocked the fire door. . . ."

"Hold on," said Lucy. "They keep the fire doors locked? Isn't that odd?"

"It's because of the wanderers, that's what I call them. The ones with Alzheimer's, you know. So they don't wander off outside and get lost," explained Dorothy. "The lock is activated by a keypad and all the employees know the code."

"So they opened the door . . ." prompted Lucy.

"Right," said Bev, speaking up. "The door opened . . ."

". . . and there was this simply awful smell. So strong, it just knocked you over," said Bitsy, rolling her eyes and fanning herself with her hand. "I was quite overcome."

Lucy looked to the others, who confirmed her report. "It was the worst thing I ever smelled," said Bev, wrinkling her nose.

"I think," offered Dorothy, in a speculative tone of voice, "there was something dead in there."

"That's what it must be," agreed Lucy. As a country-woman, she was familiar with the scent of death, and knew only too well that the body of a tiny little gray house mouse could cause a terrible stink, and that stink could linger for days if said mouse happened to meet its mousey maker inside a wall from which it was impossible to be removed. Larger animals, like raccoons and skunks, created even worse smells, which

164

for some reason Libby found terribly attractive. Many times Lucy had come home from a walk in the woods with a very stinky dog who had found some dead animal and proceeded to roll around in its horrible malodorous remains.

"I think it must be something fairly large," suggested Dorothy. "Though I don't understand how a wild animal could get in that stairwell. It's always locked."

"Maybe someone forgot a bag of garbage," said Lucy, who also was familiar with what happened when Bill forgot to take the household trash to the town disposal area and it sat in the back of his truck for a week or two. "Even the recycling stuff can get pretty ripe if it's warm."

"I think that must be what happened," said Bev, trying to offer reassurance but not sounding quite convinced.

Spotting Miss Tilley and Howard exiting the building, Lucy made her apologies and trotted across the grass circle to meet them. "Are you all right?" she asked, noticing that Miss Tilley was a bit unsteady and was leaning heavily on Howard's arm.

"Fine, I'm fine," insisted Miss Tilley as they headed for the chairs that staff had begun setting out on the lawn area. She chose a cushioned Windsor armchair borrowed from the lobby, and Howard perched beside her on a wheeled office chair.

"Tell me what happened," said Lucy.

"I'm not at all sure," said Miss Tilley, making a rare admission. "Howard and I were at the back of the line. All I know is there was some sort of commotion when they opened the door to the emergency stairs."

"I was told they keep those doors locked, is that correct?" Lucy directed her question to Howard, who nodded in reply.

"I know it seems counterintuitive," said Howard, rubbing his chin. "It has to be that way because of the folks with dementia. There's a keypad on a lot of the doors around here, but they all operate on the same code, and those of us who can remember four digits know what it is. And, of course, it's the first thing new staff members learn."

"The front door is always open," said Lucy.

"True enough, but the memory care wing has a keypad, and all the emergency exits, too. There's usually someone stationed in the lobby except at night, and then the doors leading to the lobby are locked and can only be opened with the code."

"Right," said Lucy, who had been writing

this all down in her reporter's notebook. "So you didn't get a whiff of the smell?"

"Oh, yes, we did, didn't we?" said Howard, with a nod to Miss Tilley. "Even at the back of the line."

"Any ideas what it might be?" asked Lucy.

"Bigger than a mouse," said Miss Tilley. "I'm guessing a raccoon, maybe even a bear cub, something like that."

"Or a human," said Howard bluntly. "I don't see how a bear cub could get in there. I think it had to be someone with fingers who could remember five-three-seven-nine."

"Show-off," teased Miss Tilley. "Are you sure it's not seven-three-nine-five?"

"Don't try to confuse me," retorted Howard. He smiled at Lucy. "She's such a minx."

"I'm sticking with the forgotten bag of trash theory," said Lucy, unwilling to consider the possibility that some animal, or even worse, some person, could have become trapped in the staircase. Those emergency doors all had panic bars and opened outward to avoid just such an eventuality; you needed the code to get into the staircase but not to get out. But she did wonder how many people could have known the emergency code. "Do they tell you the code? Or do you have to get a staff member to tell you."

"You mean 'loose lips sink ships'?" asked Howard, going on to explain. "It's not exactly a state secret, but the numbers do get around. It's easy enough to watch one of the staff members punch it in, anyone familiar with a keypad can figure it out."

True enough, thought Lucy, who remembered taking Elizabeth to her summer job as a mother's helper in a nearby gated community. She and Elizabeth had joked at the time, laughing at the ridiculous simplicity of the one-two-three-four code, which Lucy declared anyone could have figured out.

"No, Mom," Elizabeth had said, giggling as she corrected her. "My boss actually forgot it and had to call me to ask for the code."

Lucy remembered laughing and observing that money didn't necessarily equal brains, to which Elizabeth had solemnly replied, "I don't think Doug married her for her brains, she's thirty years younger than he is and was a Miss Florida runner-up. She has a giant photo of herself in her sash and swimsuit on the living room wall."

Lucy realized how much she missed her oldest daughter and decided she really ought to give Elizabeth a call since she hadn't spoken with her in quite a while, when Felicity stepped outside, megaphone in hand.

"Thank you all for your cooperation and your patience," began Felicity in a booming, amplified voice. "Unfortunately, we've had an unforeseen problem that requires calling off the fire drill. I'm going to ask you all to return to your living quarters, staff members will assist you." Hearing this a few impatient residents began moving toward the entrance, and Felicity quickly cautioned them, holding up a hand. "Remember, no pushing or shoving, we want a safe, orderly transition."

She might have saved her breath, Lucy decided, as the group surged forward as if rows twenty and above had just been called at an airport gate, some residents even using their walkers to clear their path. A large, uniformed orderly leapt into the fray to restore order, and once the ambulatory residents had made their way inside, staff members began the slow process of moving the frailer folks in wheelchairs and gurneys. Soon all the residents were back inside but the rescue vehicles remained, which indicated to Lucy that Howard's suspicion might indeed be correct. That was confirmed moments later when the state medical examiner's van arrived, along with state police. It wasn't a forgotten bag of trash, or an animal that had been discovered in the stairwell, it was a person. Once Lucy had reached that conclusion she took the next logical step. Could it be Agnes's body?

No, she told herself. No, no, no. By all reports Agnes was smart and physically fit, there was no way she could have become trapped in an emergency staircase. But what if she fell, wondered Lucy, her mind running away along dark pathways she didn't want to follow. What if she was in the habit of using the staircase because it was handier, for example, when she went out early in the morning to bird-watch? Maybe she didn't want to disturb other residents and preferred to slip away quietly, speculated Lucy. And what if she fell and couldn't call for help, or maybe she slipped and broke her neck, or hit her head, sustaining a fatal injury? She stood there, watching, as the ME's assistants unloaded a gurney and wheeled it into the building, and came to an inescapable conclusion: whatever had happened, it didn't look good for Heritage House. The fire drill designed to showcase the facility's expert elder care had become a public relations nightmare.

No sooner had that thought occurred to

Lucy than she noticed a white satellite van from the Portland TV news pulling into the parking lot. Of course, she realized, the mutual aid call had gone out on the regional emergency network which was constantly monitored by media, and reporters eager to get the story were already arriving. She was well known by her colleagues and a small knot of eager newshounds soon surrounded her.

"C'mon, Lucy, what's up?" demanded Bob Mayes, the stringer for the *Boston Globe,* not hesitating to impose on their long acquaintance.

"Did some old dear take a tumble during the fire drill?" asked Phil Arnold, familiar from the evening news.

"Nah, I heard they found a body," insisted Bob. "That's why the ME is here, right?"

Lucy, who wasn't about to give away information she'd gathered while on the scene, simply shook her head and shrugged. "I don't know any more than you guys," she said. "The fire drill was going according to plan but was suddenly called off and the ME showed up."

"I dunno," speculated Bob, "these old folks probably pop off pretty regularly, right? I mean, is this really a story?"

"Don't forget the fire drill angle," cautioned Jackie Jones, who was on the Portland news station's I-Team of investigative reporters. "It might be worth looking into what the state regs are and how often these places are supposed to have fire drills."

"I bet this place isn't cheap," opined Jared Katz, who was a cub reporter for the *Portland Press Herald* and whose starter salary probably made him eligible for food stamps. "This sort of thing can't be good for their reputation."

"Yeah," offered Bob cynically. "We're talking thousands of dollars a month to take care of Granny and something like this happens, it makes you wonder."

"What I wonder is what really happened," fumed the I-Team reporter. "I don't have all day, I'm working on that state police overtime scandal."

"Hold on, hold on, it looks like somebody official is about to make a statement," said the I-Team cameraman, pointing to Felicity Corcoran, who had appeared in the doorway along with the police chief.

That set off a small stampede as the reporters all dashed across the drive to meet them, shouting questions as they went. Jim Kirwan planted his feet firmly and stood his ground, stepping protectively in front of Felicity. He held up his hands in a cautionary gesture and waited for the media scrum to settle down.

"I have an announcement," he began. "I'm Tinker's Cove police chief Jim Kirwan, and I am accompanied by Felicity Corcoran, who handles PR for Heritage House, who will make a brief statement. We will not take questions at this time."

Good luck, thought Lucy, who knew the reporters would continue to demand answers despite Kirwan's warning. For the moment, however, the group was quiet, anticipating the chief's announcement.

"This morning, at approximately eleven-fifteen, while a fire drill was in progress, a body was discovered in an emergency staircase. Pending a positive ID by the medical examiner, we believe it to be the body of Agnes Neal, who was last seen ten days ago."

Hearing this, Lucy found herself reeling and grabbed Bob's elbow for support. "Easy now," he whispered as the chief continued, saying that Felicity Corcoran would make a statement. They waited attentively, along with the others, for her to begin.

After taking a few steadying breaths, she began speaking in a shaky voice: "On behalf of the management and staff at Heritage House, I want to extend our deepest sympa-

173

thy to the family of Agnes Neal." Clearly upset, she was determined to maintain a professional demeanor and continued, saying, "All of us here at Heritage House take great pride in the high-quality care we offer our senior residents and we will be cooperating fully with local authorities to investigate this tragic development."

No sooner had she folded the little piece of paper she'd been reading from than the reporters began pelting her with questions. "Is the body definitely Agnes Neal?" "How come it took so long for it to be discovered — she disappeared over a week ago, right?" "What systems do you have for keeping track of your patients?" "Have you spoken to Agnes's family members? How do they feel?" "How are the residents reacting? Are they shocked? Upset?" "Yeah, are they talking about moving out to other facilities?"

Felicity quailed under the onslaught and began to step backward under the pressure of the advancing crowd, and Jim Kirwan took her arm, offering support. "Back off, guys," he ordered. "That's all for now. We'll keep you posted as the investigation proceeds."

A couple of officers from the department came forward and neatly inserted themselves in front of the chief and Felicity, blocking the crowd's access. The two hastily disappeared inside the building, while the two cops guarded the door.

Like the others, Lucy stood a moment, studying the faux-Colonial red-brick building with its classic portico and neatly manicured plantings. It's very appearance promised safety and security, a worry-free, gracious lifestyle that offered comfort and care to the seniors entering the last phase of their lives. Turning and heading to her car, she wondered how much of that promise was actually true. "Something," she suspected, recalling a line in one of her girls' favorite childhood books, *Madeline,* spoken by Miss Clavel, "something is not right."

Indeed, she decided, something was very wrong at Heritage House and she was determined to find out what was going on. What negligence, or even worse, what criminal act, could possibly have caused Agnes Neal's death?

CHAPTER ELEVEN

Back in her car, headed for the office, Lucy struggled to sort out her emotions. What a horrible, horrible way to die. It was almost too much to bear, too hard to think about. But her mind wouldn't let it go, as she realized she was approaching fifty on Telegraph Road, where the posted speed limit was twenty-five. She tapped the brakes a few times, resolving to get her emotions under control, and approaching the stop sign, braked hard. She sat there too long, resting her forehead on the steering wheel and taking deep, calming breaths. She was startled into alertness when she heard someone tap their horn; checking the rearview mirror she noticed she'd created quite a tie-up. She stuck her arm out the window in an apologetic wave and proceeded through the intersection, careful to observe the speed limit.

Determined as she was to concentrate on

her driving, her mind insisted on straying back to Agnes's death in the stairwell. As a girl she remembered how upset family members had been when a great-uncle was discovered, by the mailman, semiconscious at the bottom of the cellar stairs where he'd fallen. Uncle Chet was a retired farmer, living alone on the acre of land he'd reserved for his brand new Cape-style house when he sold his dairy farm. The mailman had noticed when he hadn't picked up the previous day's mail and went to investigate, saving Uncle Chet's life. Lucy remembered her mother dragging her along as a reluctant teenager to visit him in the rest home where he lived out the remainder of his days, no longer able to fend for himself in the modern home that had been his pride and joy. Bits and pieces of his story came out, as her mother chatted with the nurses, and it seemed he'd been in and out of consciousness but unable to call for help. He'd sustained himself, they said, by gnawing on a loaf of bread; it seemed he may have been coming home with a bag of groceries and fell as he tried to carry them up the stairs.

Lucy wondered if something similar had happened to Agnes. Had she lain there in the stairwell, alive but injured and unable to call for help? Had she been in pain? Had she tried to pull herself to safety, crawling to one of the stairway doors and calling or knocking faintly, unheard by the people busy on the other side? So near to those who could help her, but unable to attract their attention. And if that was the case, how long did it take before she died? Thirst was supposed to be the usual cause in such situations, but she might have bled to death, if she'd had a severe injury like a broken bone that severed an artery. What would it be like to suffer an injury and, unable to summon help, watch your precious lifeblood spurting out of your body?

Lucy shook her head, determined to clear her mind and free herself from these disturbing images. She was on Main Street, she discovered with a bit of a shock, unable to remember how she'd actually got there. She pulled into a free parking spot near the office, grabbed her bag, and headed inside to write up the story.

"Is it true?" demanded Phyllis, looking up as the little bell on the door tinkled, announcing Lucy's arrival. "Was Agnes Neal in that stairway all this time?"

Ted looked up from his desk, the antique rolltop he'd inherited from his grandfather, and offered a rare bit of sympathy. "Tough morning, hunh?"

Lucy stood there, arms hanging limply at her side, unable to think what to do next.

"Here, let me help you with your jacket," offered Phyllis, levering herself up from her seat by pressing her hands on her desk. "You've had a shock. Would you like some tea? Coffee? How about a lollipop?"

"I'm sorry," said Lucy. "I've covered a lot of bad stuff, but this is really getting to me."

"Here, suck on this," said Ted, unwrapping a cherry lollipop he'd taken from the supply kept on hand for young visitors.

Phyllis took her bag and set it on the desk, then eased Lucy out of her barn coat and led her to her desk, where she pulled out the chair and turned it so it faced the room. "I'll make you some tea," she said, bustling over to the beverage station.

"I'm okay, really," Lucy protested weakly.

"No, no," said Ted. "Take it easy. You've got all afternoon to write the story."

"You're all heart, Ted," said Lucy, clearly beginning to recover. "What if I have a complete nervous breakdown? Do you still want the story?"

"Darn tootin'," he replied. "You were right there on the scene, an eyewitness. And believe me, this is going to be a big story. *Body of resident missing for ten days discovered in stairs at top-rated senior living facility.*

179

It doesn't get better than this . . ." he continued, then realized how callous he sounded and added, "from a news stand-point, I mean."

"Do you think Heritage House can survive this?" asked Phyllis, bringing Lucy a cup of hot, sugary tea. "If my mom was there, instead of neatly tucked into her grave beside the Community Church, God bless her, I'd be moving her out as fast as I could."

"It does seem irresponsible, at the very least," ventured Lucy, licking her lollipop. "They searched, right, when she was discovered missing? It's hard to believe they didn't check the stairs."

"I suppose they were locked, because of the folks with dementia," suggested Ted.

"That's crazy," observed Phyllis, settling herself back at her desk and smoothing her favorite spring-themed sweatshirt over her ample bosom. "An emergency stairway shouldn't be locked, it doesn't make sense."

"The doors have keypads and all the employees know the code and are trained to open the doors in case of an emergency. However, from what my sources tell me, most everybody in the place knows the code. It's four digits and anybody familiar with a keypad could figure it out just by watching someone use it."

"Well, that's pretty sloppy security," said Ted. "I'm with Phyllis. I wouldn't keep my mom or dad there for one more minute." He scratched his chin. "And at those rates . . . any idea what they're charging?"

"No, but I'm definitely going to find out," promised Lucy, sipping her tea. She turned her chair around to face the desk and fired up her computer, trying to decide how to approach the story. She was tempted to begin with Geri, but hesitated, deciding her reaction deserved more than a quote or two. She thought Geri deserved an entire story, and decided to interview her in person rather than over the phone. But not right away, even if Ted was pressuring her. She wanted to give Geri time to get past the initial shock, time for her complicated flood of emotions to settle into the resolute demand for answers that she needed and deserved. Answers that Agnes would have insisted upon. And as for herself, she didn't want Heritage House to wiggle off the hook, she was determined to ask the difficult questions and to get answers. She wasn't going to let Felicity spin Agnes's death as an unfortunate accident, and she knew Geri's voice would be a powerful force demanding accountability.

And she didn't want to get the usual PR pablum from Felicity, either. Nope, she decided, remembering Peter Novak's appearance at the Easter bonnet workshop, she was going straight to the top. And if he didn't have anything to say, well, a "no comment" or, even worse, a failure to respond to a request for a comment, would speak volumes. Dialing, she didn't really expect Novak to take her call, but the automated system informed her that if she wanted to speak to Peter Novak she should press two and when she did she was surprised that he picked right up.

"Lucy Stone at the *Courier*," she began, identifying herself. "I'm obviously calling about the discovery of the body in the stairwell. Do you have any idea how such a thing could happen?"

"Thanks for calling, Lucy. I appreciate the opportunity to express my deepest sympathy to Agnes Neal's family. . . ."

"I wasn't aware that the body has been officially identified. . . ."

"True, not officially, but the staff members who discovered the body were quite certain it is indeed that of Agnes Neal. They recognized her clothing and certain belongings that were discovered with her."

"Would it be possible for me to talk with

the staff members who discovered Agnes's body?"

"Perhaps at a future date. They are very upset, as you can no doubt imagine. But I do want to make it quite clear that we at Heritage House are cooperating with investigators; no one wants to get to the bottom of this more than I do."

"That's quite understandable. Something like this could be a devastating blow to Heritage House's reputation. . . ."

Novak was quick to respond. "Absolutely. We are very proud of our four-star rating which reflects the excellent level of care we provide to our valued senior residents. At this point all I can assume is that Agnes's death was a tragic accident, and I want to make sure that if there is some flaw in our system, it is corrected so that nothing like this ever happens again."

In spite of herself, Lucy found herself warming to the sincere tone of his voice, and his slight accent, perhaps Swiss, which gave his statements a certain weight. It seemed to betoken a sort of European sophistication and worldliness which was not commonly found in a small coastal village like Tinker's Cove. Recalling her determination to put Novak on the spot, and to get real answers about Agnes's death, she resolved not to be seduced by this smooth talker and reached for the printout she'd made of the findings from the recent state evaluation.

"Heritage House does have an enviable reputation," she began, flipping through the pages, "but the state inspectors found several violations as recently as last month. Staffing, for example, is below the expected level, and several accidents were noted that resulted in injuries to residents in the skilled nursing section. One lady was actually ejected from a wheelchair, fell on the floor, and was severely bruised. I understand that accidents will happen, but taken with Agnes' death —"

"I am aware of that particular incident," said Novak, cutting her off. "The staff member involved was a new hire and hadn't completed training. Like most similar facilities in the state we have difficulty finding enough qualified staff members. We conduct extensive in-house training and have co-op agreements with the community college, but it's a constant struggle. The population is aging in this state and there are not enough young people to fill the available jobs."

Lucy knew there was some truth to what he was saying, but she also wondered if perhaps offering higher wages and better benefits might attract the needed workers.

"I can assure you," continued Novak, "that all the deficiencies in the recent inspection were corrected."

"Nevertheless," said Lucy, "that didn't prevent Agnes Neal from suffering a terrible accident."

"True, and we're going to conduct a thorough internal investigation and do everything we can to make sure it never happens again." Novak sounded genuinely sorrowful.

Lucy's mind was following another track, however, wondering about the state of Heritage House's finances. The place charged a small fortune, but was known as a stingy employer, paying little more than minimum wage. Where was the money going? "I wonder if you could clear something up for me. I'm not sure of your actual position. Are you the manager? The owner?"

"No mystery. I am the CEO."

"Who actually owns Heritage House? A corporation? An LLC?"

"It's privately owned," said Novak, sounding the slightest bit defensive. "I'm afraid I cannot disclose further details, it's a question of privacy."

"It seems to me that your clients, customers, whatever you want to call them, are entitled to that information. . . ."

"I am so sorry, Lucy, it's been lovely talking to you, but I'm afraid there's another call that I must take. If you need more information, please feel free to contact Felicity Corcoran."

"I just have one more question," said Lucy, aware that she was getting the brush-off.

His voice was firm. "Really, I have to go."

Lucy knew when she was beaten. "Thanks for your time," she said.

"No problem. Have a nice day."

Well, well, well, thought Lucy. Peter Novak didn't mind discussing the results of the state inspection or staffing problems, but he wasn't about to divulge who actually owned Heritage House. That information must be available, businesses had to pay taxes and file for permits, all of which involved statements of ownership. But how could she access that information, which was probably filed away in some obscure state office?

"Hey, Phyllis," she began, as the wheels began to turn and produced a dim memory. "Didn't Elfrida work at Heritage House a while ago?"

Elfrida, Phyllis's knock-out gorgeous niece, was the single mother of a lively brood of five children, all apparently the result of her inability to say no at critical moments. It was the accepted view in town that Elfrida was simply too kind and generous with her favors, for which she could certainly not be faulted, especially since the kids were well cared for and invariably polite.

"Briefly," said Phyllis. "She worked in the kitchen. She took the job because she wanted something year-round, but said in the end she could make more waitressing for a couple of months in the summer at the Lobster Pound."

"What did she think of Peter Novak?" asked Lucy, wondering if he'd put any moves on her.

"Count Dracula? That's what she called him."

"Did he try to bite her?" inquired Ted, suddenly interested in the conversation.

"No. It was just the accent, I think."

Lucy found herself chuckling. She found Novak's accent sophisticated and charming, but to Elfrida, he was a blood-sucking creature from Transylvania. It was easy to attribute Elfrida's reaction to xenophobia, but maybe it was worth further investigation. Maybe it wasn't only his accent, maybe Peter Novak's behavior had inspired Elfri-

187

da's name-calling.

"Is Elfrida working these days?" she asked Phyllis.

"Yup. She's a lunch lady at the elementary school." Phyllis adjusted her reading glasses. "She started at the high school but it seemed her presence there got the boys a bit too excited, teen hormones and all, so they transferred her to the elementary school."

Lucy smiled, checking the time, which was almost two, and decided Elfrida was probably done for the day and would have time to chat before her kids got home from school. "Do you have her number?"

"Sure, same as it's always been," replied Phyllis, rattling off the digits while Lucy punched them in.

"Hi, it's me, Lucy," she began when Elfrida answered. "Do you have a minute? I just have a quick question."

"Uh-oh, you're not going to put me in the paper, are you?"

"No. This is kind of a background thing. Phyllis told me you worked at Heritage House for a while. . . ."

"I just heard about the body! I can't believe it!"

"It was awful," said Lucy. "Everybody's pretty shaken."

"Poor dears," cooed Elfrida. "Those old folks must be beside themselves. I suppose they'll be handing out extra tranqs tonight."

Lucy was shocked. "Is that what they do? Dope the old folks?"

"Don't quote me, I don't really know. I worked in the kitchen, but there were rumors. . . ."

"What about Peter Novak?" asked Lucy. "What did the rumor mill have to say about him?"

"Not much, but I have to say he gave me the willies."

"What do you mean? Did he put any moves on you? Anything inappropriate?"

Elfrida laughed. "No. That was the weird part. He's not married, you know, an older single man who lives with his mother. I would've expected him to notice me, chat me up, maybe ask me out. Most men do. But he never did, which was fine with me, because I really thought he talked like the Count, you know, that *Sesame Street* puppet. Weird."

"So the puppet, not the blood-sucking vampire Count Dracula who sleeps in a coffin?"

"Wouldn't put it past him," said Elfrida. "He's definitely got something going on, some secret, I think." She paused. "Maybe

189

he's gay, though I don't know why that would be a big secret."

"It would explain his lack of interest in you," suggested Lucy.

"I suppose," admitted Elfrida, but not sounding convinced. It was a simple fact of life to her that no man, gay or straight, was immune to her charms. "Well, gotta run, I see the school bus coming down the street," she said, ending the call.

Lucy sat at her desk, phone in hand, wondering what it would be like to be Elfrida. She thought of herself as fairly attractive in a wholesome, all-American sort of way. Good teeth, freshly shampooed hair, clean nails. She'd had boyfriends, but she'd never attracted the sort of male attention that Elfrida did. She was trying to decide if she'd like to be a curvaceous sex kitten, maybe just for one day, when her phone started its cheery little ringtone. A glance at the screen told her that the caller was Rachel.

"What's up?" she asked, by way of greeting.

"Bad news," began Rachel. "It's Miss T."

Once again, Lucy's heart sank like a stone, and she felt as if the breath was knocked out of her. "Oh, no. Is she okay?"

"She took a tumble. She collapsed in her

apartment. I think that whole mess with the fire drill was too much for her."

"Did she break anything?"

"I don't think so. She's back in skilled nursing, under observation but resting comfortably. That's the official line anyway."

"Have you seen her?"

"I can't, that's why I called you. I'm prepping for my colonoscopy tomorrow and have to stay close to my bathroom. I was hoping you could check on her for me."

"Will do," promised Lucy, standing up and gathering up her things. "Good luck with the um . . . procedure?"

"They say the drugs are good, if you survive the prep," said Rachel, sounding resigned to her fate.

"Where are you off to?" asked Ted, observing her departure.

"Heritage House. Miss T took a tumble."

"Things really seem to be going south there," mused Ted. "What's going on?"

"I dunno, but I'm going to do my best to find out," vowed Lucy, grabbing her jacket and heading for the door.

Chapter Twelve

After the morning's excitement, Lucy found a somewhat eerie afternoon calm had settled on Heritage House where everyone seemed to have disappeared. There were no signs of life when she pulled into the driveway apart from a handful of official police vehicles that were parked in the circle out front, indicating that the investigation into Agnes's death was already underway. Lucy parked in the side lot and made her way inside, wondering how extensive the investigation was going to be. At a bare minimum she guessed a forensic team would examine the stairwell in an attempt to discover evidence indicating the manner of Agnes's death, and investigators would interview the residents for information about the days leading up to her disappearance. There was no indication that there was anything suggesting foul play, so Lucy figured the investigation would be rather perfunctory, a matter of dotting i's and crossing t's.

The sense of a deserted ghost town contin- ued when she went inside and found the cozy chairs and sofas in the lobby, normally occupied by a handful of residents awaiting rides or greeting visitors, were unoccupied. Security had been stepped up, however, and the receptionist apologized but insisted on checking her ID and making a note of her arrival before allowing her to enter. Con- tinuing on through the hall to the skilled nursing section she didn't see a single soul, everyone seemed to have holed up in their own private units and shut the doors tightly behind them. Finally reaching the skilled nursing unit, Lucy presented herself at the nurses' station where two aides were whis- pering together.

"Hi, I'm Lucy Stone, here to see Miss Tilley," she said, startling them. They sud- denly pulled apart, staring at her wide-eyed. "Can you tell me which room is hers?"

"Oh, certainly," said one, checking a list. "I don't see her here," she confessed. "Are you sure you've got the right section? This is skilled nursing."

"You must know her," said Lucy, puzzled. "She was here on this floor until just a few days ago. She was transferred to assisted living but had a fall and came back here, maybe an hour or so ago. . . ."

"We're both new, we're still trying to learn the ropes," explained one CNA. "We do have a new arrival, but I guess her paperwork hasn't come through. She's just down the hall, in two-oh-five."

Lucy trotted off and found the room, the door closed like all the others. Weird, she thought, remembering how the doors were usually left open for the convenience of caregivers and to welcome visitors. Faced with the blank expanse of blond wood, Lucy knocked.

"Come in," someone invited, and Lucy cautiously pushed the door open, unsure what she would find. "We're just getting settled," announced Juliana Gutierrez, tucking a blanket around Miss Tilley, who was reclining in the bed. She turned to greet Lucy, revealing a growing bruise on the right side of her face and another on her right arm.

"My goodness," exclaimed Lucy, shocked at the extent of the ugly purple bruising. "What happened to you?"

"I slipped in my bathroom," said Miss Tilley, speaking with some difficulty. "One moment I was reaching for my toothbrush and next thing I knew I was smack flat on the floor."

194

"If you ask me," observed Juliana, "you had no business being in assisted living. Not when you're having spells of vertigo."

Lucy's eyes widened. "Is that true? You've been having dizzy spells?"

"Only now and then," said Miss Tilley defensively, with a wave of a similarly bruised hand. "Nothing to worry about."

Juliana shook her head. "Listen to her. She was supposed to ask for assistance when she needed the bathroom, it's right here in her file," she insisted, pointing to her e-notebook. "She's not supposed to move about without help."

"Pish-tosh," protested Miss Tilley. "I rang but nobody came and I knew I could manage just fine. . . ."

"Except you didn't," said Juliana. "You need to be patient. Sometimes it can take a while before someone has a minute to answer your ring."

Lucy sat down in the visitor's chair next to the bed and reached for Miss Tilley's good hand, giving it a squeeze. "What I don't understand is what she was doing in assisted living if she was having dizzy spells and wasn't supposed to move about on her own."

This got a snort from Juliana, who was hanging Miss Tilley's clothes in the closet.

"It's money, they only get Medicare rates for the rehab patients, the ones who are over sixty-five anyway. As soon as they can, they move them into the temporary assisted living apartments which are private pay."

From time to time Lucy had written about health care for the paper, but was aware that she had only scratched the surface of a very complicated subject. The tangle of private insurance, Medicare, and Medicaid, all providing different coverages with varying deductibles, co-pays, and coinsurance, whatever that was, had been beyond her. She couldn't even decipher her own family plan, which cost a lot but didn't cover much thanks to the high deductible that made it almost affordable. "You mean her expenses are covered in skilled nursing, but not in assisted living?"

"Right," said Juliana with a curt nod. "Medicare covers a certain number of days following a hospitalization."

"Did you know that?" she asked Miss Tilley. "Did they explain to you that assisted living isn't covered?"

"Someone might have mentioned something, I really don't remember," said Miss T, looking confused and anxious.

Lucy reached for her hand again and patted it, struck with her old friend's uncharacteristic behavior. Was old age really catching up with her? "Well, you're in the right place now. You can relax and concentrate on getting well."

"That's right," added Juliana. "Can I get you something? Some juice maybe? Or ice water?"

"Water will be fine," said Miss T, covering a yawn with her bruised hand.

"You're tired. I'll let you rest," said Lucy, standing up. "And I'll give Rachel a full report."

Miss Tilley didn't speak, simply nodded as her eyelids drooped to half-mast. Lucy followed Juliana out of the room, turning to her in the hallway. "What's going on here?" she asked. "Are there a lot of accidents?"

"Too many," said Juliana, with a sharp nod. "There's not enough staff, and they want everybody to work overtime, lots of overtime. So there's too much work, and people are tired. I'm tired all the time. I hate it, I want to take good care of my people, they're old and they deserve respect and care, but sometimes I'm just so tired."

"I did see some new faces at the nurses' station," said Lucy.

Juliana rolled her eyes. "Temps. They're almost more trouble than they're worth. We've got to train them and that takes time

197

away from the patients." She sighed. "But after Agnes Neal's *incident,* that's what we're supposed to call it, Novak and Hostens knew they had to do something fast so they quickly brought in a few people from an agency, and I heard they're going to increase overtime, too. That means I'll be working even longer hours."

"Can't you turn it down?"

Juliana shook her head wearily. "No. If I don't work the patients will suffer. They'll be neglected, especially the very sick ones, the ones too weak to complain and who don't have family visiting. They're the ones who suffer the most, they don't get washed, their meals get delivered but they don't get help to eat them, it's terrible."

"Well, I'll be back tomorrow," promised Lucy. "I'm going to make sure my friend is okay."

"Good," said Juliana, with an approving smile. "She needs you."

Back in her car, Lucy began to fire off a furious text to Rachel about the deplorable situation at Heritage House and detailing Miss Tilley's condition, then had second thoughts about worrying Rachel. She erased the furious tirade and wrote instead that **she's resting comfortably, the situation is under control but bears watching.**

Rachel quickly replied, **Thanks, Lucy. I gotta run!**

Somewhat amused by Rachel's abrupt dash for the bathroom, Lucy headed to the office to finish writing her account of the fire drill and the discovery of Agnes's body. Phyllis greeted her with news that Ted had left the building and gone to the Gilead office, which he claimed he preferred due to its spacious modern interior and a fake rubber tree plant he seemed to think connoted an uptick in status. "I dunno," speculated Phyllis. "Do you think he likes the people there better than he likes us?"

Lucy was thoughtful, considering this new idea as she shrugged out of her jacket and hung it on the coat stand. "Why would he like them better?" she asked, thinking of her colleagues at the former *Gilead Gabber,* now incorporated into the county-wide *Courier.* They were all solid, small-town journalists but in her estimation they lacked a certain inquiring set of mind.

"Well, admit it, you and I are kind of mean to Ted sometimes. Do you think we pick on him?"

"Why do you say that?" asked Lucy.

Phyllis fidgeted with the chain that held her reading glasses. "I wanted to watch this show about the Me Too movement last night and Wilf," she said, referring to her husband, "said he was sick of screaming women in pink hats. So we watched *The Guns of Navarone* instead." Phyllis shrugged. "Well, he did. I gave up after about twenty minutes and took a bath and went to bed, but I couldn't sleep because I was thinking that maybe I have become too menopausal or something. I don't want to be one of those bitchy women."

Lucy thought Wilf was indulging in pretty typical male behavior, but Phyllis seemed so upset she offered some comforting advice. "You couldn't be bitchy if you tried, Phyllis. Wilf's probably just going through a phase, he probably just needs some extra TLC," she said. "Maybe Ted does, too. Come to think of it, you and I have been working with Ted for eons, I guess we do kind of boss him around, and he probably thought I was a bit too emotional this morning. There's a lot more guys over in the Gilead office, I can see why he likes to hang out there." Lucy sat down at her desk and fired up her computer. "But except for high school sports, which I admit the Gilead guys kind of have a lock on, I'm the one who wins the press association awards every year." The computer began its slow routine of pings and groans and Lucy turned to

Phyllis. "So what are you going to do about Wilf?"

"I've got a pot roast in the slow cooker," said Phyllis. "And I'll pick up an apple pie for dessert."

"Don't forget the ice cream," advised Lucy.

Phyllis laughed. "Wouldn't dream of it."

That reminded Lucy that she needed to come up with something for dinner. It had been a tough day, she decided, a day that called for pizza, and plenty of chianti!

Lucy woke with a headache on Saturday morning, she had definitely gone a bit overboard with the chianti. But at least she had all day to recover, until she got a message from Ted informing her that the ME's report had come through and he wanted her to post it online as breaking news. Somewhat doubtfully she checked her emails and found the autopsy had been completed much sooner than usual. Somebody had definitely been putting the pressure on, she thought, eagerly opening the file. It proved disappointing, however, when she checked the space provided for *cause of death* only to discover it had been filled with the word *inconclusive.*

She grabbed the phone, which was quickly

201

answered by Suzie Zapata, the state pathologist's assistant. "What took you so long?" inquired Suzie sarcastically. "I've been sitting here, drumming my fingers on the desk, waiting for your call."

"I just saw your email. What gives?"

"Advanced decomposition, that's what."

"What about her bones? Were any broken?"

"Oh, yeah. Her hip, smashed. And an arm. Consistent with her age and a fall. But survivable, not enough to cause her death if she'd received prompt medical care."

"Which she didn't."

"Right. And the heat in that staircase was extreme, some problem with the system, they said. So she kind of cooked and bubbled and liquefied. . . ."

"No need to go into details," said Lucy, feeling rather queasy. "Do you think she was conscious?"

"The skull was intact but she could have suffered a concussion that rendered her unconscious. Maybe a cerebral hemorrhage, that could've actually caused the fall and death, as well. Or a heart attack. Doc says there wasn't enough physical evidence to make a determination."

"Not like TV," said Lucy. "Those guys always come up with a broken hyoid bone."

"Real life's a lot more complicated," said Suzie.

A series of chimes on her computer announced the arrival of another new email from Ted, marked urgent. Lucy sighed, it was Saturday and she had been hoping he'd be satisfied with a quick recap, but Ted had other plans for her; he wanted her to write Agnes Neal's obituary. She didn't want to bother Geri so soon after the discovery of her mother's body, but she did need some basic information. She put in a quick call to Geri, apologizing profusely and promising only a few quick questions, but Geri surprised her by promptly suggesting an interview. "The sooner the better," she said, and Lucy agreed to come right over.

Lucy knew that friends and relatives tended to gather after a death, but she found only Geri's car parked in the driveway of her tidy ranch house on the outskirts of town. After ringing the bell she noticed that a small clump of daffodils by the front door was the only planting on the otherwise barren yard; Geri clearly didn't share her mother's enthusiasm for all things natural.

"I'm so sorry," began Lucy when Geri opened the door.

"Thanks. Come on in." Geri stepped aside and led the way to an extremely neat living room where a number of photos and newspaper clippings were piled on the coffee table. "I've been looking through some stuff about Mom — you might find some of it useful," explained Geri, indicating that Lucy should seat herself on the couch. "Do you mind if I sit beside you?"

"No, no. Then we can go through these together."

"That's what I thought," said Geri, sighing and seating herself.

"This must be very hard for you," offered Lucy in a sympathetic voice as she opened her reporter's notebook. "Let me know if you want to take a break, or stop altogether."

Geri exhaled. "I was expecting this, right from the start. Mom wasn't one to wander off like everybody said, and as for disappearing to start a new life, well, she'd already sort of done that. She'd made a conscious choice to give up working as a foreign correspondent. She was happy with her life here in Tinker's Cove."

"Okay, I have a difficult question so let's get it over with," began Lucy. "Do you blame Heritage House for your mother's death?"

Geri stared out the picture window that was opposite the couch, watching as a pickup truck made its way down the road. "I find it inconceivable that she apparently fell in the stairway and lay there for at least nine days, maybe ten, and was only discovered because of a fire drill. I think it indicates a shocking level of neglect that does not meet the expected standard of care." She shook her head. "But on the other hand, Mom loved it there. She was one of the first to move in after it opened and was thrilled with her apartment and all the amenities. She said it was like living in a real fancy hotel."

"Why was that such a big deal for her?"

Geri shrugged. "I guess she'd done a lot of roughing it as a correspondent and enjoyed being pampered. She went on and on about the convenience." Geri paused. "She loved that big grand staircase, said it made her feel like Scarlett O'Hara every time she went down." Geri paused. "I don't really know, but I suspect she was a bit claustrophobic. Hated elevators, any sort of small, enclosed spaces." She bit her lip. "Just a quirk, I guess."

"So you think she would have avoided the emergency staircase?"

Geri was surprised by the question and took time to think it over. "Come to think of it, it does seem odd. There must have been some reason she went there." She snorted. "Maybe avoiding one of those chatty old crones. She had no patience for most of the other residents."

"What else can you tell me about her?" asked Lucy. "What kind of mother was she?"

Geri snorted. "Not much of a mom at all, in fact. She left me as a baby to be raised by an aunt and uncle while she went gallivanting all over the world, covering wars and disasters. For most of my childhood I only knew her from newspaper stories she wrote and pins we put on a map, to track her travels."

That explained a lot, thought Lucy, who didn't like to judge but had been struck by Geri's unemotional attitude. She would have expected a few tears and maybe a sniffle or two. "Did that change when she took the job in Portland?"

"Not really. Mom was in bad shape emotionally then, very withdrawn. She kind of had PTSD, at least that's how it seems to me now. I was in college then, pretty much on my own because my aunt had died and my uncle, sweetheart that he was, didn't have the foggiest idea what to do with a difficult teen. And like I said, Mom was dealing with her own troubles. I ended up taking classes in the summer and even with spending a year abroad managed to graduate in three years. I really felt like I was on my own, I needed to get a job and take control of my life."

Lucy thought of her own kids, and their somewhat paradoxical need for emotional and sometimes financial support when they began to establish their independence. "That must have been a tough time for you. So when did you grow closer to your mother? Or did you?"

"Not until a few years ago, really, when she retired and moved into Heritage House. She said she knew she couldn't make up for lost time, but said she wanted a relationship with me before it was too late." Geri picked up a recent photo of herself and her mother smiling and standing arm in arm at the Quissett Point lighthouse and studied it. "I wasn't terribly excited, to tell the truth. I figured she was just getting old and didn't want to be all alone anymore. But looking back, it was a good thing. I got to know her and understand the choices she made, and really, I didn't have much to complain about. Aunt Sally and Uncle Mort were great to me, they were childless and thrilled to bits to have a little girl. I have lots of happy memories."

"So tell me what you can about your

mother's life, starting with the basics. Parents, education, surviving relatives . . ."

Geri obliged, describing her mother's childhood in Akron, Ohio, and her education at Ohio State. Influenced by the civil rights movement she began working for alternative media in the 1970s which eventually developed into her notable career as an international journalist. As she spoke, she showed Lucy various photos of Agnes receiving prizes, including a Pulitzer for her coverage of the end of apartheid in South Africa, as well as reports she'd filed from hotspots like Iraq, Bosnia, and Northern Ireland.

"As for survivors, there's just me and Uncle Mort," she said, putting down the most recent clipping. "She was a newsmaker, I've got to give her that. Even in death."

"You're right about that," said Lucy, noticing that a white TV van was rolling slowly down the road. "This is a big story, I hope you're ready for what's coming."

"Maybe I'll do a Mom," said Geri with a mischievous smile. "I can always pack my bags and head for parts unknown."

"I hope it doesn't come to that," said Lucy. "Thanks for taking the time to talk to me."

"No problem. You were out there with me in your duck boots, helping me look for Mom. I won't forget that. I'm really grateful."

"I had an ulterior motive," admitted Lucy. "If we found her it would have been a big story."

"It seems you're just like Mom," said Geri.

"Not a bad way to be," said Lucy, ending the interview.

CHAPTER THIRTEEN

When Sunday finally arrived Lucy woke with a sense of relief and excitement. Relief because she didn't have to go to work and excitement because Zoe had surprised her by asking her to go apartment hunting in Portland and the day had finally arrived. Sometimes, she told herself as she threw back the covers, you simply needed a break. A distraction. Something entirely different from the usual routine, which in her case occasionally meant attending the early service at the Community Church or more usually spending most of the morning cleaning house, and spending a long afternoon catching up on the Sunday papers while Bill alternately cheered and groaned along with whatever sports team was in season. Bored as she was by the sports, she could never quite relax because she was constantly aware that her phone could go off at any moment and require her to drop everything to cover a breaking story. But if she was out of town, in Portland, she'd be out of reach of Ted's calls.

Feeling that it was rather a special day, she took some extra time washing and getting dressed, choosing her good black slacks, low-heeled booties, a cashmere turtleneck, and topping it all off with an antique gold lavaliere necklace inherited from her grandmother.

"Wow, what's the occasion?" asked Bill, who was sitting at the kitchen table with a cup of coffee, the sports section of the paper, and a plate smeared with the yellow remnants of a couple of fried eggs.

"Did you forget? Zoe and I are going apartment hunting in Portland." She filled a mug from the half-full drip pot. "I want to make a good impression."

"It's Zoe who needs to make a good impression," said Bill. "She's the one who needs an apartment."

"She'll probably need a co-signer," said Lucy, sitting down at the table, "landlords being the suspicious sorts they are."

"Who can blame them?" said Bill, who'd heard plenty of tales of woe from clients who had hired him to repair their rental units. Units that had often been damaged by careless tenants who had added insult to injury by leaving town abruptly while owing back rent.

"That's why I'm trying to send the message that we're responsible, upstanding folk."

"So where's Zoe? Or are you going alone?"

Lucy sighed, took a big swallow of coffee, and went upstairs to rouse her sleepy-head daughter.

Zoe, it seemed, wasn't nearly as excited about spending a day apartment hunting as her mother was. "I had this all organized," she grumbled, as they settled themselves in the car. "If only Leanne hadn't bailed on me. I'll never find a place I can afford, not a decent place."

"Don't be silly. Portland's a big city, I'm sure there are lots of apartments. And I think you have an advantage as a single young woman rather than a group of room-mates who'd be more likely to party and make a lot of noise."

"Mom, why must you rub it in?" groaned Zoe. "I'm going to be all alone, eating frozen diet dinners and listening to sad music."

"What you do is up to you," said Lucy, determined to remain cheerful as they zipped along Red Top Road on the way to Route 1. "It's not that hard to cook yourself a nice dinner, maybe a chop or a piece of salmon and a nice salad."

"I'll have to eat alone, Mom. And how will I meet people? If I had a roommate, we could go out together to one of those craft breweries, or a club." They were passing a marsh and Zoe was staring out the window, but blind to the great blue heron picking its way along the winding creek. "I can't go by myself, I'd feel weird."

"Make a date with Leanne and her pals," suggested Lucy.

"No way. That's over. I hate her."

"Have it your way," said Lucy with a shake of her head.

The first place on Zoe's list was a basement apartment in a two-family house near the medical center, and was no longer available. "Prime location," said the owner, apologetically. "I guess I didn't need to advertise. I had a little sign in the window and I swear, I no sooner taped it up when I had a nice young resident knocking on the door. And she wasn't the only one."

Lucy looked up and down the pleasant, tree-lined street. "Do you know of any other rentals nearby?"

"Sorry," said the owner. "There's plenty of new apartments going up out by the highway, why not try there?"

Back in the car, Zoe consulted her list, then unfolded a map. "It's kind of out of town," she said, stabbing a finger at the grid of streets. "But the rent is affordable."

"Well, you've got a car. Let's check it out."

Lucy put the address in the GPS system and they followed the directions, finding themselves driving past what was clearly a run-down, low-income housing project.

"This doesn't look very promising," said Lucy as they passed discarded sofas left on the sidewalk and billowing newspapers sailing down the street along with discarded fast-food wrappers.

"You're such a snob, Mom," said Zoe, determined to press on.

They found the address a few blocks beyond the project, above an empty storefront.

"No way," said Lucy as Zoe hopped out of the car. She was already knocking on the door beside the storefront, which was eventually opened by a man in a torn and faded Guns N' Roses T-shirt, sporting an unkempt beard.

"You're here about the apartment?" he asked as Lucy hurried to join her daughter on the front step.

"Yes, can we see it?" asked Zoe.

"Sure," said the guy, looking them over.

"Rent's gone up, though. It'll be nine hundred fifty dollars."

"But it was advertised at eight hundred fifty dollars," protested Lucy, following him up the filthy, creaky wooden stairs.

"That was wrong," insisted the guy, pausing in the tiny landing at the top of the stairs and pushing open the door. Stepping aside, he invited them to enter with a bow and a flourish of his arm.

Lucy's first sensation was the smell, which was musty and caused her to sneeze. Next she noticed the grimy windows, the amateurish orange paint job on the walls, and the absolutely filthy kitchen area, where the stove and counter were dotted with mouse droppings.

"Uh, sorry, but I don't think this will do," she said, reaching for Zoe's arm and intending to make a quick retreat.

"Don't be so quick. Just needs a little elbow grease."

Which, thought Lucy, was really the responsibility of the landlord, not that she was going to mention that fact to Mr. Guns N' Roses. Glancing out the window, she noticed two young men not even attempting to conceal the fact they were involved in a drug deal.

"The rent's a little high," said Zoe. "Do

you think you could come down?"

The guy narrowed his eyes and looked Zoe over, scratching his chin. "Mebbe. Depends on what you'd be willing to do in exchange."

"We're out of here," said Lucy, grabbing Zoe's hand and yanking her along.

"Mom!" she protested, as Lucy dragged her down the stairs. "It was huge, so much space, I could've shared with a couple of roommates. I bet I could've even got him to come down on the rent. He seemed really eager to negotiate."

"Yeah, if you were willing to let that jerk prostitute you."

"He didn't mean that," insisted Zoe, reluctantly climbing into the car. "You always see the worst in people."

Lucy didn't reply but started the car, terrified of the dangers the city presented to her innocent daughter. How naïve was Zoe? How was she going to survive? "What's next on the list?" she asked, hoping it was in a different neighborhood.

"Well, there's this loft conversion downtown, in the arts district."

"Sounds expensive," said Lucy.

"C'mon, Mom, what do you want? If it's affordable you don't approve and if it's upscale you assume it's going to be too expensive."

"How about something in the middle," suggested Lucy with growing exasperation. This wasn't how she'd envisioned a rare day spent with her daughter to unfold; she'd foolishly thought Zoe would appreciate her advice and support.

"I dunno, Mom. I think we've got to deal with what's available." She shrugged. "The studios in this place aren't too expensive, and I'd save on gym membership, car, all that stuff."

"Okay, okay," said Lucy as they pulled up in front of the freshly rehabbed red brick mill, complete with a neon sign announcing the address and a gleaming modernistic steel structure overhanging the door. True to the ad, the building was indeed located among a cluster of art galleries and boutiques. Lucy came to a quick decision, realizing that sometimes you had to let your little chicks try their wings. "You go on in, I think I'll sit this one out."

"Are you sure?" asked Zoe, suddenly flummoxed.

"Yeah," said Lucy, ready for a break. She was tired of being the bad guy, taking the blame for the tight rental market in Portland. She hoped that by removing herself from the situation, Zoe would get a healthy dose of reality. She remained sitting in the car for a few minutes, then, becoming restless, decided to take a little walk down the street. She climbed out of the car and straightened her good coat, slid her handbag onto her shoulder, and slipped into her city attitude. She was a city girl after all, she'd grown up in New York City, even if she had spent decades in quaint old Tinker's Cove. She strolled down the sidewalk, glancing at the storefronts and stopping in front of a gallery that had a single painting in the window, a portrait of a woman that reminded her of her daughter Elizabeth. On impulse she opened the door and went in.

"Welcome," said the smiling gallerina, who was seated at a Parsons table that was bare except for a laptop computer and a guest book. She was a young woman with long, black hair, wearing a slim black dress accented with a chunky blue necklace. "Would you like to sign our guest book?" she invited.

"Sure," said Lucy, glancing around and finding herself disappointed to discover that most of the artwork on display was of the usual lighthouse and rocky coast variety. "The painting in the window caught my eye," she said, picking up the pen and writing her name and email address.

"Ah, that's beautiful, isn't it? It's by Aurore Sonnay."

"I didn't notice a price . . ." said Lucy.

"Twenty-five."

"Hundred?"

The gallerina chuckled. "Thousand. Her work has become increasingly sought after since her death last year. That painting is of her daughter, which perhaps explains why it's so especially beautiful. It was painted with loving eyes."

"Hmm," sighed Lucy. "A bit out of my reach." She turned to go, but the gallerina spoke up. "If these paintings aren't to your taste you might enjoy the photographs we've got on display downstairs. They're by Matthieu Colon. . . ." she said, emphasizing the photographer's identity.

"Should I recognize that name?" asked Lucy.

The gallerina cocked her head and smiled. "Perhaps he's not a household name just yet, but his reputation is growing. And now's the time to buy before he really takes off. . . ."

"How can I resist?" laughed Lucy, following the gallerina's directions to the display area in the gallery's lower level.

Rounding a corner at the bottom of the stairs she was confronted by a large black-

and-white poster featuring a portrait of the photographer, who was much older than she'd expected. He was clearly well into his sixties, perhaps even his seventies, with a gray beard and a full head of hair, wearing a military-style jacket with lots of pockets and a checked scarf, and holding a camera. She paused, studying his face, trying to figure out what exactly she found so fascinating and decided it was his eyes: deeply hooded, with bags beneath, they seemed to express an entire world's worth of weariness and sadness.

Intrigued, she continued on into the exhibition where she encountered a display of news photos from the Bosnian War. No wonder he seemed so resigned, she thought, studying the photos of destroyed buildings, uncovered mass graves, and portraits of rape victims. All caught in perfect, clear focus, as if Colon was determined to capture each and every horrible detail. A child's shoe, abandoned in the rubble of a bomb attack. Two bodies sprawled on a blood-smeared street, a man and a woman, who had struggled to touch hands in their last moments. A mosque, blown to bits with several prayer rugs still in place. A bearded father, his face blackened with dust and smoke, holding the limp body of his young child.

Lucy moved slowly from photograph to photograph, unable to turn away and struggling to understand why they held such a terrible fascination for her. It was hard for her to comprehend why people would do these horrible, destructive things to one another, to their towns and places of worship. What was the reason behind it all? Why so much hate? What was it that turned people into monsters, bent on destroying each other?

Finally, she decided she'd had enough and left, and returned to the cheery, sun-filled main gallery where lighthouses stood on rocky promontories and colorful sailboats bobbed in sapphire seas.

"It's a very powerful show, no?" asked the gallerina.

"It certainly is," agreed Lucy with a sigh.

"Here's a little information about the photographer," she said, offering Lucy a brochure.

"Do people buy those photographs?" asked Lucy, who couldn't imagine living with one of the grim images on her wall.

"Oh, yes. Colon is a master of light and shadow, composition, he's clearly on the rise," she said, speaking authoritatively. "His work has real meaning and it's beautifully crafted. He's truly a master, and his work is a good investment, it will surely appreciate in value."

Lucy smiled, amused by the sales pitch while tucking the brochure into her bag. Glancing out the window she saw rescue was at hand, noticing Zoe leaning against the parked car. "There's my daughter, I've got to go. Thank you."

"Come again," invited the gallerina as Lucy exited onto the street.

"What took you so long?" demanded Zoe, clearly disgruntled to discover that her mother hadn't waited patiently for her but had gone off to pursue her own interests.

"I popped into that gallery," explained Lucy. "What did you think of the building? Any good apartments?"

"Oh, Mom, they were fabulous. Exposed brick, stainless steel appliances, granite counters, fabulous bathrooms, and huge windows. Oh, and the wood floors were gorgeous, cleaned up and polished but showing signs of age. Patina, they call it. Dings and paint spatters, they tell a story."

"Sounds like you had a very good sales rep," observed Lucy, seating herself behind the driver's wheel. Zoe was easily impressed and didn't have her powers of resistance.

"He was amazing," continued Zoe enthusiastically, sliding onto the passenger seat.

"He knew all about the people who worked in the factory. They had these big black-and-white photos opposite the elevators showing the looms and the people who worked back then. Women in long skirts with their hair up in buns, and cute young boys in high-water pants."

"People who worked long hours for little pay in dangerous conditions," said Lucy. "All to make the mill owners rich."

"Mom," exclaimed Zoe, rolling her eyes, "you don't have to get all political. I know about the industrial revolution, and it wasn't all bad. Those mills enabled young people, especially girls, to leave the drudgery of life as unpaid labor on family farms and to come to the city, where they could be more independent."

Lucy shook her head. "So what is the bottom line?"

Zoe's face fell. "Nearly two thousand for a studio, Mom. I can't afford that, no way." Zoe cast a mournful parting glance at the desired but unattainable building. "It's so unfair. There was a pool and a gym, and a rooftop patio with grills and tables. It would be so much fun to live there but instead I'm going to have to settle for some grungy basement hole like Sara's place."

Lucy started the car. "How about some

lunch," she suggested, hoping to distract Zoe from her litany of complaints.

"I'm not really hungry," she said, "but if you want to eat it's okay by me."

"Uh, thanks," said Lucy, wishing that Zoe hadn't made her feel like quite such a glutton. "Well, I do want a sandwich or something and I don't think you should characterize Sara's place as a grungy hole. She's made it really cute."

"She's just got a bunch of stuff picked up at estate sales and hand-me-down pots and dishes. It's like she took the cellar with her."

"She's gradually replacing the old stuff with new things," said Lucy, defending her thrifty daughter, who lived in Quincy and worked at the Museum of Science in Boston. "She wants to know if you want her kitchen table; she doesn't need it anymore."

"That old thing? No way." Zoe was staring out the window. "I just can't believe Leanne. We were all set, that place was going to be so cute. She was bragging about the furniture her mom was going to give us, she works at Thayer's Furniture, you know, and is always changing up her place." Zoe turned and looked at Lucy. "Not like you, Mom, who never parts with anything."

"I like my house, why would I change it?" Lucy had spotted a sandwich shop and was pulling into the driveway. "Are you coming in or are you going to skip lunch?"

"I'll come in," moaned Zoe, as if she were doing her mother a huge favor. "Maybe they've got salads — I need to lose a few pounds."

As it happened, they did have salads and Zoe opted for a huge Cobb salad loaded with hard-boiled eggs, blue cheese, nuts, and creamy dressing, which Lucy was amused to see she devoured with dispatch. Lucy stuck with her usual BLT, limiting herself to only a few of the accompanying potato chips. After seeing the photos of people whose homes and lives had been ravaged by war, and watching Zoe chow down after complaining bitterly all morning about her situation, Lucy felt a word of correction might be in order. "You know, you're really very fortunate. I think you should stop feeling sorry for yourself and start counting your blessings."

Zoe's eyes widened in surprise as she popped a cherry tomato into her mouth. "You just don't get it, do you?" she challenged her mother. "I'm not like you and Sara. I'm not into estate sales and clipping coupons — I want more!"

Lucy stared at her, shocked at this revelation. "Well, I think you'll find that there's more to life than granite countertops and stainless steel appliances." She signaled for the check. "You know those quaint old-fashioned folks in the factory photos? Do you have any idea of their living conditions, when they were working twelve hours a day in that mill?"

Zoe stood up. "Yeah, Mom, I do in fact. I've been to the Tenement Museum, you dragged me there, remember? But that was then and this is now and I am not a factory girl."

Mother and daughter were quiet on the ride home. Zoe was scribbling away in a notebook adding up columns of figures in an attempt to make her starter salary stretch to cover the rent in the desirable loft building. Lucy, on the other hand, kept replaying the photos she'd seen at the gallery. One in particular stuck in her mind; it pictured a jumble of bodies piled atop one another in the bottom of a charred stairwell.

She remembered Geri saying that her mother had developed claustrophobia after covering a war somewhere and she wondered if she'd seen something similar. It was hard enough to look at a photograph in a neat, clean gallery miles from any conflict; it would have been devastating to witness firsthand. But if Agnes did have claustrophobia, no matter how it started, it was hard to see how she might have ended up in the emergency staircase at Heritage House. Why did she go into the stairs? That was the question that Lucy wanted to answer. What was Agnes up to in the last days of her life? What had she learned or discovered that made her determined to overcome her fear of small spaces so she could venture into the enclosed space that she would have been inclined to avoid?

Since she'd worked on Saturday, Lucy had some free time on Monday morning so Lucy paid a visit to Miss Tilley at Heritage House, and was encouraged to see that her old friend was moving about more easily, but her face and arm were still darkly bruised. She found her in one of the seating areas provided for residents and guests in the skilled nursing section, where she was sitting with Howard White.

"This is nice," said Lucy, taking in the upholstered sofa and armchairs tucked into a niche off the hallway, "much pleasanter for visits than your room."

"A change of scene is always good," said Howard.

"And that hospital room is rather small," said Miss Tilley, agreeing. "I'll be glad when I can go home to my little house."

"Any idea when that might be?" asked Lucy.

"It can't be soon enough for me," complained Miss Tilley.

"You need to relax and be patient to give your body time to heal," advised Howard. "Let nature take its course."

"In my experience, nature hasn't always been my friend," snapped Miss Tilley. "I'm beginning to think it wants to be done with me."

"Now, now," said Howard, patting her knee. "There's plenty of fight left in your old bones. And like me, you're too nosey to give up the ghost, you want to know what's going to happen next."

Lucy smiled at this insight and nodded. "You know, I was wondering about Agnes, she was very curious, too, wasn't she?"

"And I suppose you've been wondering if it was her curiosity that led her into that stairwell?" asked Howard, raising an exuberantly bushy gray eyebrow.

"It has been bothering me because her daughter said she was claustrophobic. Why would she go into the stairwell?"

"Maybe she was trying to avoid someone," said Miss Tilley. "Poor Howard is always dodging that Bitsy creature."

"Now, now," protested Howard. "Bitsy is

a very dear person. . . ."

"You told me she's practically your shadow, that you can't get away from her."

"Well, she is a bit clingy," admitted Howard. "And I have to admit that if I see her first, I do my best to avoid her, but I try to be subtle about it. I don't want to hurt her feelings."

"Was there anyone in particular that Agnes usually avoided?" asked Lucy.

"Not really," said Howard, thoughtfully scratching his chin. "If anything, it was the other way round. She could be quite brusque, she didn't suffer fools gladly, and people tended to avoid her."

"I'll have to try that," said Miss Tilley with an approving nod. "Cut 'em off at the pass, before they have a chance to tell their boring stories for the hundredth time."

Howard chuckled and shook his head. "I don't think you're cut out for life in a senior residence."

"That's the truth," agreed Miss Tilley, slapping her veined hands on her thighs.

"Oddly enough, Geri said her mother loved it here," said Lucy. "She liked the carefree lifestyle."

"I think she did. She made it work for herself," said Howard.

Lucy glanced down the hallway to the

229

nurses' station, watching as the elevator door opened and an aide pushed out an enormous cart loaded with patient meals. "Lunch is on its way," she said. "I should be going."

"It will keep," said Miss Tilley with a sigh. "If it's Monday, it's gluey macaroni and cheese."

"Well, I don't want to keep you from that," laughed Lucy. "But I have been wondering about Agnes's last days. Did she behave any differently?"

"Ah-ha," crowed Miss Tilley. "You think she was onto something? Something that wasn't quite right?"

"She was an investigative reporter, after all. And it's hard for people to change old habits," admitted Howard. "Now that you mention it, she did have a special little spring in her step the last time I saw her. I even mentioned it to her, I asked her if she was excited about the hat contest and if she had another winner up her sleeve." He sighed. "Now I wonder . . ."

"How did she reply?" asked Lucy.

"Oh," he said, shrugging, "she said she wasn't going to enter the contest this year. 'Been there, done that,' she said."

"So you have no idea what she might have been excited about?"

"Sorry," he said, shaking his head.

Lucy stood up, picking up her bag and jacket. "I'll let you get to your mac n' cheese before it gets cold."

"Oh, goody," said Miss Tilley, getting slowly to her feet. Howard took her arm and they walked off together down the hallway.

Lucy turned and headed for the elevator, wondering what had so interested Agnes. It certainly wasn't the hat contest.

CHAPTER FOURTEEN

The day continued bright and clear, though the chilly temperature and the brisk breeze coming off the cove were proof that winter wasn't quite done. Lucy was cheered by the sunny day, and also was looking forward to spending the afternoon conducting an interview. She loved interviewing local people about their various and sometimes surprising pastimes and today she was going to meet Vesna Varga, an older woman who crafted elaborately decorated Easter eggs called *pisanica.* She'd learned about Vesna from Pam, who met her when she signed up for the yoga class Pam taught at the senior center. "She's remarkably flexible for someone her age," Pam had reported, noting that "she must be eighty if she's a day."

Lucy wasn't sure whether she was more interested in Vesna's Easter eggs or her remarkable youthfulness, but suspected it was the latter. Maybe she had some secrets to share about fighting the aging process, which Lucy had noticed was beginning to take its toll. She'd been dismayed lately when one of her knees began to ache after a long walk, and there were those crow's feet around her eyes, and worst of all, gray hairs appearing in her brunette pixie hairdo that necessitated a monthly touch-up at the Kut'n'Kurl salon.

She felt a bit as if she were on holiday when she drove along Shore Road, where the breakers crashed on the rocks below, and parked in the driveway at Vesna Varga's house. She had a fleeting suspicion that perhaps Vesna's reported youthfulness was one result of a well-padded bank account; the house was one of the huge McMansions that were now a feature of the pricey coast road, popping up among the older shingled cottages. She paused a moment after getting out of the car, noting the driveway was made of expensive Belgian pavers, and admiring the million-dollar water view. Studying the overblown brick house, with its entrance hall designated by a huge window that revealed a showy chandelier, she doubted she was worthy of entering through the front door. Spotting a side door with a decorative WELCOME sign, she chose that more modest entrance. She had no sooner rung the bell than the door was opened by a tiny, but very well-preserved woman who was dressed in an oversized white shirt and slim black pants. There were no gray hairs on her head, dyed in a merlot shade that Lucy knew, thanks to Laurie at the Kut'n'Kurl, had enjoyed a brief popularity a few years ago. "Ah, so you are Lucy. Do come in," invited Vesna, speaking with a charming European accent.

Entering the kitchen, she was first impressed by its size, then took in the elaborate chrome-bedecked French stove, gorgeous custom cabinets, and a massive island topped with an enormous piece of natural stone. A basket filled with the decorated eggs sat in the middle of a round table tucked into the windowed breakfast nook. Vesna asked if she could take Lucy's jacket, which she hung up in a handy coat closet, and then invited Lucy to seat herself at the table. Lucy slipped into the custom-upholstered banquette, and took her reporter's notebook out of her bag, which she then tucked beside her. Noticing her phone in the bag, she turned it off so she wouldn't be interrupted during the interview.

"These eggs are simply gorgeous," she began, amazed at the complex designs and rich colors, which shamed the homemade eggs she had dyed every year with the kids when they were young. While they had scrawled their names in crayon before dipping the eggs, or double- and triple-dipped them in various cups of dye resulting in muddy colors, these eggs were works of art with sharply delineated geometric designs worked in amazing deep shades of purple, green, and red.

"Ah, yes," said Vesna, "these *pisanica* are a tradition in my old country. The mothers make them at night, when the children are asleep, so they have a surprise on Easter morning."

Lucy studied the eggs, marveling at the skill required to create the intricate designs. "How do you make them?" asked Lucy.

"First, we make a tiny hole and empty the eggshell, we blow out the yolk and white, but" — she raised a cautionary finger — "we don't throw it away. No. We make an omelet or cake, something like that. Then we use many colors, we make dye from onion skins, beets, flowers . . ."

Lucy's jaw dropped. "No kit from the grocery store?"

Vesna's delicately arched brows were raised in shock. "Absolutely not. I make the dye myself."

"And how do you create these magnificent designs?"

"With wax. I have special tools, some I made from feathers, and I use them to apply the wax. Not too much, not too little, just right. Then I dip the eggs in the dye. The wax preserves the color below. And so on. Many times. Until I'm happy with the design."

"Are the designs traditional?" asked Lucy. "Do they have meaning?"

Vesna considered the question. "I don't really know. I make the same designs that my mother made, and my grandmother. Some of these eggs are very old, we treasure them."

"Like Christmas ornaments that we bring out every year," offered Lucy.

"Yes. Some of the eggs are gifts, we always give the best one to the village priest. Some we take to the graves of family members, especially if the person died since last Easter." She smiled, revealing a perfect set of very white teeth. "And if a girl likes a certain boy, she might give him an egg."

"I suppose it's sort of a fertility thing," ventured Lucy.

"More about rebirth, I think. A reminder of Christ rising, and the promise of immortal life in heaven," she corrected Lucy, raising her eyes to the glorious firmament high above the ceiling and the second story and the roof.

"Oh, of course," said Lucy, somewhat chagrined. "So I know you're not native to Tinker's Cove, but your English is very good. Have you been in the States for long?"

"Ah, yes. I love America. I came here about twenty years ago, I think."

"Why did you leave . . . ?" asked Lucy, fishing for the identity of Vesna's native country.

Vesna merely smiled. "Like everyone who comes to America, I wanted a better life."

"And have you found it?" asked Lucy.

Vesna waved her arm, sweeping it like a model revealing the prize on a game show. "Oh, I think so. No mud, no smoky wood-stove, no chickens in the house; instead I have all this."

Indeed, thought Lucy, "all this" seemed to be rather a lot. Those diamonds in the many rings on Vesna's fingers were huge, she was wearing a heavy gold necklace and matching earrings, and that designer white shirt reminded her of one she'd once seen in the window of an expensive boutique on Newbury Street in Boston. Remembering the purpose of the interview, Lucy asked, "Is a photo okay? Perhaps you could hold the eggs?"

"Just the eggs, I think," said Vesna, smiling coyly. "I'm not at my best today."

"You look great," coaxed Lucy. "Not a wrinkle. I can't help wonder what your secret is?"

Vesna smiled. "American face products not very good, lots of advertising but don't work. I make my own creams."

"You wouldn't want to share the recipe?"

"No. Big family secret."

"I understand," said Lucy, smiling. "But how about that photo?"

"No, no." Vesna was not about to be flattered into posing. "Just the eggs."

"Of course," said Lucy, producing her phone and snapping a couple of photos. "It's been lovely meeting you. Thank you so much for your time."

"I've enjoyed our talk," said Vesna, handing her an egg. "For you."

The egg was light, it weighed nothing at all and Lucy was afraid it would be crushed if she tucked it in her purse. Instead, she carried it in her hand and set it carefully on the passenger seat in her car. For the briefest moment, she imagined seat-belting it in. Then, smiling to herself, she drove very carefully to the office and carefully carried the little treasure inside.

"Ah, there you are!" exclaimed Phyllis, when she arrived. "You've got a distress call from Miss Tilley."

Lucy stared at Phyllis, relieved to see she'd abandoned her flirtation with beige and was wearing a colorful sweatshirt trimmed with a sequined design of a brimming Easter basket. "A distress call?"

"Yeah." Phyllis nodded. "She sounded really upset. I tried to call but you didn't answer. Where were you?"

"Interviewing this lady who does fancy European Easter eggs." She held up the egg. "See?"

"Ah, one of those Russian ones?" Phyllis held out her hand and Lucy gently passed the egg to her. "Yeah," said Lucy, as the missing puzzle piece slipped into place. "Russian."

"My gosh, she makes these?" asked Phyllis, impressed by the intricate design.

"Yeah. You can read all about it when I write the story." She held out her hand for the egg, which Phyllis returned to her.

"Well, you better give Miss T a call. Something's upset her and she said you're the only one who can help."

"I'm on it," said Lucy, taking the egg over to her desk and placing it among the paper clips she kept in a little china bowl. Then she plopped into her desk chair and reached for her phone.

"About time," snarled Miss Tilley when she got Lucy's call.

"I was interviewing someone," explained Lucy. "What's the matter? Are you well?"

"Never better, but my bank account is going to expire."

"How so?" Lucy knew Miss Tilley relied on her monthly Social Security check, supplemented by some investments in railroad and lumber stocks her father had made years ago. Rachel had complained she'd tried to convince her to update her portfolio but Miss T had stubbornly refused, insisting that her father would not rest easy in his grave if she made any changes.

"I can't afford to stay here, Heritage House is going to ruin me. You've got to come and take me home."

"Have you called Rachel?" asked Lucy, aware that her deadlines were fast approaching and she was behind in her work.

"No answer there, either," fretted Miss Tilley. "When you need people, that's when they disappear on you."

"Okay, okay. I'm on my way."

"I'll start packing," said Miss T.

"No. Don't do anything rash," cautioned Lucy. "I'm sure we can sort this out."

When she reached Miss Tilley's room, she found her pulling clothing out of her closet and throwing it on her bed, all the while muttering to herself.

Lucy took her by the hands and led her to her big chair, saying, "Now. Calm down and tell me all about it."

"It's this bill! I can't possibly pay it," she exclaimed angrily. Then her face crumpled in confusion. "I don't know what I did with it."

Lucy noticed a sheet of paper poking out of the nightstand drawer and pulled it out. "Here it is." She shoved the pile of clothes aside and perched on the foot of the bed, studying the invoice. "Well, this is for the days you spent in assisted living," said Lucy, noting the hefty sum at the bottom of the page. "Medicare doesn't cover that."

"Well, that's very odd because this woman, wearing a lot of heavy perfume, came in and told me that they're billing Medicare, too, because I went into assisted living and I wouldn't be eligible for coverage now that I've returned to skilled nursing because Medicare only pays for care after a hospital-ization, that's what she said. So they're go-ing to pretend I was in skilled nursing the whole time, but the Medicare payment doesn't cover the whole cost of assisted living which is why I got this outrageous bill. I don't believe a word of it, I think it's fraud." She set her chin stubbornly. "If Medicare is paying I don't see why I have to pay, too."

"That does sound like double billing," said Lucy. "I think you should call Medicare."

"Of course. That's the first thing I did, but they said the wait time was one hour and fifty minutes. Can you imagine?"

"Actually, I can," admitted Lucy. She noticed that her old friend was hyperventilating, struggling to catch her breath, and took both her hands. "Calm down. It's just a piece of paper. For now, your priority is to get better. You need to relax and rest, okay?"

"I'll try," said Miss Tilley, seeming to shrink into the big recliner.

"Put your feet up," said Lucy. "I'll put these things away." She began to replace the clothes in the closet, all the while chattering to distract Miss Tilley. "You know, I interviewed this Russian lady today, she makes gorgeous Easter eggs. It's some sort of old country tradition. Did you dye eggs when you were a little girl?"

"No." Miss Tilley shook her head. "My mother would never have done anything so frivolous, wasting good eggs. Papa wouldn't have approved."

Miss Tilley seemed to be relaxing a bit so Lucy continued to ask her about her childhood. "Did the Easter Bunny bring you a basket of candy?"

"Oh, no. No candy. But I did have new clothes for church on Easter morning, and maybe a fresh ribbon for my hat."

A different world, thought Lucy, putting the last shirt on a hanger. "Are you planning to attend the Easter bonnet contest? Maybe you should make one?"

"I wouldn't know where to begin," claimed Miss Tilley, recovering her normal, independent attitude. "I was a librarian, not a milliner."

"I bet some of the other ladies would help you, what about Howard's fan club? They seem nice enough."

Miss Tilley's eyebrows shot up. "The Gang of Three?"

"You still call them that?"

"Why not?" Miss T shrugged. "They're always together."

Lucy closed the closet door and went back to her spot on the foot of the bed. "They're not friendly?"

"If they want something, they can be nice," said Miss Tilley. "They were sticking very close to Agnes until she disappeared. I think they were trying to get her to reveal

243

her design for the hat contest. You know she won last year? A bird's nest I think it was."

"But Howard said Agnes wasn't planning to enter the contest this year, didn't he?"

"He did, but they didn't believe it. She did seem to be onto something, but Howard doesn't think it was the contest. Now that I've got this bill, I wonder if she had discovered something sinister."

"Here at Heritage House?" asked Lucy, thinking that this was a theme she'd been hearing a lot lately.

"Well, she was an investigative reporter, you know. It's like me being a librarian. You can't teach an old dog new tricks and I confess all my books at home are organized according to the Dewey system." She sighed. "I'm getting distracted. We were talking about Agnes, and I suspect she was trying to show that these Heritage House people are crooked, which they absolutely are."

"We don't know that for sure," cautioned Lucy. "And I wouldn't go about making claims that might not turn out to be true, if I were you."

"Or claims that turn out to be true," insisted Miss Tilley. "I bet that's what happened to Agnes. She uncovered something nefarious. . . ."

And ended up dead, thought Lucy, quickly interrupting Miss Tilley. "You don't know that for sure. Medicare's very complicated with all sorts of rules and we don't know what's covered and what isn't. I'm going to take this bill and check it out. Now, I don't want you to worry, I want you to rest and get strong so you can go home. Okay?"

"I'll rest after I sort out that mess you made in my closet. I like to have like with like, light to dark."

"So do I," confessed Lucy, realizing that in her hurry she'd hung up the clothes willy-nilly. "Never you mind, I'll fix it." Lucy spent a few minutes sorting out the clothes and when she turned to get Miss Tilley's okay, she discovered the old woman had dozed off in her chair. Lucy pulled a flannel blanket from the bed and covered her, then quietly tiptoed out.

Making her way to the lobby, Lucy noticed a sign pointing the way to the social worker's office and impulsively decided to make good her promise to Miss Tilley and pay her a visit. The placard on the door read JOYCE ZIMMER, LSW, and as soon as she opened the door she was assailed by the heavy fragrance Miss Tilley had complained about. Joyce Zimmer was seated at a large gray steel desk and looked up with interest as

Lucy entered. "How can I help you?" she asked. Lucy noticed that Ms. Zimmer was wearing a maroon polyester suit, a dotted blouse that had a bow instead of a collar, and had thick, dark hair pulled back in a messy chignon. She was wearing a lot of makeup, including an unflattering mauve lipstick outlined with contrasting lip liner that Lucy itched to wipe away.

"I'm here for my friend, Julia Ward Howe Tilley. She's upset about a bill that she just received."

"Oh, Miss Tilley, she's a character, isn't she?" said Joyce, throwing in an indulgent chuckle for effect.

"She's quite old-fashioned," admitted Lucy, "and pays her bills the day she gets them. Unfortunately this one exceeded her current assets and she's quite upset. Perhaps you could explain it to me so I can help her devise a payment plan."

"Are you by chance her next of kin?" inquired Joyce.

"Just a friend, but she asked me to check on this matter for her."

"Perhaps you have a POA?" Seeing Lucy's confused expression she hastened to clarify. "A power of attorney?"

"No," admitted Lucy, who was beginning to understand where this was leading.

"Then I'm afraid I can't help you," said Joyce, shaking her head sadly. "We have strict privacy policies, I'm sure you understand. I'll pay Julia another visit and see if I can't clear things up for her."

Lucy was beginning to feel a bit nauseous from the heavy scent that filled the small office, and, aware that she wasn't going to make any headway with Joyce, decided to save her energy. She wasn't about to give up the fight, however, as she thought it might be worth investigating further for a possible story. "Thanks for your time," she said, beating a hasty retreat. Once outside the office, she took a deep breath of what she hoped would be fresh air, only to discover that whatever the stuff was that Joyce doused herself with, it was now clinging to her. As soon as she got home she was going to head straight for the shower.

After giving herself a good scrub, and putting on fresh clothing, she threw all her scented clothes into the washer. This load called for hot water and heavy-duty agitation which caused her to laugh, thinking that Joyce's perfume should be called Hot and Heavy. Feeling somewhat giddy, she set up her laptop on the kitchen table and pulled up the state attorney general's website. There she found a phone number for health insurance inquiries and dialed it.

"Assistant AG John Williams," said the young voice of the person on the other end. "How can I help you?"

"I have a theoretical question," began Lucy. "My old friend is currently in a nursing home and she's received a very odd bill. She claims the social worker insists she owes a balance, even though they're also billing Medicare."

"Perhaps she misunderstood?" asked Williams. "Dementia perhaps?"

"No chance. She's smart as a whip." Lucy paused, remembering what Miss Tilley had told her. "According to this social worker, she's being charged for assisted living at the same time they're billing Medicare for skilled nursing. The reason is supposedly that Medicare only pays for continuous care and since the skilled nursing was interrupted by a few days in assisted living, they have to pretend she was in skilled nursing the entire time. Do you understand?"

"If this is actually the case, it sounds pretty fishy to me. What nursing home is this?"

"Heritage House in Tinker's Cove." Lucy heard the sound of a keyboard clicking. "Any chance you can tell me who owns Heritage House?"

"Sure. That's public record," said Williams. "I've got it here. TaraCare Holdings."

"Like in *Gone with the Wind*?"

"Maybe." He chuckled. "Maybe they want to imply that Heritage House is like living in a fancy Southern plantation house."

"It is pretty upscale, including the prices," said Lucy. "Do you have the names of the principal shareholders?"

"Sorry. I think you'd have to get that from the secretary of state's office."

"But it's public record?"

"Should be," said Williams. "I'll poke around a bit and see what I can turn up. Want to give me your name and number?"

Lucy obliged, thanking him for his interest. "Sorry to say, I wouldn't get your hopes up," he cautioned her. "If I were you, I'd start with Medicare. They have a strong fraud department."

"Thanks, again. I'll do that," said Lucy, hanging up. She pulled up the Medicare website and dialed the 800 number, learning as Miss Tilley had that the wait time was presently one hour and forty-six minutes. It seemed she'd have to pin her hopes on Assistant AG John Williams.

It was better than nothing, however, and she called Miss Tilley to let her know that she'd spoken to a helpful official in the AG's office who had promised to look into the matter.

"Well," said Miss T with a sigh, "I suppose that's better than nothing."

"And I'm going to stay on it, too," promised Lucy. She knew from previous investigations that it was often some insignificant bit of information that turned out to be an important clue that led to the truth. Perhaps this was the loose thread that, if pulled, would unravel and reveal what had really happened to Agnes.

CHAPTER FIFTEEN

The next few days were increasingly hectic as the annual town meeting was approaching, at which the interested citizens of Tinker's Cove gathered in the high school auditorium to vote on changes and additions to the town bylaws and, more importantly, approve the town budget. The meeting was always contentious and advocates for and against various articles all wanted to air their arguments, especially the school committee, which was advocating for a 5 percent increase in the school budget. That meant Lucy was busy dealing with a flood of phone calls at the same time she was trying to complete her weekly budget of stories. She was uneasy about some of her stories, worried that she hadn't had time to do her usual fact-checking, so she wasn't at all surprised when she got a call from Olga Skulsky, who taught Russian at nearby Winchester College.

"It's just a little thing," began the professor, "but the Easter eggs aren't *pisanica* as you wrote, but are properly termed *pysanky,* that's the plural, and the singular is *pysanka.* One egg is a *pysanka,* a basketful are *pysanky.*"

"Um, how do you spell that?" asked Lucy, glancing at the decorative egg on her desk and assuming she'd misunderstood Vesna. Or perhaps Vesna had mixed up a few letters in the translation. English was her second language, after all, and she admitted she'd been in the US for more than twenty years. Her Russian had probably got a bit rusty during that time.

Olga provided the proper spelling, and was quick to assure Lucy that she'd enjoyed the story. "Don't get me wrong, I thought you did a great job. You caught the spirit of the Easter holiday, which means such a lot to the Russians and really all Eastern Europeans. It's the time of year when the weather warms up and things start to grow and you can imagine what a relief that is after the long winter."

"Or a Maine winter," said Lucy, glancing out the window at the snow flurries that were blowing in off the ocean.

"Some weather we're having," agreed Olga. "I don't know if it's worth a correction. . . ."

"Of course it is, I'll write one right up," said Lucy. "It's important to me to get things right and I don't mind admitting when I've made a mistake."

"That's a very refreshing attitude," said Olga. "I wish my students felt that way. Somehow when they get a poor grade it's my fault."

Lucy chuckled sympathetically. "I have four kids, so I know what that's like. Thank goodness they've mostly flown the nest."

"I know your Zoe, she's terrific," offered Olga. "I worked with her on the Take Back the Night demonstration. You should be very proud of her."

"You're too kind," protested Lucy, who wasn't about to admit how pleased she was. "She's going through a difficult time, trying to get started in Portland."

"She'll be just fine," promised Olga.

"Thanks," said Lucy. "I'll have that correction in next week's issue."

True to her word, Lucy quickly wrote up the correction, then grabbed her jacket and bag, pulled a wooly hat over her hair, wrapped a scarf around her neck, and headed into the ocean effect snow squalls to drive over to Heritage House for the Easter bonnet contest.

As soon as Lucy stepped inside the foyer at Heritage House she heard the buzz of excitement filtering down the curved floating staircase that led to the second-floor lounge area. She hurried up and paused at the top, taking in the scene. Folding chairs had been added to the usual upholstered furniture and almost every seat was filled, mostly by chattering women who were all holding hatboxes on their laps.

"Nice touch," thought Lucy, noticing the Heritage House logo on the top of each hatbox, indicating they had been provided to the contestants to add a sense of drama as each entry was revealed. She looked about for Miss Tilley, but was not surprised to see she'd skipped the event, probably choosing instead to read or work on one of her crossword puzzles. A few men were scattered among the women and seemed to be there under duress, waiting impatiently for the event to start. Lucy found an empty chair at the back of the room and plopped her bag on it, then began to divest herself of her outdoor clothes. Once she'd arranged them to her satisfaction on the back of the chair, she picked up her bag and seated herself. First order of business was snapping some photos, which she did, then opened up her reporter's notebook and

waited for the contest to begin.

Exactly on the specified hour, CEO Peter Novak made his entry, and was greeted with a smattering of excited applause. "Well, well, it's great to see you all here today," he began, charming everyone with his handsome good looks and exotic foreign accent. "The weather outside is frightful, as the song says, but we know that Easter is on its way, a sure sign of the warm spring weather to come. I'm very pleased to see that so many of you are participating in our Easter bonnet contest this year and I can't wait to see what you've all come up with. But first, Felicity is going to describe the prizes."

"Thank you, Peter," began Felicity Corcoran, stepping up to the mic. "If you will turn your heads to the left, you will see the giant chocolate rabbit generously provided by Fern's Famous Fudge."

The group obliged, oohing and aahing at the sight of the magnificent chocolate bunny, and Lucy hastened to snap a photo of the chocolate rabbit, which was at least two feet high.

"I want to remind you all," continued Felicity, "that this is not one of those hollow, air-filled chocolate bunnies. Oh, no. This fellow is solid milk chocolate through and through. Plenty to share with your friends" — she paused, smiling, as some of the contestants shook their heads — "or not. It's entirely up to the winner. But," she continued, "Choco-Peter there isn't the only prize. There are also gift cards from Country Cousins, everyone's favorite emporium selling everything from fine local cheddar cheese to comfy flannel nightwear: one hundred dollars for first place, fifty dollars for second, and twenty-five dollars for third. Not too shabby."

This announcement also got a healthy round of applause, which halted when Felicity held up her hand for quiet. "But the prize that I suspect most of you are most excited about is getting your picture, in your winning hat, on the front page of our local newspaper, the *Courier*." This announcement got a hearty round of applause, which rather surprised Lucy, who thought Felicity must surely be exaggerating. "And our intrepid reporter is here today, ready to take that picture. Will you stand up, Lucy?"

Lucy got awkwardly to her feet, somewhat embarrassed by the attention. "Don't despair, even if you don't win," she began, "I know my editor wants to run a two-page photo spread of the entire event, so chances are everyone will be included in the photos. Just to remind you, the *Courier* comes out on Thursday, but the photos will also run in the online edition."

"Thank you, Lucy," said Felicity, "and now I'm going to hand the mic over to our MC, Mr. Peter Novak."

"Let's get this party started," said Peter, getting excited applause. "Perhaps this would be a good time to introduce our judges," he said with a wave of his hand, indicating the three people seated at a nearby table. "First off, we have our dedicated social worker, Joyce Zimmer, who has judged all of our Easter bonnet contests. Next is one of our most esteemed residents, Howard White, a former prosecutor and judge. And finally, Elvira Hostens, our nursing supervisor." The judges got a nice round of applause from the hopeful contestants, which ended when Peter raised his hand for silence. "So let's begin. As usual, each contestant will have the opportunity to unveil her creation, and explain why she chose that design, and how she actually made it. So first up, we have in alphabetical order, Bess Abbott. Come on up, Bess, and tell us all about it."

Bess, a tiny woman who barely came up to Peter's chest, came forward and set her hatbox on the table provided for the purpose. Lifting off the lid, she displayed her hat, and leaned forward to speak into the mic. "My theme was an Easter basket," she said, setting the hat on the head of the prepared dummy. "I took an old basket and cut away the bottom, so it would fit on my head. I sewed in a fabric liner, and as you can see, I've filled it with cello grass and plenty of real candy."

Everyone applauded, and Bess offered one final word. "So even if I don't win, I'll have plenty of chocolate to share."

That got plenty of laughter and more applause. "Thank you, Bess, and good luck. Next up is Bitsy Baker," he announced. "Come on up, Bitsy."

Bitsy was aquiver with excitement as she carried her hatbox up to the display table, where she paused to flutter her heavily mascaraed eyelashes at Peter. Lifting the lid with a flourish she produced a fascinator-style hat, which tied under the chin with wide pink satin ribbons. Perched atop was a large pink plastic egg that had cracked open, revealing a fuzzy yellow chick inside. "It was simple, really," explained Bitsy. "My daughter sent me this big egg last year filled with candy and as soon as I saw it I thought, I can do something with this." She lifted the hat up and set it on the display stand. "And this is what I came up with."

Again, the crowd applauded and Bitsy beamed, making sure to give Peter a big smile as she replaced her hat in the box and went back to her seat.

"Moving right along," said Peter, consulting his list, "we have Florida Dawkins. Let's see what you've got, Florida."

Florida was a plump Black woman, who seemed to bristle with energy as she made her way to the front of the room. "I took a different approach," she began, lifting her hat out of the box and getting some oohs of surprise. "I grew up in the South, you see, and my father was a sharecropper who grew cotton. So this hat" — she pointed to the straw farmer's hat trimmed with branches of actual cotton plants, all dotted with fluffy white balls — "is a tribute to my hardworking father. The band is actually from a bandanna that he wore when he was working in the fields."

It took a long moment for the audience to absorb what Florida had said, but then Dorothy urged on Bitsy and Bev, and the crowd followed with a hearty round of applause.

"Wonderful, wonderful," said Peter, as Florida packed up her hat. "It just goes to show the amazing creativity of our residents. And now . . ."

The demonstrations went on until each

contestant had a chance to display her entry, and Lucy was careful to snap a photo of each and jot down the contestants' names and stories. Time flew by and before she knew it, it was time for the highlight of the event, the Easter Bonnet Parade. Felicity got the music going, the ladies all donned their millinery creations, and they sashayed around the room proudly, for all to see. At their table, the judges were hunkered down, making careful notes and conferring with one another.

When the music stopped and all had returned to their seats, Peter asked the judges if they'd chosen the winners. Howard White stood up and said they had, prompting Felicity to play a drumroll on the music system.

"Third place," began Howard, "goes to Florida Dawkins. We were very impressed with her cultural reference and her tribute to her father. Well done, Florida."

"Step up and receive your prize," said Peter, producing an envelope and a small cello-wrapped chocolate bunny.

"I can't believe it," said Florida as she advanced to the front of the room and accepted the prizes. "Thank you so much."

When she had gone back to her seat, Howard prepared to announce the second prize winner. It was Helen Nowicki, whose creation Lucy had loved. She'd taken a straw boater with a broad brim and added three stuffed dachshunds, each with a small Easter candy in its mouth, chasing one another round and round. "As judges, and dog lovers, we found it hard to resist these adorable dachshunds," said Howard.

Helen beamed with pride as she received her prize and a round of applause, then all fell silent in readiness for the big moment, the announcement of the first-prize winner.

Lucy had a feeling she knew who the winner would be, and she was right. When the drumroll ended Peter announced Bitsy Baker's fascinator had taken first prize. "Oh my, oh my, I never thought . . ." exclaimed Bitsy, popping to her feet and rushing to meet Peter. "What a thrill, this is amazing," she continued, batting her eyelashes furiously and hanging on to Peter's hands when he presented her with the envelope. "You're too kind, too fabulous," she cooed, looking up at him. "Oh Peter, you're the first one I'm going to share my chocolate with."

"Ah, very nice, very nice," said Peter, patting her on the shoulder. "Felicity, the rabbit, please."

A photo was quickly arranged of Bitsy in her hat, proudly holding the giant chocolate bunny, with Peter and Felicity behind her. Lucy took another, of just Bitsy, with the bunny, but Bitsy didn't look at the camera, her eyes were fastened on Peter Novak.

Preparing to leave, Lucy wanted to congratulate Howard on a job well done, but found he was surrounded by several residents Lucy recognized as the avid bridge players. No doubt lobbying for him to join them, she thought, looking out the window and discovering that the snow was still falling. Making her way to the door she paused to congratulate Bitsy, who was clearly delighted with her win.

"I can't help it, I'm so excited. I've never won anything, and to receive my prize from Peter, well, that was just the icing on the cake."

Bev and Dorothy shared an amused glance, but Bitsy continued. "I know he's nice to everyone, but I think he really likes me."

Bev smiled indulgently and said, "I think you might be right. He was certainly impressed by your hat."

"It's his job," protested Dorothy. "Keeping us old biddies happy is all in a day's work to him."

Bitsy shook her head and turned to Lucy. "Sometimes I call her Dorothy Downer,"

262

she whispered, pursing her lips and raising her eyebrows. Then she turned back to her friends. "Come on, ladies, we don't want to be late for lunch. And don't forget to wear your hats!"

The group slowed at the doorway, where Florida had paused to accept a friend's compliments. "Such a clever idea," cooed the friend.

"Well," began a tiny, red-haired woman who was clearly frustrated at the delay, "you know she only won because she's Black."

"Like my grandson!" volunteered her companion, a rather plump woman with her gray hair scraped back into a tight little bun. "He was passed over for a job at the fire department because they wanted more diversity! They hired a Black guy who scored lower on the exam!"

"Typical," agreed the red-haired lady.

Suddenly, Florida whirled around and confronted the two women. "What are you talking about? Do you really think your sorry old hat deserved to win?" She focused on the red-haired lady. "Why, yours was nothing but a bunch of fake flowers stuck on a paper plate!"

"Well, I never!" huffed the redhead.

"The nerve of you!" added the woman with the bun.

Sensing a disturbance, the two CNAs were quick to intervene. "Now, now, ladies," said Juliana, inserting herself between the disputants, "it's time to move along."

"That's right," said Vera. "You don't want your lunch to get cold. I understand it's chicken pot pie today."

"With ice cream sundaes for dessert," added Juliana, stepping aside so the group could proceed through the doorway and on to the dining room.

Lucy, who was at the back of the scrum, paused to chat with the aides. "My goodness, racism rears its ugly head at the old folks' home. Does it happen a lot?"

"It's a funny thing," said Vera. "They get set in their ways and lose their inhibitions. They've said some terrible things to me. One lady refused to let me help her dress, said she thought I'd try to steal her jewelry!"

"And I've heard comments about my English. They're surprised I can speak it so well. I mean, my family brought me here when I was two. I can hardly speak Spanish."

"They're tough on each other, too," said Vera with a chuckle. "There's one lady here who's kind of fat, and has a big bum . . ."

"They're absolutely awful to her," said Juliana, rolling her eyes. "They think they're whispering but, I guess because they're hard of hearing, they're actually rather loud."

"What have they been saying about Agnes's death?" Lucy asked, truly curious. "Are they upset?"

"I haven't heard much," volunteered Vera.

"Yesterday's news," added Juliana. "They're mostly interested in their next meal."

"Have the police been questioning people?" asked Lucy, pressing the issue.

"Yeah. We've all been interviewed," said Vera, "and the staff's all been talking about it, but nobody seems to know much. It's really kind of awful, we all feel terrible about it. I hope she wasn't suffering in there for days before she died."

"Poor lady. I always liked her," said Juliana. "She seemed younger than the others, more interesting."

"Do you remember anything out of the ordinary, in the days before she died?" asked Lucy.

"Well, now that you mention it, there was something that surprised me. I saw her in the hallway with those three ladies, Bitsy and her buddies. I never saw her with them before, I got the impression that she tended to avoid them.

"And that was the last time you saw her?"

asked Lucy.

Juliana nodded. "I told the cops, but they didn't seem to think it was important."

"Nobody takes these old folks seriously," said Vera. "If you ask me, it's a big mistake. They can be trouble!"

"It sure sounds like it," said Lucy, chuckling. "It's been very interesting talking to you."

"Time for us to get back to work," said Juliana.

"Have a nice day," said Vera as the two aides got busy tidying up after the departed contestants.

Lucy was considering waiting a bit in order to ask Bitsy and her friends about their meeting with Agnes, but she had no idea how long the three lingered at lunch. She suspected it might be a good while, since she didn't imagine they had busy schedules. She was wandering in the direction of the dining room, just to see how the meal was progressing, when her phone rang. Checking the screen she saw it was Ted.

"What's up?" she asked.

"Bears, that's what. Bears at the Quik-Stop."

"Gassing up?" she asked facetiously.

"Probably dumpster diving," said Ted. "But it's worth a story."

"I'm on it, boss," she said, surprised to find herself somewhat relieved to leave Heritage House behind, at least for a while. Bears somehow seemed preferable to the quarrelsome, aging inmates of the senior residence.

CHAPTER SIXTEEN

The snow squalls had settled into a steady, light snow that was beginning to accumulate on the ground, making walking slippery. Driving would be, too, thought Lucy, as she got in her SUV and started the engine. Winter was over, according to the calendar, but somehow Mother Nature hadn't got the message, and Lucy wondered if it would be a snowy Easter. It wouldn't be the first time, she thought, remembering Easter egg hunts that had to be moved indoors due to snow, sleet, or impossibly muddy conditions. Other years, however, the kids had worked up a sweat, running about in strong sunshine that blazed down through the still leafless trees that offered no shade.

The drive to the Quik-Stop was short, it only took a few minutes, and when she arrived at the combination gas station and convenience store she found people were already gathering to see the bears. The small parking area was full of pickup trucks and cars, so she parked along the side of the road and walked over to join the cluster of onlookers gathered at a respectful distance from a tall pine tree growing at the edge of the parking lot. Wiggling through the crowd in an effort to get a better view, she apologized, saying she was from the *Courier*. People were in a good mood, enjoying this little bit of excitement.

"The cubs are up there," one woman told her, pointing upward.

Lucy looked up and, sure enough, two fuzzy little bear cubs were clinging to the tree. Below them, their mother was pacing nervously and keeping a watchful eye on the crowd.

"Ooh, they're soo cute," exclaimed a little girl. "I want to take one home."

"I don't think her mother would like that," cautioned her mother, keeping a tight grip on the little girl's hand.

"Yeah, that sow is getting antsy," observed a man in a plaid shirt-jac.

True enough, Lucy didn't like the way the mother bear was beginning to huff as she paced back and forth.

A couple of teenage boys had begun tossing small pebbles at the mother bear, which seemed to confuse her. She glared in their direction, then continued pacing. The boys, pleased with her reaction, chose some larger stones, getting a growl in response. They were moving closer at the same time the crowd was beginning to edge backward. The two were left in a sort of no-man's land between the sow and the crowd, and it was then that the mother bear made a more determined charge, coming within a whisker of the boys.

"Whew, that bear's breath stinks!" exclaimed one. The other, shaken by the near miss, was pulling his friend back, but the friend was resisting, reaching for an even larger rock. It was then that the state wildlife agent arrived and quickly took charge.

"Everybody back," he ordered. "These are wild animals, not teddy bears. We don't want anybody to get hurt." He glared at the boys. "That means you, in case I didn't make myself clear."

"Okay," grumbled the boy, dropping the rock. The two joined the crowd of onlookers, which had now been moved away from the tree by two more uniformed wildlife agents.

Lucy was busy snapping photos and got a nice series of shots illustrating the little drama. First off, the mother bear was tranquilized and transferred into a large

crate using a special wheeled dolly. Once
she was confined, the agents turned their
attention to the cubs, trying to lure them
down with tempting suet cakes. When that
didn't work, they set up nets at the base of
the tree and shot the cubs with tranquilizer
darts, causing them to drop safely into the
nets. Once the whole snoozing family had
been united in the crate, it was carefully
lifted and eased onto a truck with a forklift.

Lucy needed to get the whole story, so
she approached the head agent and identified herself. She got the names of all three,
and learned that they had a history with
this particular mother bear. "She did the
same thing last year, over in Goshen," he
said. "She's figured out that there's easy
pickings in dumpsters."

"Yummy," said Lucy, smiling. "So what
are you going to do with her?"

"We'll release her in the back woods; you
can assure your readers that we'll take good
care of her and the cubs."

"What about those boys?" asked Lucy,
indicating the two who were now lobbing
pebbles and pinging them off the crate.

He narrowed his eyes. "I'll have a word,"
he said, marching over to them.

"Hey, you, what's the matter with you
two? Are you idiots? Cut that out!" He

looked them over, then pulled out a note-book. "Hey, what are your names? I should report you to the truant officer."

Lucy chuckled, watching as they ran off as fast as their feet would carry them. Then she hopped into her SUV, heading straight to the office, eager to file her breaking news story. As luck would have it, Ted was in the office when she arrived and was eager to see her photos of the bears. Both he and Phyllis looked over her shoulders as she displayed them on her phone.

"What a pair of cuties!" cooed Phyllis.

"Well, Mama wasn't so cute. Especially when some kids started teasing her, throwing pebbles at her. It could have gotten nasty real fast," said Lucy.

"Yeah, but this shot of her at the bottom of the tree, looking up, that's going on page one," said Ted.

"What about the Easter bonnet contest winner," protested Lucy. "Those ladies take the whole contest very seriously, especially getting their photo on the front page."

"C'mon, Lucy. You know as well as I do that kids and animals sell papers, old ladies not so much."

"Look at Bitsy Baker, isn't she adorable? She took first prize with her fascinator."

Ted glanced at the photo and shook his

head. "She's got a giant egg on her head."

"Okay, that one is pretty silly. But Florida, here, with her cotton ball hat, made her entry a tribute to her father, who was a sharecropper."

Ted studied the photo of Florida's beaming face and relented. "Okay, okay. Bears get priority, but I'll put the three winners on the front page, below the fold. It'll be good to show we've got some diversity in Tinker's Cove." He paused.

"All one percent of it," snorted Phyllis.

"And I've got plenty of photos of the other contestants," offered Lucy. "There were some pretty creative bonnets, and the ladies were so enthusiastic. Take a look at this one: an Easter basket!"

Ted took her camera and scrolled through the photos, eventually shaking his head. "No. I'm going with the bears. It's a nice little photo essay, and a good reminder to people to leave the critters alone if they encounter them. Public service, you know?"

"I can't believe this," sighed Lucy. "I spent hours at that old folks' home getting all the details, all the names, and now you don't want it."

"In a perfect world, Lucy, sure, but I've got space considerations. You can post the contest online, how about that? Just photos

273

with captions, mind you, not a big story."

"Felicity Corcoran will kill me," groaned Lucy.

"Well, we are putting Florida and the others on page one. That's more than enough."

"Okay," grumbled Lucy, "you're the boss."

"Damn right," said Ted, grabbing his jacket and heading for the door.

"Just like a man," muttered Phyllis, watching him.

He whirled around at the door and challenged her. "What do you mean?"

"You're such a typical man," began Phyllis, rolling her eyes. "When the going gets tough, you go out the door. It's like my grandma used to say about Grandpa, how when any little thing bothered him he'd lay down the law and then he'd put on his hat and leave."

"Male prerogative," said Ted, grinning and grabbing the doorknob, setting the little bell to jangling.

"One of these days . . ." muttered Phyllis.

"What?" asked Lucy.

"One of these days I'm going to slap my hat on my head and leave."

"Sounds like menopause talking," said Lucy.

Phyllis lowered her head onto her desk and groaned. "You're right. I don't know what got into me." She raised her head. "Ted's going to kill me."

"No way, he's probably already forgotten," said Lucy, getting busy uploading her photos of the hat contest and writing snappy little captions; she wanted to get that little chore out of the way before she tackled the bear story. "It's kind of pathetic, isn't it," she said, studying one aged face after another. "These old dears put on their lipstick and got their hair done, and made their pretty little bonnets . . . You've got to admire their spunk. They're probably mostly all widows but they keep on keeping on. They've had major losses in their lives, and most of them have health problems like arthritis and diabetes, but they don't give up. Bitsy, the lady who won, she's a real flirt. She's a bit of a social butterfly, she's a force to be reckoned with at Heritage House, but even she looked kind of sad and dejected during the fire drill the other day. Get them outside and they suddenly look so frail and old. They kind of shrink."

"How do they treat them there?" asked Phyllis. "Are they getting the most out of their golden years?"

Lucy considered, staring at Bitsy's photo and trying to come up with a clever, but not condescending, caption. It was a struggle, everything she thought of seemed to demean Bitsy's achievement. In the end, she admitted to herself, she'd made a hat out of a big plastic Easter egg and it did look rather ridiculous. "I dunno if it's golden," she admitted after playing it straight in the caption, merely noting Bitsy's name and the fact she'd won first prize by recycling a gift from her daughter. "In a place like that you must feel as if you're in death's waiting room. Just killing time before it kills you."

"That Agnes Neal, she seemed different," said Phyllis. "She got out and about, she remained pretty independent."

"And look where it got her," said Lucy. "If she'd played it safer and made an Easter bonnet instead of gallivanting about, she might still be alive. You know, she won the contest last year."

"Do you think that's why she died?" Phyllis's eyes got big as she indulged her fertile imagination. "Maybe she was murdered in an effort to wipe out the competition?"

Lucy gave Phyllis a look. "You can't be serious."

"Not really," she admitted, shrugging, "but maybe, just a little. I noticed that when my mother started losing it, she had dementia, you know, she really changed. She

276

started swearing, which she never ever did, and she started stealing things. If we went shopping I'd have to check her pockets before we left the store. One time I found a sirloin steak in her handbag. What a bloody mess that was."

"They don't all get dementia, though," said Lucy. "The problem is that they all get treated as if they can't think for themselves anymore, they get treated like children and, sadly, a lot of them become childlike." Lucy sighed. "Maybe it's better to die young and stay pretty, like the song says."

"No. Not for me. I'm going to hang on for as long as possible, drink my Ensure, and join the Tai Chi class at the senior center."

"Good for you," laughed Lucy, picturing Phyllis in her bright pink tracksuit, practicing her moves. "You'll be a standout in the class."

"You betcha," agreed Phyllis.

Lucy's phone was ringing. It was Sandy Francona, the head librarian at the Broadbrooks Free Library. "Hiya, Sandy, what can I do for you?"

"Hi, Lucy. Well, I want to ask a big favor. I'd love it if you'd cover this talk at the library on Sunday afternoon. He's really kind of a big deal and I'm afraid we won't get a good turnout."

"Well, give me the information and I'll run a preview online. Any chance you've got a photo?"

"Plenty of photos, the speaker is a Pulitzer Prize–winning news photographer known for his intimate, candid shots. There's even photos of royal weddings and inaugurations."

"I meant one of him," said Lucy. "But I guess it could be one of the pics in the show? Or is it a talk?"

"Both. It's like an old-fashioned slide show, except nowadays you can cast the photos onto a TV from any device."

"Have you got a photo I can use? Or have him send me one?"

"Sure, Lucy. I've got one I can send right over. His name is Matthieu Colon, and the presentation is at two o'clock on Sunday afternoon."

"That name sounds familiar," mused Lucy.

"He's big, very big. You've probably heard of him. It would be great if you could write it up, he's an interesting guy."

"I'll try," said Lucy, unwilling to make a promise. She wasn't at all sure she wanted to work on Sunday afternoon. Maybe she'd prefer to relax with a magazine and a cup of tea, or even make a stab at catching up on the laundry.

But when she opened up Sandy's email, she recognized the work of the photographer she'd seen in the gallery in Portland. Impressed once again by Matthieu Colon's work, and intrigued by the promise of images she hadn't seen like the candid portraits, she decided the presentation was worth a story and put it on her calendar.

It was starting to get dark when she finally left the office for home. It had stopped snowing, but the trees and streetlights were coated with snow, making everything look magical. It was toasty in the car, with the heated seat turned on high, and Lucy almost felt a bit sad that winter was drawing to a close. Just a teeny bit sad, she told herself, as she was really looking forward to warm weather and planting her garden and being able to leave the house without wrapping herself up in warm clothes like a mummy.

The lights were blazing in the old farmhouse at the top of Red Top Road, a sure sign that Zoe was home. Bill's pickup was also parked in the driveway, and Lucy felt her spirits lift as she made her way to the house. It was Friday and the weekend was ahead. Maybe just this once she'd fulfill her dream of lingering in bed with coffee and the Sunday papers.

But first, she realized when she opened the door, it seemed she'd have to referee a disagreement between Zoe and her father. Both were seated at the kitchen table, confronting each other, voices raised.

"What's going on?" she asked, dropping her bag on the bench by the door and unwrapping her scarf.

"Dad's being a jerk," said Zoe, glaring at Bill.

Bill rolled his eyes in response. "First off, don't call me a jerk. I'm your father and I deserve a bit of respect. And second, I'm just trying to keep you from making a big mistake."

Lucy shrugged out of her jacket and hung it up on a hook, then joined them at the table where a bunch of papers were spread out. Picking one up, she saw it was a lease for an apartment in the rehabbed mill Zoe had visited last weekend. "You can't possibly afford this," said Lucy, zeroing in on the figure at the bottom of the page.

"I could if you guys would help me," said Zoe. "A lot of parents do, you know. They help their kids get started."

"But I thought you wanted to be independent, make your own way," said Lucy, parroting Zoe's earlier claims. "Not be beholden to anyone."

"Okay, okay. I'll do it on my own. I can afford the rent, I really can."

Bill shook his head. "The figures don't work out. Believe me, I'd like to see you in a nice place but this is not affordable. The guideline is thirty percent of take home, ideally twenty-five percent, for rent. This is more than half of your take-home."

"Yeah, but I won't need much more money because I'll be saving, like they say in the brochure. I can walk to downtown, I won't need a gym membership, everything is right there. It's just steps from restaurants and shops. They even pick up and drop off your dry cleaning."

"Which you certainly won't be able to afford," chuckled Lucy.

"And there are stiff penalties if you're late, or miss a month," added Bill, jabbing a finger at the lease. "Have you read the fine print? The least bit of damage, say one of those cheap refrigerator bins cracks or something, and you're liable for an exorbitant sum."

"I'm not a savage, you know. I'll take care of the place."

"Stuff happens," said Lucy, remembering holes in the drywall when Toby and one of his friends got in a wrestling match, and a broken window when Sara and Elizabeth had been practicing field hockey in the backyard.

"You'd also be locked in for a year," added Bill, "you couldn't move if you found someplace more affordable, or that you liked better."

"Or even get a roommate, or a pet," said Lucy, pointing to a clause in the lease.

"That's crazy. It's just a piece of paper. People break leases all the time."

"And sometimes they get slapped with a lawsuit," said Lucy, who had been immersed in the fine print. "I'm going to call Bob, get his opinion on this. I'm not convinced this lease is even legal."

"Take a photo and send it to me," advised Bob after they'd exchanged greetings. "I'll take a look at it, but I'm warning you, it's probably perfectly legal. These development companies know all the ins and outs of the law and make the most of it. I've heard of people getting burned pretty bad when they had disputes with landlords. The law is usually on the side of the property owner, sad to say."

"While I've got you," began Lucy, her mind taking a detour down a similar path, "have you had any clients with claims against Heritage House?"

"A few, nothing very serious. Mostly disputes over surcharges, things like that. They've always backed down, been eager to settle and keep their residents happy."

"No Medicare fraud? Anything like that?"

"Not that I know of," said Bob. "And by the way, don't let Zoe sign anything until I look it over."

"Righto," promised Lucy, giving Zoe a look. "Bob says it's no-go until we hear from him. Okay?"

"Okay," grumbled Zoe. "So what's for dinner?"

Bill looked at Lucy, and Lucy looked at Bill. Neither seemed to have any ideas. Finally, Lucy reached for the phone. "Pizza?"

CHAPTER SEVENTEEN

Lucy got busy Saturday morning, taking advantage of a quiet news period to tackle some spring cleaning. After fueling up with a hearty bowl of oatmeal she started by swapping the flannel sheets on her bed for crisp percale and vacuumed up the dust bunnies that had gathered beneath the bed. She took down the curtains, tossing them in the basement washer along with the flannel sheets, and had just climbed back upstairs when Zoe appeared in the kitchen, still in pajamas and with rumpled hair and phone in hand. She didn't speak but grabbed a yogurt from the fridge and disappeared into the family room.

Lucy bit her tongue, vowing not to antagonize her lazy daughter by criticizing her for sleeping so late, and decided to give the downstairs a quick vacuum before putting the machine away. She began in the living room, which was the least used room in the house despite its cozy fireplace, where the family gathered to open stockings on Christmas morning. The dining room saw more use, as the table was large enough for the whole family, but now that only Zoe remained at home, they tended to eat at the kitchen table except for holidays and special occasions. It didn't take long for Lucy to zip through those rooms with the vacuum, then it was on to the family room. The family room got a lot more wear, thanks to the comfy sectional sofa, Bill's recliner, and the huge flat-screen TV that was Bill's pride and joy. He had been lobbying for one for years, and Lucy had resisted as long as she could, but when the Patriots went to the Super Bowl, which everyone had foolishly thought would be Tom Brady's last Super Bowl, she relented. Truth be told, she admitted to herself as she dragged the vacuum through the kitchen, she also enjoyed the big TV for watching movies.

When she reached the family room, she noticed an empty yogurt container on its side on the coffee table and Zoe, sprawled on the sectional, watching cartoons and scrolling through her phone. "Aren't you a bit old for cartoons?" she asked, plugging in the vacuum.

"No." She glared at Lucy. "You're not going to vacuum right now, are you?"

"Uh, yeah," said Lucy. "Unless you'd like to do it for me?"

Zoe's eyebrows shot up at the very notion. "Me?"

"Yeah," began Lucy, finally losing her patience. "You live here, you leave yogurt containers on tables, and I see several pairs of shoes scattered about, not to mention this. . . ." She picked up a crumpled Winchester College hoodie and displayed it. "At the very least you could tidy up after yourself."

"You know, if I had my own place this wouldn't be a problem. What you didn't see wouldn't bother you. I could leave half-empty coffee cups and clothes and takeout containers anywhere I wanted." She paused for an enormous yawn. "I'd only have to clean up if you were coming to visit."

Lucy narrowed her eyes. "But you are living here now and I want this stuff out of here."

"Gee, Mom, I was only joking," she grumbled, making no move to get up, but reaching for the remote and turning off the TV. "Mom, I don't think you and Dad realize how serious this is. I'm supposed to start work in a couple of months and I don't have anywhere to live. I can't commute from

286

here, it's too far. I'm going to have to sleep under a bridge or something." She got to her feet slowly and picked up the yogurt pot and spoon, then paused to glance at her phone. "Not that you and Dad care what happens to me."

"We care," snapped Lucy. "We just don't want you to make a big mistake that will cripple you financially for years when you're just starting out."

Zoe made her way listlessly around the room, still holding her phone and picking up her things as she went. "I am trying to get a roommate, you know," she said, pausing with her arms full of shoes and clothes to indicate her phone. "If I had a roommate we could split the rent."

"Any takers?"

"Not so far, but you never know."

"A studio would be too small for two people, wouldn't it?"

"I'm looking for a roommate who's already got a place," said Zoe, implying by her tone of voice that her mother was an idiot.

Lucy decided to let it pass. "Good idea," she said, switching on the vacuum and proceeding to push the machine back and forth. When she turned toward the doorway, she saw that Zoe had gone, leaving behind a dirty sock that she'd dropped. She snatched it up before the vacuum sucked it up, then tried to decide what to do with it. It was definitely time for Zoe to move out, she decided, carrying the stinky sock to the cellar door and dropping it down the stairs. She'd grab it on her next trip down to the washing machine.

Zoe made herself scarce for the rest of the day, apparently holed up in her bedroom while Lucy did some grocery shopping, gassed up her car, and mailed an Easter package to her grandson, Patrick. She remembered to tuck in a bag of Toby's favorite candy-coated chocolate mini-eggs, too. Zoe went out just before dinner, saying she was going to meet some friends at the diner that had become a popular hangout for the Winchester crowd, so Lucy and Bill enjoyed a rare dinner by themselves.

"I think I'll open a bottle of wine to go with that steak," suggested Bill.

"Good idea," said Lucy, reaching for two glasses.

"But only if you promise not to talk about Zoe or any of the other kids," he said, smiling naughtily and brandishing the cork-screw. "Let's just talk about us."

"You've got a deal," said Lucy, accepting a glass of wine and smiling at him. "Do you have any special plans for after dinner? Since we've got the house to ourselves?"

Bill lifted his glass and they clinked, then took a sip. "You bet I do," he said with a certain gleam in his eye.

On Sunday the weather turned gray and gloomy, and Zoe was pacing back and forth in the kitchen like a caged wildcat. "Can't you find something to do?" asked Lucy, who was seated at the table working on the Sunday crossword. She was trying to think of a seven-letter word for a choral composition without much success.

Zoe dropped into a chair and propped her chin on her hand. "I'm bored. And look at the weather. It's depressing."

"This time of year always is," said Lucy, penciling in *otter* for "weasel's aquatic cousin." That gave her a *T* for the fourth letter of the musical composition. "Can you think of a seven-letter musical composition with a 'T' in the middle?"

"Cantata," said Zoe, gazing out at the birdfeeder, where pugnacious little gold-finches were fighting it out over the thistle seed. "Wow, those guys are really going at it."

"Mating season's coming," said Lucy, a slight smile playing on her lips. "Listen, I'm going to a talk at the library this afternoon that I think you'd enjoy. The speaker is a prize-winning news photographer and I saw some of his work at a gallery in Portland. He's been all over the world covering wars, earthquakes, inaugurations, even royal weddings."

Zoe stared at her. "That's supposed to cheer me up?"

"The weddings . . ." began Lucy in a hopeful tone.

"Precisely my point. Outdated rituals celebrating a bunch of overprivileged nincompoops. Not to mention the way they exploit women. Those girls are like flies walking into the spider's parlor, just think of Princess Diana."

"So I guess you don't want to be a princess," said Lucy.

Zoe gave her a disgusted look. "No way." Then she pushed herself up off the table and dragged herself into the family room, scrolling through her phone as she went.

But after lunch, when Lucy was getting ready to leave for the library, Zoe surprised her by suddenly deciding to join her. "Beats watching hockey with Dad," was her explanation. And when they arrived at the library and seated themselves in the book-lined downstairs meeting room, Matthieu Colon didn't disappoint. With his full head of flowing gray hair, his craggy face, and a military-style vest, he was the very picture of a glamorous war correspondent. Zoe was definitely impressed, nudging her mother and whispering, "For an old guy, he's actually pretty dope." Lucy was amused by Zoe's reaction, and hoped she wouldn't be disappointed when Colon began the show with photos of Prince Charles and Lady Diana's wedding.

"All us photographers knew it would never last," he said, as a very tentative-looking Diana, swathed in yards and yards of white veiling, began her long walk down the aisle of Westminster Abbey. Gazing at the photo, Lucy thought he was right; the revealing shot didn't bode well for a long and happy marriage. "See, I told you," whispered Zoe. "They say she felt like a lamb going to the slaughter."

That was followed by a picture of President George W. Bush seated at an easel, brush in hand. "He's quite a painter," commented the photographer. "Not many people know that about him." He paused, yawning, and added an aside: "So is Prince Charles, by the way."

"And I can sing and dance like J.Lo," scoffed Zoe, rolling her eyes.

It wasn't until he began showing his war photos that Zoe really became interested. It was then that the photographer really hit his stride, becoming more emotional and forceful as he displayed scenes of terrible destruction and violence. One by one he showed portraits of terrified and tearful children, exhausted and confused old people, and sometimes weary, sometimes determined soldiers. "These were all taken in Croatia, during the Bosnian War," he said. "We've pretty much forgotten all about it, but people don't go through something like this and forgive and forget."

"How come I didn't know about this?" whispered Zoe, clearly shocked.

"It was in the nineties, you weren't born yet." Lucy replied in a whisper.

Zoe gasped when the next photo appeared, a shot of a charred and crumbling stairwell with a pile of twisted and distorted bodies at the bottom. "This is the shot that won me the Pulitzer," he said in a solemn voice. "I was with a terrific reporter, a fabulous gal, and we were in a town called Ahmići trying to reach a Bosniak commander when we came upon this hospital that had been destroyed in a fire. It was actually still smoking when we arrived and a handful of people, doctors and nurses, were trying to find survivors. They told us the hospital had been burned by Croat soldiers who were destroying everything in their path." He sighed. "They'd been off-duty, they said, when the Croats attacked, that's why they were still alive. Everyone in the hospital had been killed. They couldn't find any survivors."

After the show, and the Q and A, refreshments were offered. Zoe spotted some friends in the crowd and joined them, while Lucy approached the photographer for a word. "I really enjoyed your talk," she began, "and I couldn't help wondering if you've ever worked with a reporter named Agnes Neal?"

"Sure have! Do you know her? She was the one who was with me at the hospital." His face fell as he recalled the awful destruction, then he gave a shrug and his expression brightened. "Those shots got me the Pulitzer."

Lucy was both surprised and not surprised; she'd suspected Colon would have known Agnes, but hadn't realized they'd been so closely connected. "I'm afraid I've got bad news for you," she said. "Agnes died a few weeks ago. Oddly enough, her body was found in a stairwell in the senior residence where she was living. It's not clear if her death was accidental."

Colon stared at the paper cup of mulled cider he was holding for a long time. "That's terrible news," he finally said. "Agnes was very dear to me," he said, in a husky voice, "but life took us in different directions. After Bosnia, she said she was done with wars. She wanted to settle down, and she came back to Maine. We stayed in touch, though. We used to call each other now and then."

"Did you speak recently?" asked Lucy.

"Not too recently. I was covering a space launch in Florida, I actually went into quarantine to photograph the training and preparation of an astronaut. It was really intense and I was entirely consumed, living in the bubble, and didn't reach out to anybody outside." He shrugged, and continued, "That's how I work, you know. I really get involved. But I knew I had this gig in Maine, where Agnes was living, and I was actually hoping I might see her here today. I called a couple of times, but . . ." He paused, his voice breaking. He took a minute or two to get control of himself, running his finger around the rim of the cup. "Well," he finally said, "I left a couple of messages. When I didn't see her in the crowd I thought I'd try to look her up after the talk."

"Do you remember anything from your last conversation? Anything that struck you?" asked Lucy, persisting.

"Now that I think about it, yeah. She said she thought she might have found one of the Croat officers who ordered the assault on Ahmići, that's the place with the hospital. She was real excited, said he was still wanted by the International Criminal Court, but I cautioned her to take it easy and not go making accusations."

"You thought he was still dangerous?"

"No. I didn't believe her. I thought she was going off the rails. What would a Croat officer be doing here in Maine? I was afraid she was going to make a fool of herself and get in trouble." He looked up. "Now I'm not so sure. Maybe she was onto something."

Before Lucy could reply, Zoe joined them and Matthieu immediately cheered up, clearly impressed by Zoe's youthful good looks. "And who's this?" he asked.

"My daughter Zoe," said Lucy, hastening to add, "She's twenty-two. Just finishing up college."

"Good for you," replied Colon, beaming at her. "And what are your career plans?"

"I'm going to be doing publicity for the Sea Dogs."

"Have you considered journalism?" he asked, his eyes drifting below her neck. "I'd be happy to discuss it with you. Maybe you'd join me for a coffee? Or we could have dinner?"

"I can give her all the guidance she needs," said Lucy, grabbing Zoe's elbow. "It's been lovely talking to you," she added, steering Zoe through the dwindling crowd toward the exit.

"Mom!" Zoe protested in a hiss. "I wanted to have coffee with him."

"I know. That's why we're leaving."

"But I might've got some good tips from him. Insider stuff."

"That's what I was afraid of," said Lucy as they started up the stairs.

"But he was interested in my career . . ." protested Zoe.

Lucy stopped mid-flight and looked her daughter in the eye. "Zoe, he may be a celebrated photographer but he's also an old lech. Trust me." Lucy resumed her climb up the stairs. "I know the type."

"Oh," replied Zoe, mulling over her mother's allegation. "Are you sure?"

"I'd bet the house on it."

Zoe was silent as they walked to the car, then spoke up when Lucy started the engine. "I wonder what it's like, actually being in the middle of a war."

"I hope you never find out," said Lucy, shifting into drive. "Never ever."

She was still seeing Matthieu Colon's wartime photos in her mind's eye when she went to work on Monday. Phyllis was already at the reception desk, sorting through press releases for the events listings, and dressed head to toe in baby blue. Observing her rounded shape, Lucy realized she'd gained a few pounds over the winter and repressed the notion that she resembled a very large Easter egg.

"You've got that Easter spirit," said Lucy by way of greeting. "I'm glad you gave up your beige phase."

"I tried, but I really like color," said Phyllis, peering at her over her blue cheaters. "How was your weekend?"

"The usual. I did a bit of spring cleaning." She shrugged out of her jacket. "Zoe and I went to hear that photographer's talk in the library while Bill watched the hockey game."

"Bruins are on a roll," offered Phyllis, who was a hockey fan. "I think they've got a good chance of winning the Stanley Cup."

"That's what Bill says, too." Lucy was seating herself at her desk and powering up her PC. "I'd like to write about the talk but I'm not at all sure Ted will want it."

"He's playing up the bears big-time," said Phyllis.

"Yeah. We'd have to print some of the photos, and I guess we've got too many already."

When she ran the idea by Ted his response was a groan. "No, no, no. The preview was plenty."

"How about for the online edition?"

"Nobody wants to look at old photos from a long ago, far-away war that everybody has forgotten. It's spring in Maine, we've got bears and Easter bonnets. And now" — he paused dramatically — "alewives!"

"Oh, no," said Lucy, who had covered the annual migration of the fish too many times. Visions of flopping and dying fish, circling and screaming flocks of gulls, and small children in danger of drowning in the fish ladder filled her mind. "I can't face it, give it to someone else," she pleaded.

"You're the best, Lucy. And they've just finished the fish ladder restoration project and they've got a new fish-counting device. This is news that inquiring minds want to know."

"I disagree," said Lucy. "Nobody cares."

"They do, Lucy. The alewives were endangered, the fish ladder was mostly blocked, and they couldn't get to their spawning grounds. Folks ponied up thousands of dollars to fix that ladder and save the fishies, and the least we can do is show them that their contributions are making a big difference. George Waterman says the numbers are already far exceeding previous years."

Thus it was that Lucy found herself standing beside the fish ladder in a chilly drizzle, interviewing alewife warden George Waterman. The newly restored fish ladder consisted of a series of stepped pools that enabled the migrating fish, who jumped against the current from pool to pool, to make the climb from their ocean home to their spawning ground in Blueberry Pond. "It's really a miracle every spring," said George. "You know these fish were actually born in this pond, this is where they hatched, and where they return every year. And when the ladder was blocked, well, only a few made it through. And this isn't the only ladder that needed work, there's plenty more in disrepair throughout New England. That means thousands, maybe even millions of alewives can't get back to spawn. Just think about it, thousands of potential fish that never lived." He nodded solemnly. "That's why the species is threatened."

"But I understand they're recovering, thanks to efforts like this."

George, dressed in a yellow slicker suit and muddy boots, nodded solemnly. "It's a hopeful sign, but the population is still stressed. We'll just have to see how many return to the ocean come fall, then we'll know if it's been a success or not."

His phone was ringing and he fumbled in his pockets, trying to retrieve it. When he finally got it the ringtone had ended, but the caller had left a message. "My mom," he said, apologetically. "She's got a bee in her bonnet about something." He returned the phone to his pocket, then pointed out the newly installed wire fencing. "We've fenced the ladder in, you see, it's to keep the little kids from falling in and also to keep folks from throwing stuff in. You'd be surprised how many guys think it's terrific fun to hit an alewife with a beer bottle. I've seen them making a game of it." He shook his head, reaching again for his phone. This time he got it in time.

"Look, Mom, I'm being interviewed for the paper right now. I can't talk."

Lucy could hear George's mother's voice, reacting indignantly. "So some reporter is more important than your mother." The voice sounded familiar and she realized

300

George's mother was Bev, who along with Bitsy and Dorothy made up the Gang of Three.

Amused by the mother-son exchange, Lucy looked around, noticing that the leaf buds on the bare trees were swelling, and male redwings were calling, advertising for mates. George, meanwhile, was trying to placate his mother.

"Not at all, Mom. It's just bad timing. I'll drop by at lunch, how about that?"

"I guess it'll have to do," replied his mother, throwing in a heavy, resigned sigh.

George fingered his phone after ending the call. "You know, I am a little worried. She's over at Heritage House, where that lady died in the staircase." He chewed his lip. "It's awfully expensive to keep her there and I'm not convinced it's the best place for her."

"Is she happy there?" asked Lucy.

"Used to be, but not so much now," said George, shelving his concerns for later. "Hey, let me show you the new fish counter. Computerized. It's amazing."

"I'm sure it is," said Lucy, following him up the path to the top of the fish ladder, where the counter was located. "I just check it with my phone," he said, demonstrating with a few swipes, "and voila, twenty thousand three hundred and forty-one fish have come through so far. What do you think about that?"

"That's a lot of fish."

"You said it," added George, beaming. "We're on our way to beating last year's total for sure!"

On her way back to the office, Lucy couldn't help smiling. Some folks rooted for their favorite hockey team, others preferred alewives.

CHAPTER EIGHTEEN

When Lucy was driving back to the office her cell phone rang. She pulled off the road to answer, expecting it was Bob, but discovered the caller was Assistant AG John Williams. She really hadn't expected him to follow up and was very interested to learn what he had to report.

"Thanks for calling," she began, "I can't wait to hear what you've got for me."

"Not a whole lot," he said. "I think you knew that Heritage House is owned by TaraCare and I was able to find out that the principals of that corporation are Peter Novak and Vesna Varga."

Lucy was stunned. "Are you sure? Vesna is this little old lady who makes fancy Easter eggs."

"I would guess that she's a very rich old lady who makes fancy Easter eggs," said Williams. "TaraCare is comprised of three senior care facilities in the state and is

303

valued at over twenty million dollars."

"That's a lot of eggs," said Lucy, still struggling to process this information. Of course she'd been struck by Vesna's luxurious seaside home; now it made sense. Sort of. "What exactly is a principal of a corporation?" she asked.

"It varies. It can simply be a name on a paper, or it can be an active manager. The whole purpose of a corporation is to limit personal liability, so depending on her arrangement with Peter Novak, she is likely raking in quite a bit of dough."

"Peter Novak is the CEO of Heritage House, I wonder if he's related to Vesna."

"Could be. Or it could be a partnership. That information wasn't in the paperwork I saw. She might even be the principal owner."

Thinking back to the interview, and Vesna's pride in "all this," Lucy thought that was entirely possible. "Well, thanks so much for following up. I really appreciate it."

"No big deal. I've got an inquiring mind and these senior care places are kind of the Wild West of the health care industry. Hospitals are strictly regulated but there's not much regulation or oversight in senior living outfits, or even nursing homes. Most of them are privately owned and there's a lot of money to be made."

Lucy laughed. "So I'm discovering. Thanks again."

Lucy was thoughtful as she returned her phone to her bag and got back on the road. She really wanted to have a nice, long chat with Vesna but didn't quite see a way to do that. She hadn't exactly been forthcoming when Lucy interviewed her. While she'd had plenty to say about the eggs, she'd been quite closemouthed about her life before coming to America. So Lucy could hardly believe her luck when she got to the office and Phyllis presented her with two pink "While You Were Out" notes. One informed her that Vesna Varga had called, the other indicated Bob had.

"I can't believe this, I was just thinking about Vesna," said Lucy, grinning broadly as she noted the phone number.

"Well, I wouldn't get too excited if I were you," cautioned Phyllis. "She didn't sound very happy. In fact, I'd say she was loaded for bear."

"Well," said Lucy, unzipping her jacket, "this bear has a thick skin."

As soon as she was settled at her desk, Lucy called Bob, aware that he rarely wasted any time on chatty phone calls. True to form, he got right down to business and told her the lease was watertight and he personally wouldn't advise Zoe to sign it unless she had a trust fund to fall back on.

"I wish," confessed Lucy, laughing and thanking him. She didn't look forward to sharing his advice with Zoe, and promptly shelved the matter for later since she had the more pressing business of returning Vesna's call.

Like Bob, Vesna didn't bother with pleasantries but immediately voiced her complaint. "What is this about *pysanky*? Not *pysanky*! *Pisanica!* I should know, I make them! Everyone in my little town knows, *pisanica*!"

"Sorry about the confusion," said Lucy, doing what she should have done originally and googling the term. *Pisanica,* she soon discovered, were the Croatian, not Russian version of the decorated eggs that were made throughout Eastern Europe. "My mistake," admitted Lucy as the wheels began turning in her head. "I assumed you were Russian."

"No!" snapped Vesna. "I'm not Russian. I don't like Russia. I've never been to Russia. Where did you get that idea?"

"Doesn't matter," said Lucy, who was not prepared to throw her source under the bus. "It was a careless mistake and I will be sure to correct it in the next issue. So tell me

306

about your home village in Croatia. . . ."

"That was very, very long time ago," said Vesna. "It has all changed now."

"Was it affected by the war?" asked Lucy. "Or did you leave before that?"

"We were lucky, we got out just in time. My son Peter and me."

Just as she'd suspected, thought Lucy. Peter Novak was Vesna's son. "And you came to America and started TaraCare?" suggested Lucy.

"That's my Peter, he's the genius." Vesna's tone was definitely growing warmer; Peter was clearly a favorite subject. "He was the one who came up with the name Tara because it is a famous river in Bosnia, but he says also the name of a plantation in a famous American book. Very clever, no?"

"Absolutely," said Lucy. "But why senior housing? Did he have a background in that in Croatia?"

"No. But is natural choice for him. In Croatia, we always honored the old ones. And my Peter, he takes very good care of the old folks."

He certainly didn't take very good care of Agnes Neal, thought Lucy, keeping that thought to herself. "So he does," she said, hoping to encourage more confidences from Vesna. That, however, was not to be.

"So you will print correction?" she demanded, clearly ready to end the call.

"Absolutely," promised Lucy, who had no sooner spoken than the line went dead.

As she typed up the second correction, she tried not to think about Ted's reaction. She should have done a bit of fact-checking, but hadn't thought it necessary. It was far too easy to take people at their word and Lucy feared she'd grown lazy and maybe even somewhat gullible lately. Maybe it was because she'd been dealing with all these old folks. She'd been raised to respect the elderly; she remembered long Sunday afternoons when her aged great-aunt Etta visited. She'd always been delegated to run outside and greet Aunt Etta's taxi, giving the stout and arthritic old lady her arm and helping her into the house. She'd also been expected to pass the chocolates and chat with her, uncomfortably aware that her time would be better spent studying for the upcoming week's exams than listening to Aunt Etta's reminiscences about her work as a bookkeeper for her adored employer, the very wealthy Mr. Hanselbach. Then retired, Aunt Etta had nothing but pleasant memories of Mr. Hanselbach's quirks and sometimes Lucy thought she knew more about Mr. Hanselbach than she did about her own grandfather.

That old-fashioned upbringing had had a huge influence on her, she realized, thinking how she had fallen so easily into a friendship with Miss Tilley, who was much older than her. She'd been close to retiring from her job as librarian at the Broadbrooks Free Library when they first met, but they had immediately become friends. Miss Tilley had managed to remain young in attitude, if not in body, thanks to her interest in younger people and her intense curiosity about the world. She often said she couldn't even think of dying because she wanted to know what was going to happen next. But now Lucy was worried about her oldest and very dear friend. It was more than her concern about the bill for assisted living; now she wasn't convinced that Heritage House was a safe place for her, especially since she'd learned of George Waterman's mother's concerns.

Something was definitely amiss at Heritage House and she was afraid that she might have put Miss Tilley and Howard White in danger by encouraging them to investigate. She'd finished the correction some time ago and was staring at it, remembering Colon's photos from the Bosnian War, and she thought of poor Agnes, who'd also died in a stairwell. Different circumstances, surely. But was it a coincidence? And what about Bev Waterman? She was a member of the Gang of Three, as Miss Tilley called them, which put her at the top of the Heritage House social ladder. Her son had dismissed her concerns, citing her age, but Lucy wasn't convinced. The gang members seemed pretty sharp and she feared that if they were worried, there was probably a good reason.

It was probably irrational, but she had the strongest urge to get herself over to Heritage House, just to make sure everything was okay. She knew she wouldn't be able to get any work done until she'd quieted her fears, so she sent the correction to Ted, then powered off and got up. It wasn't just that she didn't want to be around to hear Ted's angry reaction to the second correction, not at all, she told herself. Maybe it was intuition, or something rumbling around in her subconscious, but she felt she had to get over to Heritage House and she'd learned through the years that she should trust her instincts.

She was just parking her car when she noticed George Waterman in the parking lot, shaking his head as he made his way to his truck. She quickly hopped out and hailed him. "Long time no see," she began, getting a grin. "How's your mom?"

"I don't know," he said, scratching his chin. "She had some story about that lady who died in the stairwell, but I couldn't make head nor tail of it."

Lucy felt the hairs on the back of her neck rise, and pressed him for more information. "What exactly did she say?"

"It's not worth repeating, she gets confused these days."

"I'm sure they're all somewhat upset," said Lucy. "It was a terrible thing to happen and it must make them all wonder if they're safe."

Waterman bit his lip. "That's not the feeling I got. It wasn't that she was afraid, it was more like she felt guilty."

"Guilty? What on earth has she got to feel guilty about?"

"Well, last thing she mentioned was the time she borrowed her sister's dress and ruined it and that all happened fifty-some years ago, but she keeps bringing it up." He screwed his mouth into a grimace. "I did some research and it's one of the signs of dementia. They remember stuff from long ago. And sometimes she mixes up dreams and reality."

Lucy's first impulse was to disagree. She'd

never got that impression about Bev, but then again she didn't know her as well as her son. "That's too bad," she said. "Maybe she's just having a bad day."

"Ever the optimist, hunh, Lucy?"

"I guess I am," admitted Lucy. "My mother used to say there was no sense worrying about things you can't change."

"I'll keep that in mind," said Waterman, giving a little salute and continuing on his way. Eager to reassure herself that Miss Tilley was all right, Lucy hurried into the senior residence and went straight to her room, only to find it empty. Somewhat shocked, she tracked down a nurse's aide to find out what was going on.

"Oh, her friend Howard took her for a little change of scene, they're probably in the common area on the mezzanine," said the aide.

"Thanks." Lucy made her way through the corridors to the mezzanine, but there was no sign of Howard and Miss Tilley. The Gang of Three were there, however, engaged in an absorbing conversation. They were huddled so closely together, and so intent on their discussion, that they didn't notice Lucy. She spotted a nearby chair and decided to sit down and wait a bit, in case Howard and Miss Tilley showed up. In the meantime, she busied herself poking in her handbag while straining to hear what the women were talking about.

It wasn't easy to catch the drift of the conversation; for one thing, staff were busy in the adjoining dining room, setting the tables for dinner. She could hear them chattering and laughing, occasionally exclaiming when someone dropped something. She could also hear the distant hum of a vacuum cleaner being operated out in the hallway. But every now and then, she'd catch a word.

"Not your fault," proclaimed Bev, only to be quickly shushed by Dorothy.

They must be talking to Bitsy, concluded Lucy, struggling mightily to resist the urge to turn her head. Instead, she bent a little closer to her handbag, plumbing its depths as if searching for some elusive object.

She heard a sob, followed by the sound of someone blowing their nose, and guessed that whatever was bothering Bitsy had reduced her to tears. Certainly not, she thought, some ancient misdeed like spoiling a sister's borrowed dress or fibbing to a parent. No-nonsense Dorothy certainly wouldn't waste any time consoling her for such a trivial matter. No, whatever was under discussion was taking place in the here and now.

That hypothesis was confirmed when Dorothy spoke up quite firmly. "I think we should make a clean breast of it and tell the truth," she declared.

"To who? The police?" inquired Bitsy, horrified.

"I'm not sure it's a matter for the police, it's really a matter of conscience," said Dorothy. "What about Reverend Marge? We could ask her to pay a pastoral visit and tell her. See what she has to say."

"But what if she tells the police?" asked Bitsy in a quavery voice.

"Clergy have some sort of confidentiality thing, like lawyers," said Dorothy.

"I'm not so sure about that," said Bev. "Remember that movie *Doubt* they showed the other day? Meryl Streep was convinced of Philip Seymour Hoffman's guilt. She was going right after him."

"But she didn't get him. It was called *Doubt,* after all," said Dorothy. "I'm sure Reverend Marge would —"

"She might not tell the police, but what if she went to Peter? Or one of the others, like Elvira or that social worker woman? I might get kicked out! We all might! What'll we do then?"

"Shush," urged Dorothy. "You need to get a grip. Nobody's going to kick us out. We're not in any trouble."

"I guess the best thing is simply to sit tight," sighed Bev.

It was then that Lucy's phone rang and all three heads turned in her direction. "What are you doing here?" demanded Dorothy.

CHAPTER NINETEEN

The melodious ringtone continued, so Lucy held up a finger, indicating her intention to take the call, and checked the caller ID. It was Ted, probably calling about that correction, so she declined the call, figuring she'd give him time to let his temper cool. Then she addressed the women.

"I'm waiting for my friend, Miss Tilley," she began. "But I couldn't help overhearing. It seems you have some sort of problem. Is there anything I can do to help?"

Bev was quick to reject Lucy's overture. "Oh, no. It was nothing. You know how it is in a place like this. Little things get blown all out of proportion."

"I do know how that is. I've spent many a sleepless night fretting over some trivial oversight, especially if it meant I had to run a correction in the paper." Lucy gave them an encouraging smile. "I've found it really helps to talk these things over with someone neutral."

"You're just digging for news, Lucy Stone," said Dorothy. "Don't think we don't know what you're up to."

"That's not entirely true," said Lucy, her voice rising as she defended herself. "As you know, Miss Tilley is living here at the moment, recuperating from a nasty case of pneumonia, and I'm very concerned for her safety. I don't want what happened to Agnes to happen to her." Realizing her emotions were getting the better of her, Lucy took a deep breath and looked each of the ladies in the eye. "I know one thing for sure — the truth has a way of coming out. All you have to do is tell me that anything you say is off the record, and I can't use it. I can't print it in the paper. But I do believe with all my heart that oftentimes you can gain control of a situation if you go public. If something is amiss here at Heritage House you'll all be much safer when the truth is known."

Bev seemed to be looking inward, wavering, and Bitsy was dabbing at her eyes with a tissue. Only Dorothy met her gaze. "She's right," said Dorothy. "The sooner we tell what happened, the better off we'll be. We can't go on like this, scared of our shadows. It's time to face the truth."

"I disagree," said Bev. "My son said I should put it out of my mind and forget about it. He said that was the best thing."

Bitsy didn't take this news well. "You didn't tell him, did you?" she demanded, angrily shredding her tissue.

"Well, I . . ." began Bev, looking very guilty indeed.

"Now you've done it. It was a secret, our secret!" Bitsy sounded like an outraged child. "We promised not to tell anyone! A double-pinky promise."

"But he's my son —"

"Doesn't matter!" snapped Bitsy.

"Bitsy's right," said Dorothy. "The cat's out of the bag. It's better if we tell what happened, exactly as it happened." She sighed. "Then we'll let the chips fall as they may."

"For now, this is off the record, I'm not writing anything down, I'm not recording anything," said Lucy, hoping to coax them into talking. She took a seat on the couch and turned her phone off, placing it on the coffee table for all to see. "You can change your minds afterward, if you want."

The three women nodded.

"So who wants to start?"

"I will," said Dorothy, taking a deep breath. "It's like this, we lured Agnes into the stairwell."

Lucy was absolutely horrified and completely stunned by this admission, but was determined not to reveal how she felt. She took a deep, centering breath, and asked in a soft voice, "Why did you do that?"

Bev closed her eyes and pressed her lips together. Bitsy emitted a sharp sob. "It was supposed to be a good deed."

"It was Peter's idea," said Bev. "You know how charming he can be and that day he sat right down on this sofa, next to Bitsy, just where you are, and asked if she would do something for him. Something that he needed help with, a sensitive matter, he said, due to the Heritage House policy that a male staff member couldn't be alone with a female resident."

Bitsy nodded. "I've always liked him, he's so handsome, and I was flattered that he was paying attention to me. And it was just a little thing . . ."

"He wanted us to find Agnes and tell her that there was a tiny little owl, a baby owl in the stairwell and convince her that he needed her help to get it to safety," said Bev. "So we went to her apartment, all three of us. Agnes wasn't convinced at first, she said it was impossible because it was too early in the year for baby owls to be hatched."

"Not hatched, fledged," corrected Dorothy. "She said fledged. That's when they leave the nest."

"Just a minute," said Lucy. "Where was Peter?"

"He said he was going to get a box so he could move the owl because the stairwell wasn't a safe place for it, so if we wanted to see it, we should bring Agnes and meet him in the stairwell, the one just down the hall from her unit. He added that he couldn't wait to see Agnes's reaction, he knew she'd want to help because she was such a keen bird-watcher and absolutely loved birds.

"So that's what I told her," admitted Bitsy. "That it wasn't every day you got to see an owl up close."

"But she still didn't want to go," added Bev.

"Then I remembered something I'd read, about saw-whet owls, so I asked her if it might possibly be one of those. That got her interested," said Dorothy, "and she agreed to take a look, just through the window in the door."

"So we all went over to the stairwell and peeked in and we saw Peter, on his knees, staring into a box that he had on the floor. He was kind of chasing the bird around in the box, trying to grab it or something, and

Agnes got all upset. She punched in the code, it took a couple of tries she was so mad, and she charged in, yelling at him to stop."

"And what did you do?" asked Lucy.

"Well, we went in, too, but Peter said maybe it was too many people, that the owl was frightened, and we peeked in and the poor little thing was huddled in a corner of the box, kind of panting. He said that he and Agnes would take care of the owl," recalled Bev, "and that's when Bitsy got upset."

"Why was that?" asked Lucy.

"I said I'd like to help, too," continued Bitsy, "but Peter was quite firm. He reminded us that it was lunchtime, they were trying out a new menu and wanted to know if people liked it, and he said he especially wanted to know what I thought. . . ."

"And Agnes was fuming in that way she had, kind of like a teakettle steaming just before it goes into a boil and whistles," recalled Bev.

"So we went off to the dining room, leaving Agnes and Peter together," said Bitsy.

"In violation of the rule?" asked Lucy.

"I actually asked him about that," said Dorothy. "I wasn't interested in lunch, I had some leftovers from the Cali Kitchen I wanted to eat, so I asked if he wanted me to stay, but he said it would be all right just this once and he didn't want to keep me from my noon meal." She paused, as if wondering if she'd done the right thing, but quickly justified herself. "I couldn't argue with him, it wasn't my place. And I was right about the owl, it was definitely a saw-whet, I looked it up later."

"But we never saw Agnes after that," said Bev.

"What about Peter? Did you see him later that day?"

"Oh, yes," said Bitsy. He always comes in when dessert is served and chats with the residents, makes sure everyone is happy. And, of course, he wanted to know what we thought of the meal. It was some sort of fake meat."

"It was supposed to be better for the planet," offered Bev.

"Well, I didn't like it," insisted Bitsy, scowling. "I don't see what's the matter with actual meat."

"Did you ask him about Agnes?"

"Actually, no," recalled Bev. "But he volunteered the information anyway. He said she was going to check out the owl, make sure it was okay, and then take it to the woods and release it."

"At first we thought she'd got lost in the woods," said Bitsy.

"But when they found her in the stairwell, we started to wonder," said Dorothy. "Not at first, but as time passed, we began to feel we were somehow involved."

Lucy pressed on. "But when you left, she was alive, alone with Peter?"

"It might've been an accident, she might've fallen carrying the box," speculated Bev. "It's tricky carrying a box down stairs. You can't see the steps."

"But there was something going on between them, you could sense it," said Dorothy. "I think that's why we've been worried."

"You said Agnes was steaming . . ." suggested Lucy. "Was she angry? Confrontational?"

"At first," remembered Bev. "But then I got the sense she was afraid."

"I didn't get that at all," countered Bitsy.

Lucy looked to Dorothy, who repeated herself. "Afraid. Definitely afraid."

"This is really important information," said Lucy. "It means that Peter was probably the last person to see Agnes alive."

"Does that mean he's in trouble?" asked Bitsy.

"I think it means the police would want to talk to him again," said Lucy.

"Lying to the police is a serious offense," said Dorothy.

"Well, for all we know, he's already told them all about it," suggested Beverly.

"Right," said Lucy, desperate to convince them to let her use this new information in a story that she believed would prompt the police to reopen the investigation. "I do think it would be best for everyone if I write this up for the paper, just the way you told me."

The three women seemed to share some private signal, and Dorothy spoke up. "Only if we all agree, right, ladies?"

Bev and Bitsy nodded their heads in agreement.

"So what do you say?" asked Lucy, trying not to sound too eager.

"I don't see the harm," said Dorothy.

"I know it would take a load off my mind," said Bev.

"Well, I disagree. We all made a double-pinky promise to keep it a secret and I don't break my promises," insisted Bitsy.

"Are you sure about this, Bitsy?" asked Dorothy.

Bitsy pouted. "Absolutely."

Dorothy looked at Lucy and shrugged. "Sorry."

"Me too," said Lucy, "but Bitsy's got a

point. A promise is a promise. I'll keep this conversation to myself, but I'm not giving up, I'm going to keep investigating. If I get similar information from another source, I will use it."

"That's fair enough," said Dorothy.

But Bitsy wasn't pleased. "You wouldn't!"

Lucy had a sudden flashback, she was suddenly back on the playground at PS 81 in the Riverdale section of the Bronx, where she grew up. Alex Richman and Linda Bruno were scoffing at her claim that she could go round the world on the playground swing. She answered back, "Oh, yes I can. Just watch me!" Fortunately for her, the bell rang ending recess and she didn't have to make good on her boast, and a spell of bad weather ended outdoor recess for several days, by which time Linda and Alex had forgotten all about her boast. She hadn't forgotten, however, and worried about being found out, because no matter how hard she tried, she couldn't actually manage the trick. Years later she learned it was actually impossible, without special equipment.

But now, here in Heritage House, Lucy was determined to find out exactly what had happened between Peter Novak and Agnes Neal. "Oh, yes I would," she said, with a sly smile. "Just watch me."

Back in her car, she was fumbling in her bag for the keys, which always seemed to fall to the bottom, when she encountered her reporter's notebook and tossed it aside. Just like she'd had to toss aside the Gang of Three's confession. It really bothered her that she couldn't use the story but she decided to jot down a few notes, for her own use, just in case. She turned on the engine to get some heat and sat there, scribbling away, getting down the women's words as she remembered them. When she'd finished, it occurred to her that Agnes was a reporter, just like she was, and had most likely had the same habit of writing things down so she wouldn't forget them, or get them wrong.

Matthieu Colon had told her that Agnes had confided to him that she suspected she'd found a Croat officer who had been involved in the assault on Ahmići — had that discovery led to her death? Was it possible that Peter Novak was actually a former Croat soldier? And had he killed Agnes to keep his identity secret? Lucy felt a growing sense of excitement, convinced that if Agnes had indeed been investigating the Ahmići massacre she would certainly have kept careful notes. Somewhere in her effects there must be a notebook or a recording, some form of documentation.

Her phone rang, it was Ted calling again, and again she ignored it. Instead, she dialed Geri Mazzone and asked if she'd saved her mother's effects.

"Well, not really," said Geri. "There wasn't much, she just had that little apartment, so I cleared it out and gave everything to the Salvation Army. I did keep a little desk, it was a family heirloom."

"Any papers? Or maybe her phone?"

"The phone's dead, she used her thumb as an ID. I took it to the store but they said they couldn't do anything."

"Papers? Notebooks?"

"Maybe in the desk. I haven't cleaned it out yet. I was waiting for my son to help me move some furniture so I can put it in my bedroom."

"Would you mind if I looked at it?" asked Lucy. "I think she may have been working on something that led to her death, but I need more information."

"It's okay by me," said Geri, "but I can't imagine what you think you'll find. Mom was definitely not a hoarder; she was a compulsive shredder. The minute she was done with a piece of paper it went into the shredder!"

Lucy's spirits sank, but she wasn't about

to give up now that she'd finally found a lead that might explain Agnes's death. If Peter Novak was implicated in the Ahmići massacre, and if he'd killed Agnes because she had discovered his guilt, it was time for the truth to come out. "I'll be right over," she said, shifting into gear.

Geri's house was on the other side of town and it took Lucy twenty minutes to get there, growing more excited with every minute that passed. She was convinced that Agnes would have saved her notes and a desk seemed like a natural place to tuck them away. Of course, Geri had warned her that Agnes was a devoted shredder, and Lucy also knew that a lot of journalists destroyed their notes once a story was published, to protect their sources, especially if the story was based on a whistle-blower's account. Those notes couldn't be subpoenaed if they didn't exist.

When she reached Geri's little ranch house, she found Geri was waiting for her in the unheated garage, wearing only a sweater that had seen better days, her arms wrapped across her chest for warmth. "Golly, it's colder than I thought. When is spring coming?"

"Your guess is as good as mine," said Lucy. "Thanks for doing this." She looked around but didn't see a desk. "Where's the desk?"

"It's here," said Geri, leading the way to a boxy shape covered by a painter's drop cloth. "I already looked through it, while Mom was still missing. There really wasn't anything of interest."

"You never know," said Lucy, resolving not to give up before she'd started. "Let's see what we've got."

"Okay." Geri dragged the drop cloth away, revealing a very petite, black-and-gold chinoiserie drop-front desk.

"That was really your mom's?" asked Lucy, shocked by the piece's feminine style. She'd expected something like Ted's prized rolltop, the enormous desk he'd inherited from his grandfather.

"Yeah, it was her mother's before it came to her, she said it was ridiculously impractical but she absolutely adored it."

Lucy noticed the detailed gold design, which featured weeping willow trees, temples, flowers, and, of course, birds. "It is a lovely piece of furniture, and I imagine it's quite valuable."

"I have no idea," admitted Geri. "I have just the spot for it in my bedroom but I have to get a big old bookcase moved out."

"Do you mind if I take a look inside?"

"Go right ahead. I'm probably going to toss out the contents anyway."

Lucy lowered the drop front, revealing a row of tiny drawers with cubbyholes on top. A ceramic figure of a bright yellow goldfinch sat in the middle cubby, but the ones on either side contained folded bits of paper and envelopes. Lucy pulled them out, discovering some old receipts and postcards, a map of the trails in the conservation area, and a few business cards. Pulling out the drawers she found some postage stamps, a few pens, and a box of paper clips.

"Don't say I didn't warn you," said Geri.

Lucy closed the slanted flap and eyed the four drawers beneath it. "What about the drawers?"

"Go ahead, but I'm warning you, they're very shallow. There's not much in them."

Pulling them open, one by one, Lucy found folded sheets of wrapping paper, a ruler, several packs of notepaper featuring birds, a handful of large manila envelopes, an address book, a phone book, and a pair of faded black-and-white studio portraits.

"My great-great-grandparents," laughed Geri, as Lucy studied the rather stern expression of a woman wearing wire-rimmed glasses and a flamboyantly musta-chioed, rather stout gentleman sporting a diamond stickpin in his striped tie. "A real fun couple. I've been told she was a member of the Woman's Christian Temperance Union."

"He more than her, I'd guess," said Lucy, chuckling. "He looks like someone who enjoyed a hearty meal."

"Family lore has it that he was very much under her thumb. He emigrated from Sweden and she insisted he lose his accent before she would consent to marry him."

"I'm not surprised," said Lucy, "she doesn't look like someone you'd like to trifle with."

"You could say my mother took after her," said Geri, replacing the photos and shutting the drawer. "I'm sorry there wasn't anything here for you." She was reaching for the drop cloth when Lucy had a sudden inspiration.

"You know, I saw a desk like this on *Antiques Road-show.*"

This caught Geri's interest. "Was it valuable?"

"I can't remember," admitted Lucy. "But what I do remember is that it had a secret compartment."

Geri dropped her hands. "Really?"

"Yeah." Lucy once again lowered the flap that served as a writing surface and carefully moved the figure of the goldfinch to

331

one corner. "See how this cubby is much shallower than the others?"

"There's a hidden space behind!" exclaimed Geri. "But how do you open it?"

Lucy gave a gentle push with one finger and they heard a little click. "Like that," she said, giggling with excitement. "Just like that."

"What's inside?"

"I don't know if there's anything," said Lucy, bending down and poking into the cubby. "There is something, I can't quite reach it."

"Use that ruler," advised Geri.

"Good idea." Lucy retrieved the ruler and poked it into the cubby, drawing out an old piece of newsprint that had begun to turn brown. It was foreign, the words were in French, but when she unfolded the brittle scrap, the photo revealed the much younger but clearly recognizable face of a man dressed in military fatigues, identified in the caption as Croat Colonel Pyotr Novak Varga. Lucy's high school French was rusty, but she understood enough to learn that he was wanted by the International Criminal Court for war crimes committed against Bosnian Muslims. Those alleged crimes included ordering massacres, systematic rape programs, and the destruction of hospitals and mosques.

Here it was, thought Lucy, staring at the aged scrap of newsprint. The bit of information that explained everything, the discovery that cost Agnes Neal her life.

CHAPTER TWENTY

"Do you know what this means?" Lucy asked, holding out the clipping.

Geri took the scrap of newsprint and studied it. "Isn't he the man who runs Heritage House?"

"He sure is, and it seems that he's an alleged war criminal. I think your mom was investigating and discovered Novak's true identity. She probably knew about him from her work covering the war in Bosnia."

Geri was suddenly unsteady on her feet and Lucy grabbed her before she could fall. "Let's go inside," urged Lucy, leading the way to the three steps that went from the garage into the house. Reaching them, Geri plunked herself down and sat, still staring at the clipping. "You think Mom was investigating this guy and he found out about it and killed her?"

"I think that must be what happened," said Lucy, sitting beside her. "I was talking to that group of three women who always hang out together, do you know who I mean?"

"Not really." Geri shook her head.

"Well, there are these three women, close friends, and they told me that Novak convinced them to coax your mother into the stairwell to see a baby owl. It took a lot of convincing, they said. . . ."

Geri nodded knowingly. "I bet. Mom hated those stairs. Any enclosed space, in fact, ever since she came back from Bosnia."

"It was only when she thought the owl was being mistreated that she agreed. Once they were all in the stairwell Novak reminded the three women that it was lunchtime, so they left, and your mother was alone with him." Lucy reached for Geri's hand, taking it in her own. "We know she never left the stairwell."

"I just can't wrap my head around this. What's a Bosnian war criminal doing running a senior care residence?"

"I don't think he put 'Supervised massacres and torched hospitals' on his visa application," said Lucy. "What I can't figure out is how he discovered that your mom was onto him. She was an experienced reporter and investigator and she knew how dangerous he could be. She would have been very careful not to tip him off."

"On the other hand, he had a guilty secret and knew she was a potential threat. I bet he'd been keeping an eye on her all along. I know her apartment was searched while she was out. She mentioned to me that somebody had been messing with her things, she'd noticed subtle changes and things moved around and she thought it might be one of the nurses. I didn't take it too seriously, I thought she was probably just getting forgetful in her old age. She eventually complained to the nursing supervisor, Elvira Hostens, who defended the staff and told her that it must be one of the other residents. She said some of the more advanced Alzheimer's folks tended to take anything they took a fancy to but staff members always made sure the items were returned to their proper owners. Mom said she gave her a look that sort of suggested she'd be in trouble if she kept making accusations, so Mom backed down."

"Elvira went on the offensive, turned the tables."

"Yeah. I'm a little surprised that Mom even approached her, much less registered a complaint. She called her Nurse Ratched, after the awful nurse in *One Flew Over the Cuckoo's Nest.* Mom always tried to stay

336

clear of her after that, she said she felt she was being watched. I think she might've been afraid to continue investigating Novak. She sure never mentioned anything about it to me." Geri stood up and brushed away a few tears. "She did seem kind of stressed before she died — I should've paid more attention." Geri brushed away her tears. "I thought it was just old age."

"You know," said Lucy, also getting to her feet, "I'm beginning to think Heritage House is just a fancy way for Piotr Novak Varga to disguise his evil past. I'm beginning to wonder why I wasn't more suspicious, why I fell for all those press releases about 'aging in elegant surroundings' and 'making the most of your golden years.' "

"Well, the place must be a golden goose for whoever owns it," observed Geri.

"That would be Peter Novak and his mother, Vesna Varga."

Geri's eyebrows rose in surprise. "The Easter egg lady?"

"The very same," said Lucy, who had been adding two and two. "They own the place outright, which means they must have had money, plenty of money, to invest when they arrived here from Croatia."

"Money they stole?"

"I wouldn't put it past them, but maybe

they were well-off and brought along their cash. Immigration policies tend to favor wealthy people. And now they are raking in the dough, for sure. For one thing, Heritage House is only one of three senior residences in the TaraCare Corporation, which is conservatively estimated to be worth twenty million dollars. I wrote a story last year about the way some businesses set up fake corporations to provide overpriced services like laundry and cleaning, so it seems as if they're losing money even when they're making a huge profit — and they don't even have to pay taxes."

"I should be surprised, but somehow it all makes sense. I was never happy that Mom was there, something about the place always bothered me." Geri shrugged and sighed. "She loved it, though, she really did." Geri grabbed the railing and climbed up onto the first step. "I don't know why she had to start poking around, looking for trouble."

"Looking for trouble," said Lucy, repeating the words and realizing she was guilty of the very same thing. "Some of us just can't help ourselves."

"Well," said Geri, taking the next steps and opening the door, "if Mom's experience tells us anything it's that if you look for trouble you'll probably find it."

"Do you mind letting me have the clipping?" asked Lucy, indicating the scrap that Geri was still holding, careful not to rip the fragile paper.

"Of course not. Here," she said, handing it over. "But promise me you'll be very careful. Novak is a dangerous man."

"I will," promised Lucy, giving her a smile and a little wave. She heard the door close with a snap as she made her way through the garage, wondering what her next step should be. When she reached her car, parked in the driveway, she had a plan. She tucked the clipping into her reporter's notebook, dropped it in her bag, started the car, and headed straight for Heritage House.

First things first, she decided, intending to get Miss Tilley out of danger and into the safety of her own home. She didn't really think Miss T was in any danger, and neither was she. There was no way Novak could know she'd learned about his past. As far as he knew, once he'd disposed of Agnes he could be confident his secret was safe. She would have to confront him sooner or later, hopefully by telephone from the safety of the *Courier* office, but not until Miss Tilley was safe in her own little house. In the back of her mind she had some niggling concern that her visit to the social worker and her inquiries about the double billing might have sent off some alarm bells. It wasn't likely, she told herself, resolving to proceed very carefully. Better safe than sorry.

The drive only took a few minutes, and she was soon crossing the lobby, purposely slowing her pace as she proceeded through the hallways as if she had all the time in the world. Finally reaching Miss Tilley's room, she found her old friend sitting in an armchair, dozing, with an unfinished crossword puzzle in her lap.

Lucy's first thought as she bent to pick up the pencil that had fallen on the floor was that dozing off in a chair seemed a bit out of character for Miss Tilley, especially if she was tearing through a crossword puzzle. Then she remembered her friend's extreme old age, the warmth of the room, and the lateness of the afternoon, and thought maybe she was wrong. So she cleared her throat and shook Miss Tilley gently by the arm, expecting her to wake right up. But she didn't.

"Wake up! Wake up!" she ordered in a sharp voice, at the same time giving that arm a good shake.

Miss Tilley's eyelids fluttered briefly, then closed. By now Lucy was truly concerned, wondering if her old friend was ill, or worse, overmedicated. Spotting the sink in the corner she dashed over and grabbed a washcloth, soaking it with cold water. "Wake up! Wake up!" she demanded, gently wiping the cool, damp cloth on Miss Tilley's face and wrists.

"What are you doing?" someone demanded in an authoritative tone of voice.

Startled, Lucy whirled around and encountered Elvira Hostens, Nurse Ratched herself, phone held tightly in a hand bare of rings with clipped nails. Even though she was dressed in street clothes, her tightly coiled French knot hairdo, starched white blouse, and trim navy pants, as well as her stiff posture, gave the impression of a uniform.

"I'm trying to wake up my friend. I'm supposed to take her out to dinner tonight."

"Really?" Elvira narrowed her eyes suspiciously. "How very odd. She didn't take her name off the dinner list, or let us know that she was going out for the evening."

"It was rather last minute," said Lucy, furrowing her brow. "But that's moot now. She seems to be, well, see for yourself. She's not responsive."

Elvira was quick with an answer. "Just napping. They all do it. It's typical of the

341

aging process, especially if they've been too active. She's got herself all wrought up, she's become obsessed about poor Agnes's accident and keeps fretting about it, talking nonstop with anyone who'll listen. She needs to decompress, let her blood pressure settle down. Just leave her be, she'll be fine. We'll take good care of her. Her dinner will be here any minute and that always wakes them up."

"I think you're wrong," said Lucy. "I think she's been overmedicated."

Just then the rumble of the meal cart was heard and, right on cue, Miss Tilley's eyes popped open. She blinked a few times, then exclaimed, "Lucy! So nice to see you. What brings you here?"

"We had a dinner date," said Lucy, making eye contact and holding it. "Did you forget?"

Realizing something was up, Miss Tilley played along. "I'm afraid I must have," she said.

"I thought you might like a change of scene," continued Lucy. "Get you out of here for some good home cooking."

"Sounds great," said Miss Tilley. "I'll just need my coat and purse."

"I really don't think this is a good idea," said Elvira, placing herself to block the doorway. "What about your special diet?"

"A lot of tosh," opined Miss Tilley, standing up and wobbling a bit on her feet. Lucy quickly stepped forward and took her arm, steadying her. "And besides, it's rather stuffy and overheated in here. I could certainly use some fresh air."

"Exactly," said Lucy, helping Miss Tilley with her coat and purse. Then, Lucy taking her by the arm, they walked the few steps toward the doorway, where Elvira continued to block their exit.

"This is not a prison," snapped Miss Tilley. "I am free to go."

The nutrition aide had appeared, standing behind Elvira with tray in hand, waiting to deliver Miss Tilley's dinner. She gave a polite cough alerting the nursing supervisor to her presence, forcing Elvira to step aside so as not to arouse the aide's suspicion. Lucy and Miss Tilley quickly took advantage of the opening to leave the room. "I'm eating out tonight," Miss Tilley told the aide, getting a smile from the pretty young woman. "I don't blame you," she said, lowering her voice and winking. "It's mystery meatloaf."

Lucy glanced at Elvira, worried about her reaction, and discovered she was busy texting on her phone. There was no time to waste, thought Lucy, beginning to think she'd made a big mistake. They were probably all in it together, Elvira, that social worker Joyce Zimmer, maybe even Felicity. She suspected Novak had cunningly involved them in defrauding the residents, using their guilt in lesser crimes to guarantee their silence and to hide his major one. She felt a sudden surge of adrenaline, an imperative to act fast and get Miss T, and herself, to safety. "I'm getting you out of here," whispered Lucy, guiding Miss Tilley down the hallway to the elevator.

"With just my coat and purse," giggled Miss Tilley. "I feel as if I'm fleeing East Berlin."

The comparison struck Lucy as particularly apt, and she was struck by Miss Tilley's insight. Also her willingness to play along, catching on quickly without posing questions or demanding answers, and she gave her old friend's arm an affectionate squeeze. Lucy wasn't happy about taking the elevator, but knew that Miss Tilley couldn't manage several flights of stairs. Their only hope was speed and, much to her relief, the elevator was waiting at their floor. They quickly got in and Lucy pressed the starred L button, saying a little prayer that it would swiftly deliver them to the lobby and a clear route out of the building.

Much to her dismay, instead of descending, the elevator went up. Her heart started racing, but Miss Tilley didn't seem worried. "It's dinnertime, a lot of people take the elevator around now."

True to her word, when the doors opened on the fourth floor, Howard and his Gang of Three joined them.

"What a lovely surprise," said Howard with a courtly nod. "Good evening, ladies. Will you be joining us for dinner?"

"Unfortunately not, Miss Tilley and I are just on our way out," she said, stressing the word *out*.

Howard raised his eyebrows and gave an approving nod, signaling he realized something was up, but the others remained focused on their supper.

"Any idea what's for dinner?" inquired Bev to the group in general. "I forgot to check the menu."

"Meatloaf," replied Dorothy, in a resigned tone, "and Brussels sprouts."

"But there's Boston cream pie for dessert!" exclaimed Bitsy.

"Bon appétit," said Lucy, feeling that the situation was a bit surreal. "Miss T is coming to my house for dinner tonight and Agnes's daughter, Geri, is also coming," she

345

added, in an effort to give Howard more information about their situation.

"That should make a nice change," observed Howard, tapping the floor with his cane.

"A dinner party!" enthused Bitsy. "What fun!"

"That's the idea," said Lucy as the elevator doors rumbled open on the dining room level, where most of the residents had gathered in the mezzanine, waiting for the doors to open. The area was crowded, as there were several people in wheelchairs, and a number of folks with walkers. But standing directly in front of the elevator were Elvira and Novak.

Peter was charm personified, indicating the wheelchair he had at the ready with a graceful wave of his hand. "My dear Julia . . ."

"That's Miss Tilley to you."

"Ah, yes. Miss Tilley. Let me take you back to your room," he invited. The wheelchair was positioned so that it blocked the others from leaving the elevator, and worse, keeping the Gang of Three from their dinner.

"Move that thing," ordered Dorothy in a brusque voice.

"Yes, yes. We don't want to be late for din-

346

ner. There's already a crowd at the door," observed Bev.

"And we like to be first so we can get the best table, the one by the fireplace," explained Bitsy in a fretful tone of voice.

"As soon as Julia, uh, Miss Tilley, is seated in the chair, the way will be clear and there will be no problem," insisted Peter with another little flourish. His voice had developed a bit of an edge, Lucy realized, and his handsome face had taken on a hawkish appearance. It was his nose, she realized, which had a decided hook, and that white streak in his pompadour reminded her of some avian pred ator. He stepped forward, intending to grab Miss Tilley's arm.

"The crowd," hissed Howard, shepherding his little fan club out of the elevator as the doors began to close. "Use them."

She understood he meant for her and Miss Tilley to join them, mingling with the throng and using the crowd to block Novak while they made their escape. The dining room doors had opened, however, and the seniors were on the move. Desperate measures were called for; it was now or never.

"Stop! Hold on!" Lucy yelled, causing a few curious heads to turn. She quickly produced the newspaper clipping and handed it to Howard. "Howard has an important announcement."

That caught the residents' attention, no doubt expecting to hear that tonight's wine would be free, or that he was treating everyone to birthday cake. Novak, however, had recognized the clipping and lunged at Howard, intending to grab it, but instead collided with Bitsy, who was determined to get her favorite table. She shrieked and clutched at the nearest person, who happened to be Novak, embracing him. That definitely drew the attention of the hungry seniors, who began to focus on the little drama that was such an interesting change from their usual dinner hour.

"Howard, would you please share this, so everyone can hear?" she requested in a loud voice.

Novak, meanwhile, had managed to shake off Bitsy. Elvira was trying to herd the group into the dining room, muttering that dinner would be getting cold, but having little success as a good number of residents had decided this unfolding drama was a lot more entertaining than a meatloaf dinner. A few waiters had even appeared in the doorway, wondering what was causing the delay.

Howard straightened his glasses and unfolded the clipping, raising his eyebrows as he scanned it. "Well, it's been some time since I've used my French but I'll do my best." He adjusted his glasses and furrowed his brow in concentration. "It seems from this that Colonel Piotr Novak Varga, pictured here, is wanted by the ICC," he began, then paused to provide a clarification. "The ICC is the International Criminal Court located in The Hague, and that court apparently, and now I'm translating rather loosely, 'wishes to try Croat Colonel Piotr Novak Varga who is accused of war crimes against Bosniaks during the war in Bosnia.' " He carefully folded the paper and gave it back to Lucy, then faced Novak. "This is a very serious charge," cautioned the former prosecutor and judge. "What have you got to say for yourself?"

There was a communal intake of breath as the residents waited for his answer. "It is absolutely ridiculous, it's Novak Varga. He's some other guy, not me," he insisted huffily. Some of the residents, Lucy noticed, were genuinely shocked, others seemed eager to believe he was innocent, and she also suspected a good number were responding to the appetizing scent wafting from the dining room and beginning to want their dinners.

"There's a remarkable resemblance, then," said Howard, stubbornly continuing even as some of the residents began to drift toward the dining room doors. "Photographs don't lie. You are definitely the man pictured in the photograph, albeit much younger."

"I'm innocent!" Novak declared. "You and Julia" — he pointed angrily at Miss Tilley, who was standing next to Lucy — "you've been listening to Agnes, she started this false lie about me. She got me mixed up with this Varga guy. I tell you, I am not him."

That declaration caused a bit of a stir among the remaining residents, which encouraged Lucy. "That's why you had to kill Agnes, isn't it? Because she recognized you. She knew all about you. She was covering the war in Bosnia, she saw the destruction and the bodies. . . ."

That got the residents' attention; there were mutterings and glances. Elvira stood by helplessly, lips pursed, watching in horror as she realized Novak was not the only one in big trouble. Once investigators began digging into the murder they were bound to discover her role in the financial irregularities at Heritage House. It would all come out, every nasty, sordid detail.

"A complete misunderstanding," said Novak, sensing he had lost the crowd and beginning to move away, no doubt intending to flee.

"Stop!" ordered Howard in a thunderous voice as he advanced toward Novak. "I am placing you under citizen's arrest. Lucy," he added, "call the police."

Novak looked nervously from side to side, then darted into the crowd, only to be tripped up by Florida Dawkins's walker. He struggled to his feet, disentangled himself, and dashed for the stairs. The crowd moved toward the mezzanine railing, which overlooked the lobby, and watched amazed as he fled through the seating area and toward the door.

"He's going to get away," said Miss Tilley, who was at the railing, along with Lucy.

But when Novak reached the door, it was blocked by the substantial form of Officer Barney Culpepper. "Where do you think you're going?" he asked, arms akimbo.

"He killed Agnes!" screamed Bitsy, leaning over the railing. "He made us lure her into the stairwell. . . ."

That got another collective gasp from the residents, and a puzzled look from Barney. "What's going on here?"

Those who were able were beginning to descend the staircase, wishing to get closer to the action in order to hear what was going on. Howard was among them and, prompted by Miss Tilley, Lucy quickly left

351

her and stepped alongside him in order to assist him on the stairs, if needed. He managed just fine, however, taking them one at a time.

"Exactly, right, Officer," said Novak, slightly out of breath and taking in the advancing crowd. "As you can see there seems to be some confusion. We can talk about it outside, let these good people have their supper. . . ."

"Well, that's what I'm here for. My buddy, retired cop Sam Friendly, invited me." Barney was eying the crowd, looking for his friend, and wondering what to do. On one hand he had the threat of an unruly crowd of seniors, and on the other he had an accused murderer who he needed to question further. It was definitely a situation that needed to be resolved.

"Barney, I'm over here," called out Sam, raising his arm.

"Hey, good to see ya, buddy." Barney took a step or two forward, and Novak advanced, clearly hoping to get past him out the door and make his escape into the night.

"You better grab that fella," advised Sam. "It seems he may have been involved in Agnes Neal's death."

Novak was turning his head from side to side, looking for an alternate escape route, as Barney had taken a step backward, positioning himself squarely in the doorway.

"It's true," declared Dorothy, stepping forward and speaking in her authoritative voice that brooked no nonsense. "He had us lure Agnes into that stairwell, and she never came out. You don't have to be a genius to figure out what happened."

Barney finally came to a decision and reached for his handcuffs. "Mr. Novak, I really think I'd better take you in to the station," he began, only to be interrupted in mid-sentence when Novak pulled a gun on him.

That started a chaotic stampede as the frightened seniors began to flee through the lobby, many heading for the nearest door, which led to the hallway beyond. That door was unfortunately locked, forcing the crowd to turn and head for the stairs, moving as fast as their old bones would carry them. They rolled on, pushing walkers and leaning on canes, surging past Elvira and forcing her against a wall where she was trapped.

Lucy turned from the mayhem just in time to see Howard swing his cane around, hooking Novak's ankle and causing him to fall. He dropped the gun, which skidded across the polished Versailles parquet floor and stopped at Bitsy's feet. She stooped and picked it up, training it on Novak, who was trying to rise. "If you think I don't know how to use this," she declared, narrowing her blazing blue eyes, "it will be the last thing you ever thought, Mr. Varga."

Novak froze, still on his knees, and Lucy watched as Barney promptly handcuffed him, then helped him to his feet.

"Lucy, maybe you better come along and explain what happened," suggested Barney. "You too, Mr. White." Then he led Novak out to his cruiser and drove off into the night.

Lucy glanced up at the mezzanine to check on Miss Tilley, relieved to find her in Vera's capable hands. "Okay," she told Howard, "I'll drive." Reaching the station, they were first interviewed by the chief, Jim Kirwan, and then State Police Detective Horowitz. Novak was detained while searches were conducted at his home, where evidence was found confirming his identity as Varga. DA Phil Aucoin handled the press conference the next day, announcing Varga's arrest and his eventual extradition to the ICC authorities. But first, he assured the gathered media, Piotr Novak Varga would face trial for the murder of Agnes Neal.

"What will happen to Heritage House?" asked reporter Deb Hildreth.

Aucoin looked stumped. "I don't have an answer for that," he said. "That is something for the state regulators to decide."

Stopping by at Heritage House later that day, Lucy discovered the residents were very concerned and fearful for their future. "What's going to happen to us?" wailed Bitsy when Lucy met her in the lobby. Determined to get answers, Lucy tracked down Felicity Corcoran, finding her in a meeting with Vesna.

"Ah, Lucy, good timing," said Felicity, welcoming her. "I think we have good news to announce."

"Yes," agreed Vesna, who was sitting behind her son's massive desk, clearly assuming his position as CEO. She was dressed in what looked to Lucy to be a black-and-white tweed Chanel suit, and her Merlot hair was perfectly coiffed. "As the major investor in TaraCare I am happy to announce that everything will continue as before. The residents do not need to worry, there will be no changes in the immediate future."

"That's great news," said Lucy, somewhat puzzled by Vesna's cool and collected attitude. If she herself had been in a similar position, if her son, Toby, had been charged with a serious crime, she would be frantic with worry. But Vesna seemed to be enjoying her newfound position of power. "If you don't mind my asking, what is your reaction to your son's arrest?"

Vesna fingered the softly gleaming three-strand pearl necklace that encircled her neck. "Peter bad boy, always bad boy," she finally said, with a shrug. "What's a mother to do?"

"You expected this?"

"Maybe, maybe not," she replied. "But money to start TaraCare, that was my money. Always my money. From cosmetics business. I wanted to start up cosmetics here, but Peter said no, too much competition. More money to be made in senior residence." She smiled. "Sometimes even bad boy can be right."

"Will you support him through the trials, and the extradition?"

Vesna's eyes widened and she gave a sharp nod. "Of course. He's my boy. With good lawyer, I think he will get off."

"And what about Agnes Neal, the woman he killed? Do you have anything you want to say to her daughter and her friends?"

"I am sorry for their loss, of course." She paused. "But we all know that accidents do happen. Stairs are very dangerous for old people."

"So you think Agnes was killed in an accident."

Vesna shrugged. "Hard to prove either way, no?" She turned to Felicity. "Now, if you don't mind, Felicity and I have work to do."

"What about the double billing, the Medicare fraud?" asked Lucy. "There will certainly be an investigation, probably an audit."

Vesna was not perturbed. "I know nothing about that," she said, giving Felicity a questioning look.

"Nor do I," insisted Felicity. "We will, of course, cooperate fully with any investigation. As to the immediate future of Heritage House, which is a matter of great concern to our residents and their families, they can rest assured that we are committed to providing them with the highest quality care." She paused. "I'll be getting a press release out to you ASAP, Lucy."

Leaving the office, Lucy decided to pay a quick visit to Miss Tilley, to see how she was doing. When she reached her room, however, she found her old friend waiting, with her bag packed.

"Rachel is going to take me home," she

said happily. "I'm finally getting out of this den of iniquity."

"That is good news," said Lucy. "How's your blood pressure after all the excitement yesterday?"

"One ten over seventy," she crowed proudly. "It seems a little excitement was just what I needed."

"A bit too much for me," admitted Lucy. She sat down on the bed, suddenly tired. "Did you know that Vesna, Novak's mother, is taking over Heritage House? She says it was her money they used to start the business, she made it in cosmetics, in Croatia."

"What's so surprising, Lucy?" mused Miss Tilley. "Don't they say that behind every successful man, there's an even more successful woman?"

"I just hope she wasn't behind his war crimes," said Lucy.

"Well, that's another reason for me to get out of here," said Miss Tilley with a knowing glance.

Lucy sighed and got to her feet, eager to relax at home. "See you later, alligator," she said, picking up her bag.

"Not if I see you first," quipped Miss Tilley, prompting Lucy to smile. Her old friend was definitely back, cantankerous as ever.

"Busy day?" asked Bill, greeting her with a wave of his spatula when she got home later than usual. Lucy was exhausted after struggling all afternoon to write up what she suspected was the biggest story of her career. "I went ahead and fried up some burgers."

"Great," said Lucy, hanging up her jacket on the hook by the door and going directly to the refrigerator where she grabbed the bottle of chardonnay. Bill handed her a glass and she filled it, then sat down at the kitchen table.

"You won't believe what happened. . . ." she began, taking a rather large swallow, preparing to tell him all about it.

"Guess what?" announced Zoe, bursting into the kitchen. "Remember that apartment, the one Leanne and I were going to share?"

"Sure," said Lucy. "The cute attic one with the retro kitchen?"

"That's it!" exclaimed Zoe. "Well, I've got it again, with a new roommate, Charlie. I just got a text. Funny coincidence, but the apartment was still available and Charlie found it and asked me if I'd like to share.

Isn't that crazy?"

"So who's this Charlie?" asked Bill, flipping the burgers and adding cheese on top. "Charlotte or Charlene?"

"Nope, it's Charles," says Zoe, smiling like a cat who found the cream. "I know him from school, we worked on a team project together. He's really cute, but," she added, with a sigh, "I don't think he's into girls."

"That's good then," said Bill, visibly relieved as he put the burgers onto their buns and set the platter on the table. "Let's eat."

ABOUT THE AUTHOR

Leslie Meier is the acclaimed author of over twenty-five Lucy Stone Mysteries. She has also written for *Ellery Queen's Mystery Magazine,* and like her series protagonist, Lucy Stone, she worked as a New England newspaper reporter while raising her three children. She is currently at work on the next Lucy Stone mystery and can be found online at LeslieMeierBooks.com.

The employees of Thorndike Press hope you have enjoyed this Large Print book. All our Thorndike, Wheeler, and Kennebec Large Print titles are designed for easy reading, and all our books are made to last. Other Thorndike Press Large Print books are available at your library, through selected bookstores, or directly from us.

For information about titles, please call:
(800) 223-1244

or visit our website at:
gale.com/thorndike

To share your comments, please write:

Publisher
Thorndike Press
10 Water St., Suite 310
Waterville, ME 04901